Praise for Book 1: *The Nightmare Room*

"Sorensen has a knack for cliffhangers that make you want to start reading the next chapter immediately."
   —*Frank Errington, Cemetery Dance Online*

"...a perfectly paced, well-plotted, and compelling haunted house tale filled with oppressive atmosphere, sympathetic and detailed characters, and only a touch of gore."
   —*Becky Spratford, Library Journal*

"Chilling and forceful, Sorensen's story of family, emotional pain, and suspense will maintain listeners' rapt attention."
   —*AudioFile Magazine*

"*The Nightmare Room* is one creepy little gem...I highly recommend this fantastic 5 star read!"
   —*Horror Maiden's Book Reviews*

"...a really well written haunted house story that's easy to follow and scary enough to leave the light on or read during the day. I loved it! This is a must have for your horror collection!"
   —*Mother Horror*

"*The Nightmare Room* is a very well written haunted house story packed with genuine scares, heart wrenching emotion and strong characters you care about."
   —*Kendall Reviews*

"*The Nightmare Room* lives up to its title."
   —*Laurie, Horror After Dark*

Praise for Book 2: *The Hungry Ones*

"Think of your absolute favorite sequel, no matter the franchise. Got it in mind? This is what Sorensen has accomplished for me with *The Hungry Ones.*"
　　—*Tracy Robinson, Sci-Fi & Scary*

"No sophomore jinx here. In fact, *The Hungry Ones* ups the ante with more scares, mystery and flat out horror."
　　—*Hunter Shea, author of CREATURE and SLASH*

"…Chris' books tell unique, horrific stories."
　　—*Gingernuts of Horror*

"Chris Sorensen is the only horror author to make me love—not one, but TWO—haunted house stories."
　　—*Rachel, Shades of Orange*

"Easily the best horror story I've read in 2019. Put on your bib and prepare for a feast—*The Hungry Ones* won't let you down."
　　—*Brian's Book Blog*

"Usually a book two indicates a bridge piece, connecting the first and third books, but *The Hungry Ones* is different. The main difference being author Chris Sorensen."
　　—*Cedar Hollow Horror Reviews*

"I finished *The Hungry Ones* last night and I can assure you all that Book 2 delivers in buckets."
　　—*Steve Stred, author of RITUAL*

THE MESSY MAN

BOOK 3 OF THE MESSY MAN SERIES

CHRIS SORENSEN

Harmful Monkey Press / Sparta, NJ

Publisher's Note: This is a work of fiction. Names, characters, places, and incidents are a product of the author's imagination. Locales and public names are sometimes used for atmospheric purposes. Any resemblance to actual people, living or dead, or to businesses, companies, events, institutions, or locales is completely coincidental.

Chris Sorensen — First Edition

ISBN 978-0-9983424-3-6

For Mom

SERIES NOTE
FROM THE AUTHOR

The Messy Man is the continuation of a story that began with *The Nightmare Room* and *The Hungry Ones,* and as such, these books are best read in order.

Should you wish to refresh your memory about the previous books in the series, I've made short synopses of *The Nightmare Room* and *The Hungry Ones* available at the end of this book.

CHAPTER 1

The girl woke to the sound of her own screams. The nightmares were back.

Ellen extracted herself from the sheet that had wrapped itself vine-like around her lower body and leaned over to open the drawer to her bedside table. She fished out the Teenage Mutant Ninja Turtles daily planner she'd picked up at the dollar store—it could have been covered in daisics for all she cared—and flipped to June 21st.

Across the top of the page, written in scented red marker, was a reminder.

June 21, 2003 - Birthday #11

Was it her birthday already? Only last month, she'd been suffering through Mrs. Haber's fifth-grade class. Old Mrs. H had a habit of letting slip bits of scripture during Science period and had once informed the boys in the class they had one less rib than the girls due to goings-on in the Garden of Eden.

But tomorrow was the first day of summer. And the nightmares had returned.

Ellen scooted up in bed and adjusted the pillow behind her back before snagging a pen from the drawer and getting down to the business of documenting her dreams.

The first—was it actually the first or just the first that came to mind?—was the least formed. Already it was seeping from her head like soapy water from a sponge. She scrunched her brow, willing the particulars to congeal, yet only managed a sketch of the thing.

> *Dream One: Fire everywhere. No air. Couldn't breathe.*

Unsatisfied, yet determined to catch the dream fragments before they flitted off, she moved on.

> *Dream Two: A split man. Bird and man. <u>Torn apart</u>. The circle, the girl, the spell. A conjuring. The man, the bird. <u>Torn apart</u>. <u>Torn apart</u> in the winter circle with the blood-red stone.*

She underlined each instance of *torn apart* as this was the predominant aspect of the nightmare. The raw horror of it, the sawing of bone and flesh and soul.

Ellen looked at the words on the page, her careful penmanship allowing them to stand out starkly. They added black solidity to the nightmare and yet were inadequate to capture the terror yet to be dispelled by the morning sunlight.

Dropping a few inches down on the page, the girl relinquished her firm grip on the pen, allowing its tip to circle almost playfully below the nightmare's description. Her fingers and wrist moved cyclically, decorating the page with a quarter-sized O. *The circle.*

"Not quite right," Ellen said to herself as she lifted the pen from the page.

The sound of laughter swooped through her head on frantic, beating wings. She stabbed at the center of the circle with her pen as if it were a button capable of shutting down the intrusive noise, but the laughter continued. And so she stabbed again. And again. And again.

"What the hell are you doing?"

The voice broke through Ellen's rising panic, causing her to look up at the woman in the doorway.

Mom. It was Mom standing half in, half out of her room, dressed only in an oversized Hawkeyes jersey.

"I'm...I'm journaling," Ellen said, her mouth suddenly dry as a bone.

"At six in the morning? Je-esus, Ellen."

"Sorry. Were you sleeping?"

"Hell, yes, I was sleeping!" Rita Gooding punctuated this with a monstrous yawn, calling to mind the Nutcracker from the ballet she had seen with her father. She had buried her face in his chest when the Mouse King appeared. Mice, rats, the hamster in Mrs. H's class—rodents of any sort—were Ellen's undoing.

"Earth to Ellen," her mom called.

Ellen flinched. Her mother had a voice like a jackhammer. So unlike her father's, which had been low and smooth; always comforting, never—

"Hey, Spooky!"

The nickname caught Ellen off guard.

"Don't call me that."

"I thought you liked—"

3

"Only Dad calls me that."

Her mother tilted her head with a warning look. Mom was in her early thirties, but when her temper flared, she seemed for all the world like a mean, old woman. The kind that pinched and slapped.

"Called," Rita said, correcting her daughter. "He *called* you that." Emphasis on *called*. Emphasis on his absence.

Sensing the stirring of her mother's ire, Ellen acted quickly to change the subject.

"It's my birthday," she said a little too loudly.

"I know that," her mother said a little too quickly. "Don't you think I know that?"

"I don't need a cake or anything."

Her mother snorted. "Of course you're going to get a cake."

"But I don't need one."

Ellen suddenly realized she had miscalculated. Instead of taking the burden of cake baking off her mom's plate, she had struck a nerve.

"Get dressed," her mother said with a snarl, and she turned and stalked out of the room.

Ellen knew better than to dawdle. Not when Mom was on the warpath—or at least edging up to it. She tossed her dream book in the drawer and quickly stripped out of her PJ's and dressed. Black shorts, orange t-shirt, green flip-flops. The shorts were a bit tight—it had been quite some time since her mother had taken her clothes shopping at the Kmart. She was still struggling with the zipper when her mom returned with a handful of crumpled singles.

"You look like an oversized pumpkin in that getup," her mother said. "Put on something else."

"Nothing else fits."

Her mom shook her head and held out the dollar bills. "Go downstairs. Pick out a cake."

Ellen took the money. "Is this enough?"

"Well, you're not buying a wedding cake, Ellen. Just a little one, okay? Sheesh!"

"Okay."

"Go on. I'm going to make some coffee."

Rita let loose with another of her monster yawns, and Ellen made a beeline for the front door.

"No chocolate," her mother called after her. "You hear?"

But Ellen didn't respond. She could always feign ignorance if a particularly tasty chocolate cake presented itself. It was *her* birthday, after all.

The bright June sunlight temporarily blinded her as she opened the door and stepped out onto the fourth-floor landing of the University Arms apartment complex.

Such a sunny day. Couldn't Mother Nature, just once, relent and send her a dark and stormy birthday? The kind of day she felt most at home in? But in Ellen's experience, relenting was not something mothers did willingly or often.

With the wad of singles clutched in her hand, Ellen rushed down the staircase that hugged the building, drawn by the enticing scent of Burke's Bakery below.

* * *

As Ellen opened the door to the bakery, rolling waves of heat and coffee and yeast hit her squarely in the face, momentarily overloading her circuits.

Even at six in the morning, Burke's was bustling with business. Twenty or so people queued up at the register—some picking up orders, others still searching the menu board. A murmur of conversation filled the place, along with the eclectic music selections of a campus radio station DJ.

"That was 'Ice Cream for Crow' by Captain Beefheart," squawked the speakers perched about the room. *"Next up on KRUI, broadcasting at one hundred watts from the Iowa Memorial Union this fine Saturday morning: a polka by Bartok."*

Ellen joined the line, the shortest customer by over a foot. As she shuffled forward, stopped and shuffled forward again, she turned inward and revisited her second dream. The circle. The man.

The bird.

Had it been the bird that was laughing? And if so, was it possible it wasn't laughter she'd heard but cawing?

"Makes sense if it was a bird," Ellen said.

"You're holding up the line, kid."

Ellen looked up. She was standing before the register, behind which stood a rather large, rather husky-looking young woman with cropped hair and cutoff sleeves.

"Cake!" Ellen shouted, caught off guard.

"You picking up?"

"Yes."

"Name?"

"Ellen."

The woman behind the counter sighed. "Last name?"

"Gooding. But my dad's name was—"

"Hold on." The woman turned to a baker's rack and searched the boxed baked goods from top to bottom. "Don't see any Gooding. When'd you order?"

"Right now. I want a chocolate—"

The woman with the cropped hair scowled. "Kid, it's the morning rush, and you're wasting my time. Could you—"

"Hey! I know you." A lanky man with an apron, a hairnet and a slight mustache raised a hand in greeting. Ellen raised hers in return.

The guy looked familiar, but that was as far as Ellen's mind would take her. People, or rather the *specifics* of people, held little interest for her. People were a messy mix of crossed signals, and unless they had some relevance to the situation at hand, they were usually more trouble than they were worth.

Still, there was something about him. What was it?

Then it hit her.

Ellen was suddenly no longer eleven but nine. She was no longer standing alone but with a big man with a barrel chest. Christmas music floated on the air.

"Should we get gingerbread cookies, Spooky?"

"Cookies are for kids."

"So should we get some?"

"Yes, please."

"Then give the man with the pencil-thin mustache our order."

"You have a pencil-thin mustache," Ellen announced.

"That's right. You remember! The man always gave me grief about my 'stache." The guy laughed. "Hey, Jazz, that's Professor Marx's kid."

The woman with the cropped hair softened. "That right, sweetie?

Ellen managed a nod. The woman, Jazz, stepped into the back and returned with a small box. She set it on the counter in front of Ellen.

"No charge. Your dad failed me my freshman year. Best teacher I ever had."

At a loss for words, Ellen blurted out, "It's my birthday."

"Happy birthday, sweetie."

* * *

Rita was pouring herself a cup of coffee when Ellen returned with the bakery box.

"What flavor did you get?"

"I don't know," Ellen replied.

Her mother raised her eyebrows. "Say what?"

The girl set the box down on the kitchen table, a wobbly thing held together with a healthy dose of duct tape. There were many things in the shabby little two-bedroom that were teetering on the brink of doom, held just this side of the dumpster by duct tape.

"I don't know what kind of cake it is. Or even if it *is* cake. The lady at the bakery gave it to me for free."

"*Woman*. The *woman* at the bakery."

"Sorry. Woman."

"Free?" Ellen's mother set her coffee mug down and tapped her nails on the table. "What, do they think we're a charity in here?"

"No, Mom."

"Because your dad didn't put a ring on it when he could, and now the university won't pay out?"

"Please, Mom."

"Those poor Goodings up on four!"

"Have some cake—"

"That poor welfare mom and her freak of a kid!"

Those last words hung like poison in the air between them. Ellen knew if she were to be the next to speak, she might soon be dodging her mother's coffee mug. Or worse.

And so, she simply opened the box, revealing the item inside—a pound cake.

"Nothing wrong with a pound cake," her mother said, a lone tear dampening her cheek. "Free, you said? Where's the money I gave you?"

Ellen set the stack of bills on the table. "Can I have some coffee?"

"You drink coffee?"

"Dad lets me. Sometimes."

"Let."

Rita plucked a second cup from the mug tree and set it in front of her daughter.

"I like milk and sugar," Ellen said. "Like Dad."

"Gooding women drink it black." Her mom poured half a mug and passed it to the girl. She got them each a fork and sat at the table opposite Ellen.

"No candles?" Ellen asked.

"Don't push it."

Mother and daughter took their first bites, and Ellen smiled. Not outwardly, but inside her secret self.

Free cake on my birthday. Because of Dad.

A knock at the door interrupted their feast.

"Shit. I paid the rent, didn't I?" Rita rose, tiptoed over to the door and peeked out the peephole. Her demeanor shifted dramatically, as if she had suddenly thawed.

"Here comes trouble!" her mother cooed.

She opened the door a crack, and Ellen could see a young man with unkempt hair that contrasted with the formality of his dress, an unlit cigarette dangling from his lip. The badge on his light blue shirt told the whole story. *U.S. Postal Service.*

"Hey, Rita," the young man said.

"Hey, Bo. Any reason why you're making a door-to-door delivery when I have a perfectly good mailbox downstairs?" Was her mom actually flirting?

Mr. Unkempt Hair grinned. "You know why."

"Shh," said Rita. "The kid."

Bo handed her a stack of mail and spoke in a lower tone. "We still on for tonight?"

"I am if you are."

"I'm a bit...light this week. Don't know how that happened, but...mind if we..."

"We can eat in." Yup. Definitely flirting, Ellen deduced. It made her stomach twist. "Ellen! Take the mail."

Ellen rose and trudged over to where her mother was making a fool of herself. She took the mail and stalked back to the kitchen, eager to be free of the cloud of cheap cologne that engulfed the one called Bo.

Was that cologne? And if so, why did they make cologne that smelled like a slaughterhouse? It was sickly sweet and heady.

As her mother continued chattering away with the young postman, Ellen absentmindedly picked through the mail. Bill, bill, advertisement, bill.

Her breath caught in her throat, and she stifled a cough. She didn't need to draw her mother's attention. Not now. Not while she was trying to make sense of the red envelope she held in her hands.

There was no return address, and the handwriting was shaky. Their University Arms address was barely legible, but it was there, as was her name.

"Hey, Ellen," her mom started.

"Gotta go to the bathroom!" Ellen cried as she pulled the envelope close and took off down the hallway.

Once behind the closed door, she double-checked the lock before sitting down on the closed toilet, her heart racing in her chest. Willing her hands to stop shaking, Ellen slowly tore open the envelope.

Just like Charlie tearing open the candy wrapper, looking for the Golden Ticket.

"Shut up," she told her wayward brain.

She carefully extracted the birthday card. A crow wearing a party hat adorned the cover.

HAPPY BIRD-DAY TO YOU!

"Don't open it," she warned herself. "Throw it away." She didn't listen.

Inside were six crisp fifty-dollar bills and a loose-leaf note written in the same handwriting scrawled across the envelope.

Ellen read the opening line and closed her eyes tight.

11

Hey Spooky, it's Dad.

CHAPTER 2

Ellen sat in silence as she gathered the courage to open her eyes. A sigh of water from the always-leaking toilet played soundtrack to her distress.

Hey Spooky...

Dad had come up with his special name for her when she was seven. They'd been walking across the autumn campus after a screening of Ingmar Bergman's *Smiles of a Summer Night*—Ellen *loved* accompanying her father to lectures, art shows, concerts, even if she was out of her depth—when she struck up a conversation with a student who had joined them on their stroll. After learning the young man's name was Treat, Ellen couldn't stop giggling.

"What's so funny, Ellen?" her dad had asked.

"Treat is such a *silly* name!"

Dad stopped walking and looked at her. "Where did you hear that name?"

Ellen turned to point at the student, but he was nowhere to be found. "Where'd he go?"

Later, her father showed her a copy of *The Daily Iowan* with a photo of the young man.

"That's Treat," Ellen said, gingerly touching the headline which read, "Dubuque Student Death Ruled Homicide."

"That's spooky," her father said.

…it's Dad.

But it couldn't be. Dad was dead. There had been no funeral, no casket, no body, but the police had been very clear about his status. His Plymouth had veered off the Mirror Lake Bridge near the Wisconsin Dells and fallen through the ice below. They'd recovered the Plymouth—not so, her father.

Ellen lifted the sheet of paper out of the card and read on.

I'm sorry I can't be there today. 11, huh? That's a big one. I'm enclosing $300. Show this card to your mom and say Uncle Don sent you $200 and give her $100.

She looked back at the card. A short birthday greeting from Uncle Don gave credence to the lie. She continued.

That way you'll have some money to hold onto for a rainy day and still have some left to get or do something you want (Mom won't bug you about your $ if she has some of her own). I'm sure something will jump out at you.

All my love,
Dad

Her father's sign-off was a panacea for all the fear and grief to which the card's arrival had given rise, and Ellen drank it in, savoring its simplicity and power.

All my love…

"I love you, too," she whispered.

"What, did you fall in?" came her mother's piercing cry.

Ellen quickly stuffed the note and two of the fifties into her shorts pocket and flushed the toilet. She placed the rest of the bills back into the card and the card into the envelope and ran a short burst of water in the sink for good measure.

"Out in a sec," she called.

"I'm going to eat up all this cake."

"Out in a sec, I said!"

Ellen checked herself out in the mirror, making sure she could mask the chaos racing about inside. On any other day, she wouldn't have to worry. It was easy to close herself off from the rest of the world, something about which her father had once, in fact, warned her.

"You can be a closed book sometimes, Ellen. Makes it hard to read you."

Good. Snap the book closed. Hide the frantic jumble of thoughts within. Snap it *shut*.

"Mmm, yummy-yummy!" cackled her mom.

Ellen relieved her face of all expression and stepped out of the bathroom.

"What's that you've got there?" her mother asked, always the eagle-eye.

Ellen set the card on the table and sat, picking up her cooling mug of coffee. "What did the mailman want?"

"First, he's a *postal worker*. And second, you didn't answer my question."

"Just a card."

"From whom?"

"You can read it, if you want."

"Don't think I won't."

Rita reached across the table so quickly, she nearly toppled her own coffee. When she opened the card, the fifties slipped out of her grip and onto the floor.

"Shit! There's money in here."

Both mother and daughter dove beneath the table and scrambled for the bills.

"Fifty…one hundred…two hundred dollars? Why is your Uncle Don sending you two hundred dollars?"

"Because he feels bad? Because he never called or sent flowers or…anything?" Ellen offered, feeding the fiction.

She was surprised how her words struck her mother. She half-expected her mom to hug the cash to her breast and shout *mine-mine-mine!* But instead, Rita held the money out to her daughter.

"You keep half," Ellen said. "I'm just a kid. One hundred bucks is enough for me."

For a brief moment, Ellen thought her mom might draw her daughter to her in a thankful embrace. Instead, Mom slipped back into herself.

"We're using this money to get you some new clothes. You're about ready to pop the button on those shorts." She gave Ellen a poke in the belly for good measure. "Let's go, birthday girl."

* * *

At first, Ellen wondered what her mom was thinking. She knew from experience Kmart opened at eight, but it was still only around seven. But when she caught her mom circling ads in the *PennySaver*, the pieces fell into place.

Garage sales. They were hitting the garage sales.

"Get in, get in! If we waste time, they'll all be picked over!" Rita called as she urged the old Chevy Nova to life. The muffler rattled underneath like an enormous cicada angered at being awakened.

Ellen hopped into the car and slipped on her safety belt, which was actually half belt/half duct tape. If the stuff was a useful workaround in the apartment, it was absolutely essential here in the Nova.

The engine sputtered and complained but eventually started, and soon the two Gooding gals were off on their Saturday morning adventure.

"That coffee made me thirsty," Ellen said.

"It'll do that. Now, pay attention. I put numbers next to the sales so we wouldn't have to zigzag all across town. What's the address of number one?"

"1105 Keokuk Street." As soon as she spoke, Ellen knew her mother was calling up her inner Garmin, testing out multiples routes in her head so as to shave off one or two minutes of drive time, and thus beat other shoppers to the punch.

Hey Spooky, it's Dad.

The police were wrong. It wasn't her father's car they found lodged in the ice along the banks of some Wisconsin river. They got bad intel.

No, it was his car. It was the Plymouth. The police had photos. It still had the *Where the Heck is Wall Drug?* bumper sticker on the back from the time they'd all driven up to South Dakota to see Mount Rushmore. Yup, it was his Plymouth. It was Dad's car.

"Asshole!" her mom shouted as she pounded the horn. The delivery truck that had strayed into her lane swerved right, and the driver stuck an apologetic hand out the window. "Get off the road!"

"That was Keokuk," Ellen said.

"I know that, Ellen."

Her mother took the next right a tad too fast, causing Ellen's seatbelt to dig into her gut.

The garage sale turned out to be more of a yard sale, with a treasure trove of items spread out across the grass—golf equipment, tools, an ancient snow blower. There were also stacks of cardboard boxes through which a collection of moms were picking.

"Dang. We're late." Her mom quickly parked two doors down in front of a house with patchy grass and a sign in the yard touting *Kerry/Edwards: A Stronger America.* She jumped out of the car and made a mad dash for the stacks of boxes, muscling in between two women sorting through floral print clothing.

Ellen took her time joining the party. She'd done this many times before, helping her mother search out a coffee maker, toaster oven or the like. Her job was to sit on the item— sometimes literally, in the case of something larger like a mini-fridge—while her mother haggled. But Ellen was in no rush to discover the look of her new wardrobe. God knew what sort of cheap, glitter-covered horrors her mom would select for her.

So instead she wandered down the long driveway to where the seller was sitting. She was a dour woman in a plaid shirt, plaid shorts, smoking menthol cigarettes. A cashbox sat on the card table that was the woman's base of operations, and next to it was a pitcher of pink lemonade.

"Can I have some lemonade?" Ellen asked.

"One dollar," was the reply.

"I'll pass."

An enormous blue tarp covered half of the two-car garage's roof, one untethered edge flapping in the breeze, catching Ellen's eye. One of the garage doors was open, and inside she could see more junk piled high and a man sitting alone in a lawn chair.

Eschewing the free-for-all out on the lawn—Mom was arguing with a woman twice her age, clearly giving her a piece of her mind—Ellen headed for the garage. As she drew nearer, the man in the chair raised his eyes. She knew at once he must be the husband of the sour woman at the card table. Probably hiding out while she lorded over her sales. He had a buzz cut and Bermuda shorts, and he gave her a little salute as she approached.

"Sale's back that way, little miss."

"I'm just looking."

"Looking's free. Nothing wrong with looking."

Ellen wrinkled her nose when she stepped into the garage. There was a wet, burnt smell that permeated the place. Still, her curiosity had been piqued by the off-limits clutter.

The man rose from his chair, retrieved a beer from a cooler and cracked it open with a satisfied *ahhh.*

"I know it's a bit early, but if you were married to that woman, you'd buy me a case."

Ellen ignored the man's complaint. She knew it was an invitation to join him in his wallowing, and she had neither the interest nor the time to do that. Instead, she began poking around the boxes—tentatively at first, then with abandon.

The man paid no attention. His eyes were trained on his wife down the drive. "Always yammering, jabbering, blabbering. Never a moment's rest. And see? Most of the stuff she's selling? *My* stuff. My hard-earned stuff."

Shoving aside a milk crate of loose, warped records, Ellen saw something that caught her eye. At first, she thought it was the case for a sewing machine or a musical instrument, but when she undid the clasp and opened it, she saw it for what it was: an old Norelco reel-to-reel tape recorder.

"Smokes like a chimney, she does. Whole house smells like a pack of Kools." The man set his beer aside, grabbed a faded-red gas container and kneeled before an old Craftsman lawnmower. "Reason I stay out here."

Ellen ran her hand over the recorder's controls. Pause, Rewind and an intriguing little button labeled Trick.

I'm sure something will jump out at you.

Next to the Norelco sat a paper bag half-filled with tapes of various sizes. Some in cases, some not.

"Got that at auction over in Roseville, Illinois," said the man. "Come with a bunch of bibles and choir books, it did. I like auctions. Gets me out of the house."

"How much?"

20

He thumped the red container down hard, splashing a bit of gasoline on the cement floor in the process.

"I don't want to sell that. Hell, I don't want to sell anything. That damn woman. I should really—"

Ellen fished one of the four fifties from her pocket and held it out. "This for the recorder? And the tapes? You can keep the bibles."

The man considered her for a moment, then took the fifty, folded it in half and slipped it into his pocket. "She don't need to know about this."

Ellen nodded and put the cover back on the recorder. It was heavier than she had imagined, and getting it and the bag of tapes to the car without the woman at the card table seeing took some effort. She was aided by her mother, now bickering with the woman, who sat back in her chair, sipping her one-dollar lemonade.

She stashed the recorder and bag in the back seat and then quickstepped it to where her mom was paying for her finds.

"There you are. I got you tons of good stuff."

Taking stock of her mother's purchases, Ellen could see that pink and purple were to soon make up the bulk of her new wardrobe.

As Rita disputed the amount of change she had coming, the scent of smoke once more hit Ellen's nose, and she instinctively glanced back at the garage.

Instead of being covered by a tarp, the garage's roof was ablaze, fire dancing and reaching toward the sky. The man in the Bermuda shorts was dancing as well. Engulfed in flames, he hopped about like a wounded bird, arms flapping as he burned.

He caught Ellen staring, paused momentarily and gave her another little salute before returning to his grisly dance.

"I'm so sorry about your Jonathan," the next customer in line said. "Just awful. My condolences."

The woman at the card table took an extra-long draw on her smoke. "Damn fool nearly burned the whole house down. That clock's priced wrong. It's ten bucks."

Ellen shuddered. The tarp was back, the garage door was down. No, the roof was on fire, and the man was dancing. The man was burning.

"C'mon," said her mother, giving her a little shove. "A few more stops, and we should have you set for the year."

She followed her mom to the car at a distance, eyes still glued on the garage where the man danced. And didn't.

Danced.

And didn't.

CHAPTER 3

Rita stashed her purchases from the second garage sale of the day in the back seat. "Where the hell did this come from?" she asked, pointing at the recorder.

"I bought it."

"No, you didn't."

"Yes, I did."

"I didn't see you."

"Well, I did."

Her mother stared at the bulky contraption. "How much?"

"I got a bag of tapes too."

"How much did you pay, Ellen?"

"Fifty."

Rita's knees buckled. "Are you kidding me? Fifty dollars? For that crappy thing?"

"I wanted it."

"Haven't I taught you anything? *Never* pay full price."

"I know."

"I could have gotten that for ten…five bucks!"

"Probably."

"Then why—"

"It's my birthday." The phrase was coming in handy in a pinch. This time, it shut her mom up. The woman was still steaming, but at least the scolding had stopped. For now.

They drove in silence to their next stop, Ellen trying hard *not* to think of the burning man. It was no use. She had seen too much. And even though she'd been quite some distance from the man's flaming flamenco, she could still see the fire consuming his skin, his eyes cooking in his head...

Stop it.

His wide grin stretched across his charred face, teeth exploding like popcorn in his mouth, white bone appearing through the fat of his sizzling jowls.

"Stop it!" Ellen shouted.

"Stop what?"

For a second, Ellen had no reply, so strong was the memory of the burning man. But she quickly redirected her thoughts.

"Stop *not* talking."

"You say I talk too much."

"But it's worse when you stop."

"What do you want to talk about?"

"I don't know," Ellen sighed.

"How about we talk about the shrink your school counselor wants me to take you to? Hmm? Those sessions aren't cheap, you know."

This shut Ellen up. Better talking about nothing than the subject her mother had broached. It wasn't Ellen's fault the counselor had called her mother. It wasn't her fault the girl she shoved in the hallway was about to walk through a dead janitor. Who'd want to walk through a ghost? But her considerate act was labeled "unprovoked aggression," and therapy was the counselor's requested remedy.

Best to steer clear of everyone, the living and the dead.

24

"Gimme the next address," her mother said. "I think it's on East Market."

* * *

The remainder of the morning consisted of limited conversation and too much time to think. Whenever Ellen thought she had swept aside the memory of the burning man, fresh details would emerge that would make her belly clench. At the final garage sale—a pitifully picked-over assortment of baby clothes and cheap figurines—she'd had to beg the owner of the house to let her use the toilet, that bad were her vision-induced stomach cramps.

When they returned to the University Arms, Ellen's mother made her help haul the plastic bags of musty used clothes up the three flights of stairs before letting her go back to retrieve her recorder.

"Keep that thing in your room, you understand? I don't want it taking up space in the living room."

"I got it, Mom."

"If it trips a breaker when you plug it in, out it goes."

"Okay."

Ellen hauled the reel-to-reel to her room and set it on the bed. She wouldn't test it out, not just yet. Mom was still too watchful, and Ellen didn't want to risk losing the thing should it let loose with a *buzz* or a *zap*. Her father's money had paid for it, after all. It was, in essence, his birthday gift to her.

The rest of the day was much like any other Saturday except for the inordinate amount of laundry they had to do, thanks to her mother's garage sale finds. The two of them shuttled back and forth between the laundry room down the hall and the kitchen table. By the time the last load was dried and folded, the piles of clothes looked like a small mountain range.

"Purple mountain majesties," Ellen said.

"What's that supposed to mean?" When she got no answer, Rita handed her daughter the first stack. "Try them on. Whatever fits, we keep. Whatever doesn't—"

"I know. eBay," Ellen said.

She retreated to her room and began the painful process of trying on other people's clothes. Painful because every now and then she got a whisper of something when the fabric hit her skin. A stray memory, a single word. While putting on a pair of blue jeans that actually fit quite well, she distinctly heard a girl's voice behind her shout *NO!* She hurriedly kicked them off and placed them in the eBay pile.

When it was over, half of the clothes made it to the dresser, the other half back to the kitchen table to be photographed, priced and stowed in cardboard boxes. The one bright spot of the ordeal was an oversized black sweatshirt that swallowed Ellen whole when she put it on.

"How'd that get in there?" her mom moaned.

"I like it."

"Of course, you do. Not a normal bone in your body, is there?"

Ellen regarded the cluster of boxes her mom was slowly filling. "Where are Dad's boxes?"

"Hmm?" Rita said, laying a beige sweater on the table, smoothing its wrinkles and taking a photo with her flip phone. *Snap.*

"Dad's stuff. All the stuff he kept here. His books, his typewriter, his—"

"People will buy just about anything online."

Ellen puzzled a bit before landing on the sorrowful conclusion. "You sold it?"

"Gotta pay the bills." *Snap. Snap.*

"All of it?"

"Most of it."

"Didn't you keep *anything?*"

"I kept *you.*"

Ellen stiffened. Her mother turned from her chore, realizing the line she'd crossed.

"Sorry."

The apology cost her mom, but Ellen didn't care. She hugged the black sweatshirt tightly about herself and slunk off to her room. She ignored her mother's call for lunch and then, later, dinner, preferring to remain curled up in bed, staring at the *Sleepy Hollow* movie poster on the wall across the room.

"I can microwave you some meatballs," her mom said through the door.

"I'm not hungry."

"Last chance. I've got company coming over. You know that."

Resigned, Ellen opened the door and slipped past her mother. She gathered some cheese, crackers and hot sauce from the fridge and retired once more to her room.

"Okay. It's Mama's private time."

"I got it," Ellen sighed. *The last thing I want to do is catch you and that mailman...postman...whatever...making out on the sofa.*

As if on cue, she heard a knock at the front door and the creak of the hallway floorboards as her mother went to answer it.

Ah, well. Time to get acquainted with the Norelco.

* * *

With no manual to guide her, navigating the workings of the old device proved trickier than Ellen had anticipated. Having set the device in the middle of her bed, she went about detecting how to turn it on and off, where to insert the jack for the boxy microphone. She even managed to set up both a supply and take-up reel from her collection of tapes. She hit Play, the reels turned but the speaker offered up nothing but a muted hiss.

It wasn't until she noticed all the other reels had handwritten labels on them that she realized she was trying to play a blank tape.

Muffled laughter bled through the wall, and the stink of Bo's cigarettes snuck under the door. Ellen glanced at her alarm clock. 7:22. Mom and Bo had been entertaining each other for well over two hours, during which they had grown progressively louder. Time to get the recorder working so she could drown out the noise of their date. Drowning out noise was no easy feat for Ellen—isolating sounds was next to impossible without serious, determined effort. Most people heard the Beatles; Ellen heard John, Paul, George and Ringo in equal measure, each competing with the others for her attention.

She lifted a new reel from the bag.

Hymns (30 min).

At least this reel held the promise of actually containing something. Ellen looped the tape from reel to reel and placed her finger on the Play button.

Dad would love this.

The more mechanical a thing, the more he liked it. His old manual typewriter was a case in point. The typewriter her mom had either sold to some collector on eBay or had stashed somewhere, hidden away like the rest of their former life with him.

She pressed the button, and the speaker barked with static. Ellen quickly dialed down the volume and leaned in toward the machine.

A quavering male voice called out from the recorder, distant and echoing in whatever room this recording was made.

"Hymn 734. 'Bringing in the Sheaves.'"

A less-than-note-perfect introduction followed, hammered out on an out-of-tune piano. A small choir joined in, and although the muddle of music and voices sounded as if the recording had taken place underwater, Ellen managed to pick out the first few lines of the hymn.

Sowing in the morning, sowing seeds of kindness,
Sowing in the noontide and the dewy eve,
Waiting for the harvest and the time of reaping —
We shall come rejoicing, bringing in the sheaves.

As the hymn continued, she played with the rest of the controls, finally landing on the Trick button. As the choir warbled on, she depressed the small button.

The speaker went instantly silent.

"Damn. I broke it."

But releasing the button caused the hymn to return, same as before.

What's the trick? *That it screws up your recording?*

Ellen hit Stop, then Rewind. When she had returned a foot or two of tape back to the supply reel, she hit Play again.

…in the sheaves.

Pretty good for eyeballing it. The choir returned, and the hymn continued until the tape came to the moment Ellen had pressed the button. The moment of her *trick*.

"Damn. I broke it."

Ah! It was her voice the moment she'd held down the button. But not just her voice. The hymn continued underneath while her voice rode on top.

"That's cool," Ellen cooed, legitimately impressed by the ancient technology.

She was about to shut down the recorder and switch reels when a similar dip in the sound of the hymn occurred. A rhythmic panting rose above the choir—not an animal, but a human being. Someone either breathless or scared out of their wits.

"Ellen!"

A lone voice trumped the din of the choir, rising above it but only just. The cry had sounded so suddenly, it hadn't registered as either male or female to Ellen's ear. The choir followed up with a shrill rising chorus of…

Bringing in the sheaves!
Bringing in the sheaves!
We shall come rejoicing, bringing in the sheaves!

Eager to gather her wits, Ellen stabbed at the Stop button, but the tape recorder had no interest in stopping.

"Blind Rock! Ellen…Blind Rock! Ellen, you…Ellen!"

The voice was now barely recognizable as a voice at all. It was a roaring inferno of words.

"Blind Rock!"

A high-pitched scream blasted from the other side of her door, and it took a moment for Ellen to recognize it for what it actually was—the smoke detector.

She shoved the reel-to-reel away a split second before black smoke began to curl from its innards. The reels revved up, spinning so fast they whined. The take-up reel couldn't keep up the pace, and the Norelco spat its thin brown tape across the bed and onto the floor. The choir wailed—the voices rising higher and higher, their tempo increasing.

"Blind…Rock!"

The room suddenly went pitch black.

But the sun is still out.

All was silent.

No…the frightened breathing remained. And it was not her own. Someone or something else was in the room.

"Mom?"

Ellen quickly rose from the bed. She felt her way toward the door. The carpet felt different beneath her feet. In fact, it didn't feel like carpet at all—it felt like…earth. Cold, hard earth.

Her hands came in contact with the door, and she reached for where the doorknob should be, but it was gone. The door itself felt as foreign to her as the ground. It felt like corrugated metal and was freezing to the touch.

A rasping cough behind her caused her to jump and she spun around, facing the dark room.

"Hello?" Ellen called, the *hello* meaning *stay away, whatever you are, stay the hell away!*

"Who's there?" a ruined voice replied.

"Who's *there?*" Ellen insisted.

The air began to vibrate, and the thumping pressure of it assaulted Ellen's eardrums, causing her to cry out in pain. The screech of the choir returned full-force, adding to the din.

When our weeping's over,
He will bid us welcome!
We shall come rejoicing,
BRINGING IN THE SHEAVES!

"What are you doing in there?"

Her mother's voice cut through the cacophony, yanking her back from the darkness. But the room was clouded with acrid smoke, and the detector in the hallway shrieked and shrieked.

"Ellen!" her mom shouted.

Scrambling over to the outlet, Ellen yanked on the recorder's cord, the plug popping out of the socket with a concussive spark.

Rita threw open the door to the sight of her daughter on the floor, sprawled in a nest of still unspooling quarter-inch tape.

"That's it. Out that thing goes."

Yes. Get it out of here. I don't want it. I don't want it.

"You hear me?"

But Ellen was listening instead to another voice, the one that still cried out even though the recorder was dead and smoldering and would never play again.

"Ellen! Blind Rock! Ellen!"

Ellen screamed.

CHAPTER 4

The man woke with a start.

Where am I? he asked himself. This was followed shortly after by: *Who am I?*

It was cold, the kind that freezes to the bone. He was lying on a hard cot with a wool blanket that was a foot short of being useful. The room he was in was dark and cramped.

I'm in the Nightmare Room.

But as his eyes adjusted, he discovered he was not in a room at all, but a shed. Its walls were corrugated metal, its floor, winter-hardened earth.

It was night, that much was obvious. What little light there was filtered in through seams in the metal, through rusted-out patches.

The man sat up on the cot and instantly regretted the move. His muscles resisted as if he were using them for the first time. His back cramped, and he doubled over in pain. As he waited for his muscles to release their grip, he caught a gentle sound drifting in the air.

A piano. What's a piano doing out here? What am I *doing out here?*

Tentative, but ready to give it another go, he tried once more to rise. This time he succeeded, throwing off the blanket and standing. As soon as he was upright, he felt a warm, tickling breath at his ear.

"Peter. Your name is Peter."

He jerked back, startled.

"Who's there?" he croaked, finding that his throat was as clenched and rebellious as the rest of his body.

There was no reply, but the name the voice offered felt like a gift. Like something he could hang his hat on, a point of reference, a touchstone, a—

"Shh," he told himself, entreating his rebooting brain to go slowly, let him catch up.

There was a girl. And a bird, and a circle of stones. There were other things too—gnashing things, stuff of nightmares. And a horrible tearing of flesh and mind and bone and self. He placed a hand on his chest, feeling his heart beating a wild tattoo within. He was whole. There was no rending of flesh, no great gash down his center, even though that's exactly how he felt.

"I'm Peter, and I'm in one piece," he said, feeling both the truth and the lie of it. "I'm Peter…"

But the rest of his name eluded him. Peter Rabbit? Peter Parker? He could have been Peter the Great, for all he knew. Try as he might, he couldn't fit another name to the one he'd been offered. Peter Pan? Peter Tell?

Tell? Is that right? Am I Mr. Tell?

Voices joined the piano, and together they rose and fell as the wind played keep-away with the music. Snippets of lyrics caught his ear, and he found himself asking what a *sheave* was. No matter. There were no answers to be had here in this shed. It was time to leave.

The locked door thought otherwise.

The metal strained as he threw his weight against it, but the door held firm—no doubt latched and padlocked from outside. Peter searched the shed, looking for weak spots in walls where the rust had eaten through, digging away frozen dirt clods where metal met the earth. As he searched, he discovered not all of the dirt floor was in fact dirt. The cot was sitting on a series of old wooden planks covering what, exactly? A sinkhole? A well?

Leaving well enough alone—he managed a chuckle at the wordplay—he continued his inspection until he found a loose seam at the back of the shed where two metal panels met. A number of the rivets holding the two pieces together were popped, allowing him to squeeze his arm through to his shoulder.

The wind outside was rising, and ice crystals sifted through his fingers.

Time to get out. Time to get some damn answers.

Peter leaned into the opening and felt the old rivets give way. He pressed forward, pulled back and pressed again. Back and forth he went, the metal edges slicing his thin shirt, digging in his flesh, rivets popping with each thrust.

Finally, Peter birthed himself from the metal shed and fell sprawling into a drift of freshly fallen snow.

A small, wooden church, its crooked steeple doing its best to abandon the rest of the structure, sat twenty yards away. It was a plain two-story building topped by a slate roof. Where stained glass windows no doubt once lived, there were now simple colored panes of glass—red, green, yellow. A light burned within, and that was enough for Peter. He rose from the snowdrift, shook the ice from his hands and stumbled toward the church.

The wind was really picking up, and for a brief moment he lost sight of the place entirely. When the snow blinded him, he was suddenly reminded of a story about a girl caught out in a blizzard. Was it someone from *The Little House on the Prairie* books? One of the Ingalls girls?

Funny you can remember the story but not your own name.

The wind died down enough for Peter to see he had to adjust course—his former trajectory had been taking him out into the empty field.

A low rumble echoed across the landscape. Was that thundersnow?

No. Peter risked a look back and saw the shed being buffeted by the wind—so much so, the metal sheets he had forced loose were flapping wildly, thundering like an old-time radio sound effect.

The squall wreaking havoc with the shed was heading his way, following his footprints in the snow. And with it came voices. Not lifted in song, as he had heard earlier, but raised in anger. The gust of wind and snow turned tornadic, swirling and threatening as it approached, gaining on him, accusing him in its clamor.

Peter urged himself on. He was ten yards from the church. Five. One. His foot slammed into a buried step, and he fell against the heavy front door.

"Please!" he yelled as he pounded on the door, the encroaching storm drowning out his pleas even to himself. "Open up! Please!"

The whipping snow engulfed him, ice raking his hands and cheeks, robbing him of his breath.

That's it. I'm finished.

The door swung inward, and Peter fell forward. A howl rose from the window outside, angry at being thwarted of its prize. Peter hit the floor hard, and heard the door slam closed behind him. He was safe.

Panting for breath, he managed a thank you, but the words came out as a moan. He was on the verge of passing out. He *was* passing out. But before he did, he looked up.

Standing before him in the nave was a collection of children, the foremost being a willowy girl in a plain homespun dress. A black bird with watchful eyes perched upon her shoulder.

CHAPTER 5

The boy sitting across from Ellen in the waiting room kicked his legs and squirmed as if he had to go to the bathroom. He stared at her with big cow eyes. It made Ellen want to pick up one of the magazines on the table next to her and chuck it at him.

Stop looking at me, stop looking, stop looking.

The boy kept on staring and added nose-picking to his repertoire. The kid was probably six or seven, but as he was rail-thin it was hard to know for certain.

"Cut it out, Percy," said the boy's father, a nervous man who looked as if he too had to use the restroom. And to Ellen's disgust, the man proceeded to pick at his ear. The ear-picking father and his nose-picking son. Just another Tuesday morning at Striving Kids Psychiatric Clinic.

Ellen glanced at her mother. Rita was engrossed in her phone. She'd been unusually tight-lipped since the incident with the tape recorder had broken up her date. Instead of launching into her usual barrage of threats and complaints, she'd gotten busy.

First, she disappeared the Norelco. Ellen couldn't be sure, but she had a good idea it now resided in the dumpsters behind the apartment complex. Ellen had only managed to save one reel, the *Hymns (30 min)* tape, because it toppled off the recorder when her mother snatched it up. Next, her mom called up Mr. Traynor, the school counselor, and got the contact information for the child psychiatrist. Finally, she cleaned house. She cleared the fridge of junk food and replaced it with fresh vegetables from the Aldi. She attacked the pantry as well—goodbye Pop-Tarts, hello Fruit Roll-Ups. She spent so much time scrubbing the sink and tub in the bathroom that Ellen thought perhaps the fumes from the cheap chlorine cleaner she was using had overcome her, and she'd find Rita passed out on the tile floor, tongue out and eyes bulging.

Ellen knew her mom's modes well, and this was fix-it mode. She'd fixed the apartment, and now she'd fix her kid.

A solemn woman in a grey suit with hair to match stepped from the inner office and beckoned to Rita.

"Ms. Gooding? Please come in."

"Be right back," her mother said, snapping her phone closed. She followed the woman into the office, leaving Ellen alone in the waiting room with the pickers.

We shall come rejoicing, bringing in the sheaves...

She'd stopped trying to block the tune. It was an earworm, and earworms were pernicious buggers. While her mother was out at the grocery store, she'd attempted to look the hymn up on their old laptop, but the computer asked her for a password—something it had never done before. Rita must have locked it down just like she intended to lock down the rest of her daughter's life. Lock it down and put an end to all the mess and foolishness.

Nuts. Without the laptop, how was she supposed to find out what *Blind Rock* was?

Percy farted and raised his eyebrows in surprise at its volume. Ellen picked up a magazine and pretended to read. *Highlights for Children.* How engrossing.

The door to the inner office opened, and her mother emerged, red-faced. She plopped down in the seat next to Ellen and made a motion with her head Ellen couldn't quite interpret.

"What?"

"Go on in," her mother said, putting her wallet back into her purse.

"Aren't you coming in with me?"

"Apparently not."

Confused and in no small way on edge, Ellen rose from her seat and just stood there.

"Go. Go," her mother said, nodding again with her head but this time much more empathically. "I'm sure she's already on the clock."

Ellen moved slowly toward the door, past the bubbling tank with its darting goldfish and swaying, plastic sea plants. She threw a final glance back at her mother, but Rita was already busy with her phone. Ellen was on her own.

* * *

The office was sparse—a sofa, a cushioned chair with a small table next to it upon which sat an open laptop. Despite the mild June weather, a rotating space heater in the corner was up and running, making the small space as hot and stuffy as Burke's Bakery.

"I hope it's not too warm for you," said the woman as she tapped at her computer. "Raynaud's. My hands are always cold."

The image of a fox flitted through Ellen's mind, and she realized she was thinking of *Reynard the Fox*, a children's theater production her father had taken her to on campus. All the characters in the show had been animals, and Ellen thought it was a rather sad affair—the costumes were dingy and the actors lackluster. But she was particularly taken with one of the fables concerning the title character Reynard, the fox, and a crow whose name eluded her. In the story, the fox tricked the crow into singing, thus dropping a bit of cheese that the sly fox quickly snatched up.

"Ellen?"

Ellen snapped back to attention. "Yes?"

"You may sit."

"Okay."

She sat on the sofa, her still-ticking mind conjuring up an image of the woman trying to work her laptop with fox paws.

"I've spoken with your mother, and now I'd like to speak with you. Does that sound good to you?"

No.

"Yes."

"Fine. As I told you during our pre-interview on the phone yesterday, my name is Dr. Rankin, and I'm a child psychiatrist. Do you know what a psychiatrist is?"

"A shrink?"

Dr. Rankin smiled. "We don't use that term in this office. A psychiatrist is a physician who helps people learn how to deal with life's difficult situations."

"Okay."

"What sets my practice apart from that of a psychologist is that I have the good fortune of being able to prescribe medication should I think it warranted. Are you with me so far?"

"Yes." Ellen scratched at the neckline of her black sweatshirt.

Dr. Rankin smiled again. "Good. Are you sure you aren't too warm?"

Yes, I'm too warm. It's like a furnace in here, lady.

"I'm fine."

"All right. So, why don't you tell me why you think you're here?"

"Mom brought me."

"Yes, but why do you think you're here?"

The woman was already making notes on her laptop.

Laptop. Top hat. Pad paw. Fox foot.

The heater rotated and blasted Ellen's legs with hot breath.

Fox paw. Foxfire. Firefighter. Fireman. Burning man. Burning man. Burning man. Burn.

"Because I pushed a girl at school."

"Why did you do that?"

Because she was about to walk straight through another person, that's why!

"I don't know," Ellen said, opting for the less-is-more approach. "My mom said I had a fit."

"We don't use that term in this office. I prefer the word, episode."

"Like TV?"

Dr. Rankin smiled and shifted in her seat. "How about if I ask you some questions—"

"I am a little warm."

"Fine. I'll turn the heater down—"

"Can you turn it off?"

"Off completely?"

"Yes. It makes a whining noise whenever it turns counterclockwise."

"And you find that distracting?"

Yes, don't you? And you're tapping on the keyboard—tap-tap-tap. Why not use a pen and a notepad? And aren't the lights driving you crazy? They sound like angry bees.

"No."

"Then you won't mind if I just turn it down a bit. Like I said, cold hands…"

Warm heart. Where had she heard that phrase? From Dad, probably. Almost everything worth remembering was about him.

"Fine," Ellen said.

The woman rose and dialed down the heat, but the whine remained.

"Let's continue. Ellen, what were you doing right before this episode at school took place?"

"I was in the hallway."

"Yes, but what were you *doing* in the hallway?" *Tap-tap* went her keyboard.

"I was…"

"Yes?"

Ellen grit her teeth and turned her head. For besides the tap of computer keys, the whine of the heater and the buzz of

44

the lights, there was another sound working its way into the mix, and this noise was more distracting than all the others combined.

"Ellen?"

It was sobbing. At first, Ellen thought Dr. Rankin might have a second office next door where another doctor was holding a session with a patient—a patient in so much distress she could hear their cries through the wall.

"You know, sometimes we act out when we're feeling a lot of stress. Can you think of anything that might be causing you stress?"

The sobbing grew louder and louder, making it hard to concentrate on Dr. Rankin.

"Why don't I give us a jumping off point? Shall we talk about your father?"

It's her. *It's the doctor. She's the one crying.*

"Ellen? Let's talk about your father."

"What do you want to know?"

"Why don't you just tell me the first thing that pops into your head when you think of the word *father.*"

Ellen closed her eyes, and something *did* pop into her head, but it had nothing to do with her father. No, the thought didn't belong to her at all.

"Roller coaster."

"Good. What do you mean by that? Can you elaborate?"

"Up and down all the time. Like a roller coaster."

"You mean emotionally up and down?"

"Yes."

"Mood swings?"

"Yes."

Tap-tap went the keyboard.

"So, tell me, Ellen, how did these mood swings of his make you feel?"

"Like I couldn't do anything about them. Like I should be able to, but I just couldn't."

"That's understandable. But I must tell you, that as a child—"

The faucet that had been dripping inside Ellen's head suddenly gushed. "I should have been able to help him. I watched him closely, took him into my own home. Medicated him. I'm a psychiatrist, for Christ's sake."

Dr. Rankin flinched, but Ellen took no note of this as the doctor's thoughts poured from her mouth.

"He said he was feeling better. For the first time in a long time. He even started cooking again. Lasagna, my favorite!"

"Ellen…"

"Why did he have to do that? Why? And in my house, in my home! All those pills…all the mess. Daddy, I'm sorry. I'm so, so sorry!"

"That's enough!" The woman rose, shoving her chair back against the wall.

"I'm *so* sorry!"

"Let's take five," Dr. Rankin said, shutting her down. She stepped out of the room and closed the door so hard the artwork on the wall trembled.

Ellen breathed deep and shook the foreign thoughts from her head. Glad that Dr. Rankin was at least momentarily leaving her be, Ellen took advantage of the fact that the woman's laptop was open.

She slipped over to the computer, quickly clicked out of the note-taking program and launched Netscape. Fingers flying, she typed the words *Blind Rock* into the search box. Hundreds of results came back, none of them leaping out at her as relevant.

Where did the garage sale guy say he bought the recorder? In Illinois?

She added *Illinois* to her search and came up with a cluster of results that appeared to mirror each other. She clicked on the first one.

Blind Rock Interview: Pat Porter (RealMedia Format)

There was an arrow underneath that bid her click it, which she did. A deep voice sounded from the laptop's small speakers.

"The Massacre at Blind Rock remains, to this day, one of the least understood chapters in Maple City history. In 1894, the Church of the Harvest community was thriving. By 1895, they no longer—"

The audio froze. An error message popped up on the screen. No matter what Ellen did to try to close the offending webpage, it remained.

She heard her mother's voice on the other side of the door. Mom was upset—what else was new—and arguing with the doctor.

Ellen frantically searched the webpage for any other bit of info she could glean and found it in the page's title bar.

Maple City Library • Maple City, Illinois

Dr. Rankin opened the door. "Get away from my computer, please."

Ellen obeyed, wary of the stern woman but warier still of her mother who hovered in the doorway.

"Let's go," Rita snapped. "Eighty bucks down the drain."

Ellen gave the woman in the suit a final glance as she followed her mother out of the room. Dr. Rankin did not return the favor.

* * *

The ride home was even more tense than the drive to the clinic. And since there was no promise the mood would lighten anytime soon, Ellen decided to blurt out her request.

"I want to go see Aunt Tuffy."

"Fine," her mother said, eyes on the road.

"I still have some birthday money left. A Greyhound bus to Burlington only costs—"

"I said fine. I'll set it up."

It had been easier than she had thought. Not a single objection. The hard part now would be to somehow switch buses, travel to Maple City *instead* of Burlington and still make it to Aunt Tuffy's without arousing either her aunt's or her mother's suspicion…well, she'd cross those bridges when she came to them.

Having ripped off the Band-Aid, Ellen ventured a step further.

"Don't you ever miss Dad?"

Her mother stiffened. "If you wanted to talk about your father, you should have done so with the doctor."

Neither said a word for the rest of the drive, and when they got back home, Ellen pulled out her backpack and started packing.

CHAPTER 6

When Peter next opened his eyes, he was lying prone on a pew. He sat up quickly, and the blood rushed from his head, making him momentarily woozy. He dropped back down, the back of his skull hitting the wooden pew with a *thunk.*

Twin chortles of laughter answered his pained grimace.

"Clunk!" came a little girl's voice.

"Clunk!" came a little boy's.

Peter tried rising again, easing himself up this time, listening to his joints pop. He squinted and tried to adjust his eyes in the dim light.

The children—there were five in all—hovered nearby. The girl with the dark eyes, the tallest of the bunch, stood the closest keeping careful note of his every move. Her bird, however, was nowhere to be seen.

"Hi," the little boy said. He was no more than five, and he was bundled up against the chill in the room with what looked like two layers of sweaters. A girl his same age, similarly dressed, gave him a shove.

"Don't talk to strangers."

"I wasn't talking. I said *hi.*"

"*Hi* is talking."

"Quiet, you two," an older boy said. The kid was a lanky teen with a long shock of hair hanging down over his face. He kept his distance, flicking a cheap lighter on and off, on and off. The very picture of youthful angst.

A troubled moan came from behind Peter, and he turned to find a skinny boy hobbling his way. The boy sported twin forearm crutches that assisted his twisted legs. He held tight to a rope leash, the end of which looped about the neck of a scrawny, old mutt whose legs were as challenged as the boy's. The kid's head lolled to the side, his body curved into a question mark. His clothes hung loosely about him, reminding Peter of a scarecrow.

"It's okay, Curly," the older girl said. "Papa will sort it out."

The boy shot her an anxious look but nodded all the same.

The dog barked at the ceiling, and Peter looked up to find the girl's bird circling above. A slow, lazy circle like a vulture guarding its prey.

"Whisper! To me!" The girl held up her arm, and the bird descended. It swooped past Peter's head, so close in fact, he could hear the ruffle of feathers as it passed. The crow homed in on the girl's upstretched arm and alighted there, gripping her forearm tightly with its talons.

Then a curious thing happened. The bird tightroped its way up the girl's arm and stuck its beak into her hair. If Peter didn't know better, he'd think the bird was whispering to her.

"Thank you," the girl said, giving the bird a kiss on the beak.

She threw her head back. The bird squawked and bowed its head. It crumpled in on itself, dissolving in a puff of smoke, and the girl breathed in the cloud of crow.

No, she didn't, that's impossible, she didn't breathe *it in.*

"He's dirty," said the little girl, staring at Peter.

51

"He's messy," echoed the boy.

"I already said that."

"No, you didn't, you said he was dirty."

"You're dirty."

"No, *you're* dirty!"

Peter rose. The two little ones stepped back, as unsure of him as they would be of a panther in their midst. But the tall girl—a young woman actually, he noted—stepped forward.

"Where am I? How did I get here?"

"I conjured you."

"You…"

"It's her trick, you know?" the lanky boy said, seemingly already bored with the conversation. "Her thing? It's what she does."

"I don't understand."

The boy clapped his hands loudly, causing the skinny boy with the crutches to jump. "Poof! You're here. Poof! You're gone." He turned to the older girl. "Time to make him gone, Willa."

The girl, Willa, shook her head. "He's not…I didn't call him. He just sort of…showed up."

"You brought him here, you can send him back."

"I don't think I can—"

"Hey!" Peter shouted, his voice echoing off the walls. "Where am I?"

A gruff voice from the back of the church answered. "You're in the Church of the Harvest, my friend. And you are most welcome."

Peter turned, and for a second he could swear he was standing in the presence of Santa Claus.

CHAPTER 7

Much to Ellen's relief, the Greyhound station was bustling on Thursday morning. She'd been banking on a crowd to help give her cover while she pulled her "old switcheroo," as she fancied her scheme. The "old switcheroo" was a favorite of her father's. He'd tell her they were off to listen to a lecture on modern art, and they'd end up at the roller skating rink. The "old switcheroo" rocked.

Her mother remained oddly aloof as they entered the building that smelled of bus fumes and freshly-mopped floors. She even let Ellen purchase the round-trip ticket herself.

There were four agents working the ticket booths, and Ellen chose a man with enormous, wiry eyebrows. Those eyebrows would be easy to remember later.

"You traveling alone, kid?" the ticket agent asked. He was brusque man and his eyebrows danced as he spoke.

Ellen was prepared for this. "Yes. And my mom has my form. Mom?"

Her mother looked up from her phone. "What's the problem?"

"My unaccompanied form? The one you filled out?"

Rita nodded, fished a folded paper from her purse and stuck it through the slot to the agent.

"Says here you're twelve," the ticket agent said, eyeing Ellen.

"My birthday was last Saturday." Keep to the truth as much as possible when lying—that was something her mother taught her.

"This child's twelve?" the agent asked Rita.

Her mother rolled her eyes, and Ellen felt instantly sorry for the man behind the glass. After a diatribe laced with four-letter words and threats to call corporate, Rita grabbed the proffered tickets and handed them to her daughter.

As they walked to the gate, Ellen couldn't help but admire her mother's skill. But it didn't come without practice. Ellen's age had varied anywhere from nine to fourteen over the past year, depending on the situation and how her mother wanted to play it. Today, she was twelve instead of eleven, and it made her somehow feel a bit braver. Braver by one year, at least.

Her mother handed her a phone card. "You're going to call me as soon as Tuffy picks you up, you hear me?"

"Yes."

"Don't forget. You know how you are."

"I won't forget. Don't *you* forget the recycling."

"Shit."

"It's Thursday."

"Don't you think I know that?"

They approached the gate where the Burlington bus sat parked, awaiting its passengers.

"Can't believe you wore this thing again," her mother said, tugging on Ellen's new favorite black sweatshirt. "You've got your tickets?"

"Yes."

"You sure?"

"Yes."

"Tell me what you do if a stranger approaches you."

Ellen thought for a moment. "Scream?"

"No! Just tell the bus driver."

"Okay."

"Don't scream. What's wrong with you?"

Five minutes later, the driver had yet to arrive. Ellen could tell her mother was growing eager to be on her way. "Where is this guy?"

"Why don't I just get on?"

"Okay." Her mother leaned in for an unaccustomed hug before quickly stepping away. "You're going to call—"

"As soon as I get there."

Satisfied, and obviously eager to kick her child-free weekend into gear, Rita Gooding shooed her daughter onto the bus and headed back into the terminal.

Ellen scampered up the stairs and into the empty bus. She took a seat next to the window so she could wave at her mother should she look back. She didn't.

Ellen checked her watch. It was an old Rolex knockoff she'd found in the park one day, and she kept it looped about a carabiner attached to her backpack. 8:19 am. Perfect. The bus to Davenport left at 8:30 and there was only a twenty-minute wait until the connecting bus left Davenport and headed to Maple City.

She had worked out the plan—and its multiple variations—in her head over the past few days. It was a welcome relief to plot her escape to the Maple City Library. Whenever her brain went idle, the ghostly choir would set up house, droning on endlessly about their damn sheaves. And the voice that cried *Blind Rock! Ellen!* would pound behind her eyes, knocking insistently, demanding entrance.

Why was she doing this? Why not wait out the choir and the voice and let them slip back into the ether?

Because Dad sent me a birthday card.

He'd promised her she would find something to buy with his money, and boy, had she picked a winner. The connection between the card and the recorder and her bus trip were tenuous at best, but it was all she had to go on. And, in an odd way, it felt practical to her. And Ellen was all about practicality.

If I go, I'm following Dad's lead; if I don't…

She paused. What would be the consequences of inaction? Not much. The summer would roll on, she would spend half of it haunting the university library, the other half trying to avoid her mother's moods. Sixth grade would come into view, then seventh, then eighth, then…

Then Dad will fade away completely.

Ellen rose. Time to get moving.

Step One: exchange her tickets. She had the twenty to pay for the change fee ready and waiting in her pocket.

Step Two: get to a phone. She'd noticed there were fewer and fewer payphones on the streets of Iowa City, but here at the bus station they were plentiful. As were kiosks selling phone cards, laundry bags, travel-sized toiletries. Catering to the itinerant crowd.

Step Three: call Aunt Tuffy. Her mom's sister was an old softie. She let Ellen watch all the TV she wanted, kept a ceramic bowl filled with salted licorice candies—Ellen's favorite—and always slipped her a few bucks to spend at the old office supply store where she worked the register.

The schedule Ellen had snagged showed a connection between Maple City and Burlington arriving later that evening. She would call and tell her aunt the bus had mechanical problems and she'd be arriving this evening instead of this morning. And Aunt Tuffy would believe her, bless her. Her mom's older sister was the type who replied to spam and listened to door-to-door evangelists. Her niece would *never* lie to her. *Never.*

This step required a bit of faith. Mom was having Bo over for a redo of their interrupted date. Once Ellen called her from Davenport, saying she was in Burlington with Aunt Tuffy, her mother would be free and clear to do…whatever with her mailman friend.

Ellen had Steps Four, Five and beyond mapped out in her head, but getting on with the first few were of primary importance and would involve some of the most serious concentration.

She reentered the terminal and headed for the ticket booths. She paused for a moment to make sure old Bushy Eyebrows was helping another traveler before approaching a petite ticket agent who was eating a breakfast sandwich.

"I need to change my tickets. My aunt's meeting me in Maple City instead." Ellen shoved the tickets through the slot along with her unaccompanied minor form and a twenty.

The woman wiped her mouth with a napkin and looked at the tickets. "When did you buy these?"

"This morning. But my aunt just called my mom…" Ellen nodded toward a woman, her faux mother, leaning against a column reading a USA Today. "And now I have to go to Maple City, instead."

57

Do it. Do it. Come on, just do it.

"Vern!" The woman held up the tickets and waved them toward the man with the wiry eyebrows. "I have a ticket exchange."

Shit.

Mr. Eyebrows held up a finger, indicating he was busy with his current customer. Ellen's agent shook her head.

"They changed the policy about exchanges. Always changing things. I think you can change date and time, but not…hold on…Vern!"

"In a minute!" was the reply.

Ellen suddenly had to pee, something that always happened when she got nervous. The eyebrowed agent was wrapping up with his current customer, so Ellen decided to run with it.

"I've got to pee."

"Yo, Vern!"

"I gotta pee. I gotta pee, I gotta pee, I gotta pee…" Ellen strung the words together like rapid machine gun fire, demanding the ticket agent's attention.

The woman turned back to her. "Just a moment. I need to—"

"I-gotta-pee-I-gotta-pee-I-gotta-pee-I-gotta-pee-I-gotta…" Ellen's voice rose in pitch and desperation. The repetition felt good in her mouth, and she let it ride. She drummed on the counter with her fingers and let her eyes go wide.

The woman behind the glass held up her hands. "Fine. I'll just void them. Maple City, you said?"

Ellen nodded frantically. "I gotta pee, I gotta…!"

"Here." The woman took Ellen's twenty and stuffed the new tickets through the slot. "Women's room is over there," she said, pointing. "Jesus Christ."

Ellen snatched the tickets and made a mad dash for the restrooms. As she rounded the corner into the women's room, she glanced back. The man with the eyebrows was chatting with her ticket agent. And he was looking her way.

She barreled into the restroom and slipped into a stall. Her heart was racing as she peed.

Slow down. Breathe. You don't have time to panic. Blow your nose, wash your hands, get to a phone.

Ellen grabbed a wad of toilet paper and blew her nose. After flushing, she stepped from the stall and came face to face with the female ticket agent.

Busted.

"You forgot this," the woman said, holding out the unaccompanied minor form.

"Thanks," Ellen said, swiping the paper from the woman's hands and heading for the door.

"You're welcome," came the sarcastic response.

Phone.

Ellen circled around a newsstand to a bank of payphones just out of sight of the ticket counter. She extracted the phone card and scratched the strip on the back, exposing the lengthy code necessary to place a call. She punched in the string of numbers and waited for Aunt Tuffy to pick up.

"Hello, Gooding residence."

"Hi, Aunt Tuffy. It's Ellen."

"Oh, Ellen! I'm so looking forward to your visit—"

"Me too. But my bus is having problems, and they have to get a new one."

"Oh, dear."

"So, I won't be coming in until later tonight."

"Oh, dear. I was hoping I could take you to the Perkins for lunch—"

"You can pick me up at 7:45 tonight, okay?"

"That's fine. The Perkins stays open late. We can—"

"I'll see you tonight, okay? At 7:45."

"I'll be there."

Ellen hung up before the conversation could get away from her.

She stopped off at the newsstand, bought some Red Hots for the road and headed off to Gate 22, where the 8:30 bus to Maple City sat waiting. She hopped aboard with a couple of other passengers and took a window seat halfway down the aisle.

Blind Rock...

The voice was just a whisper, but it was there.

"Yeah, Blind Rock, I know. Shut up, already," Ellen said as she popped a handful of hot cinnamon candies into her mouth and waited for the bus to depart.

CHAPTER 8

Peter squinted to better see the approaching man.

"The weather's restless out there," the fellow said. "That's the only word for it. Restless."

No, the man was *not* Santa, although his bushy beard definitely gave him a Father Christmas vibe. He was wearing a bulky calfskin jacket and an old fedora. His boots were high and covered in snow, which he had tracked into the church. What struck Peter most profoundly were his eyes. They twinkled behind his wire-rimmed glasses. There was no fear or concern in those eyes as they assessed the newcomer—just curiosity.

"Papa!" the two youngest children cried as they rushed the man, throwing their arms about his legs.

"Whoa, now. You're going to knock me over." The man bent down to the young boy. "Have you been good, Huck?"

"Yes, Papa."

"And you, Jo?"

"I've been the best!"

"Well, if you say so." The man dug into his pockets and came out with a handful of wrapped candies, which the children descended upon like ravenous dogs.

Maybe I was wrong. Maybe he is *Santa.*

"You're going to rot their teeth," Willa said, crossing her arms.

"I wouldn't be so quick to scold, Willa," the man said. "I wasn't the one who let a stranger into the church."

"We locked him up!" the little girl Jo said through a mouthful of toffee.

"But he got out!" Huck added.

"Is that so?" The man approached Peter, sizing him up. "Where'd you put him?"

"In the shed," Willa said, defensively. "He shouldn't have been able to get out—"

"But he did," the lanky boy said with a sneer. "I told you that shed ain't worth shit."

"Language, boy," the man admonished. "I don't mind 'shit,' but I can't abide 'ain't.'"

The skinny boy with the crutches approached the man, the rat-haired dog hugging his side. He mouthed a few words Peter couldn't make out, but that the old fellow could obviously understand.

"Oh, she did, did she?" He turned to Willa. "So, this isn't just some passing stranger you've let into our house. This is one of your strays?"

"No, Papa."

"You didn't draw him forth—"

"Yes, I did, but…he's not one of mine. I know mine. He's something different."

"Excuse me." Peter waved his arms above his head, eager to grab the man's attention. "I'd like to go home now."

"And where might that be? Your home?" the man asked.

Peter opened his mouth and his mind went instantly blank. He felt like he was teetering on the edge of an abyss—one more step and he'd tumble into nothingness.

62

"You won't fall. I've got you."

The voice that filled the empty space inside was the same one that had visited him in the shed. The voice was reassuring.

"I don't know," Peter said.

"That might prove a bit of a problem," the man said. "And what might your name be?"

"Peter."

"My name's Fallow, Peter. But the children call me Papa, so I suppose that's Papa Fallow to you."

"Fallow."

"Don't worry. We're going to get you sorted out. Agreed?"

"Agreed."

"Good." Papa Fallow grinned. "Do you like pancakes, Peter?"

CHAPTER 9

Ellen had both seats to herself during the ride from Iowa City to Davenport, as did most passengers on the bus. She put her feet up on the empty seat, admiring the chunky shoes she'd chosen for the trip. They added a good half inch to her height and were comfy as hell. And they were black.

Her mother didn't understand black, would always ask why she preferred black to, say, green or blue or pink. Ellen would reply that black was the negation of color, that it calmed her and eased her many tics. It was and it did, but that wasn't the full story. Ellen loved black because she felt protected in it.

Ever since her chat with the dead boy named Treat, others had sought her out. Not actively, but they tended to want to hang around like pesky insects. Like the time when she went to the grocery store with her mother, and the stock boy who'd been crushed by the delivery truck followed her through the fresh produce section. Or when the cop who'd been shot while arresting a neighbor at the University Arms wandered up and down their landing, passing their door a couple dozen times before disappearing when her mother came home.

Like the young man in the John Deere cap slowly making his way down the aisle to where she was sitting.

Gimme a break, dude.

Ellen unfolded the bus schedule and pretended to read, ignoring the guy's gaze. When he finally slid into the seat across the aisle from hers, she'd had enough.

"What's your damage?" she whispered, careful not to wake the elderly woman sleeping in the seat behind her.

"That driver. I don't think he likes me," said the young man in the cap.

"So what?"

"If he liked me, he would have pulled over."

"I'm trying to read—"

"After he ran me off the road. He should have pulled over."

Ellen looked up at the man and wished she hadn't. It wasn't the fact his John Deere cap was the only thing keeping his head in one piece, or that a couple of ribs were poking out of his t-shirt. It was the needful look on his face. The desperate desire for connection she saw there.

"Sorry," she said and resumed her fake reading.

"He doesn't like me!"

Suddenly, a snapshot of the young man's death popped into her head. A ruined pickup truck and a gash in the earth at the side of the road. The pickup lay upside down, its cabin crushed, rear wheels spinning.

Ellen shoved the image aside and pointed an insistent finger at the man.

"Fuck off!"

It was not a phrase she could recall ever actually saying aloud, and she said it with much more force than she had intended, but it did the trick. The young man didn't so much disappear as he simply wasn't there anymore. Like he hadn't been there in the first place.

She caught the driver staring back at her in the rearview mirror, and heard the old woman sitting behind her stir.

"Bad dream, honey?"

"Yes," Ellen answered.

"I get them all the time. Ever since my Wendal passed. Last night's was a doozy. I remember I was flying over Chicago…"

Ellen endured half an hour of the woman's prattle, but it was a welcome relief from the dead man's company. When the bus pulled into the station at Davenport, the woman offered her a religious tract with *This Was Your Life!* on the cover along with a cartoon sketch of a man and an angel staring into the night sky.

"The Lord be with you," the woman said as Ellen stuffed the tract into her backpack.

The bus had arrived late, so she had only ten minutes to make her call and get to her connecting bus to Maple City.

She threw a glance back at the driver as she descended the stairs and thought, *I know what you did.* The driver was busy checking his phone, and so Ellen left the man and his secret behind and trotted off for the station.

The Davenport depot was more sparse than Iowa City's, and the bright-red, neon swirls on the ceiling made the place seem more like a food court than a bus station. After striking out on two out-of-order payphones, she found one that worked and called home. The trip from Iowa City to Burlington was supposed to last an hour and twenty-five minutes, so their late arrival actually worked to the benefit of her subterfuge. Even so, her mom seemed on especially high alert the moment she answered the phone.

"You got in early. Those buses are never on time."

"Well, I'm here."

"Put Tuffy on."

"She's getting the car."

"Well, tell her to go easy with the black licorice. Remember last time?"

"I remember."

"You had diarrhea for two days."

Ellen heard music in the background and a mumbled male voice. Rita had wasted no time inviting Bo over.

"I gotta go," Ellen said, adding, "I gotta *pee*." Heck, if it worked once…

"Go. Be good. Call me tomorrow."

The line went dead.

She was rewarding herself with the last of her Red Hots when, through the big glass windows, she saw the bus to Maple City shutting its door.

Ellen choked down the mouthful of candy and raced for the exit.

The driver was none too pleased to have to open up again. "Ticket," was all he had to say.

Maple City, or points farther down the route, were popular destinations here in Davenport. The bus was crammed full. Ellen managed to find an aisle seat next to a chubby businessman with salt and pepper hair who smelled of booze. The man removed his briefcase from the seat next to him with a grunt.

The bus pulled out, and they were soon crossing over the Mississippi River into Illinois, through Rock Island and the decaying burg of Milan—which locals pronounced *My-lun*—before once more hitting the highway, this time a two-lane stretch snaking into the heart of the prairie. The desolate expanse of empty fields gave Ellen an empty feeling in the pit of her stomach.

She pulled the religious tract the old woman had given her from her pack and leafed through it. It was a black-and-white comic book depicting a man's death, his judgment and his eventual redemption. And even though the story was told through cartoons, it was still profoundly disturbing. One panel showed the man clutching his chest—the obvious victim of a heart attack—while the Grim Reaper stood by, sickle at the ready. The verse below it was just as foreboding.

But God said unto him, thou fool, this night thy soul shall be required of thee.

The businessman let out a snort. Ellen looked over at him and saw he had fallen asleep with his head pressed up against the window. His mouth hung open, evidence of his liquid breakfast condensing on the glass.

Ellen unzipped her backpack to stuff the tract inside when a glint of plastic within caught her eye. She reached in and touched the lone reel of tape she'd recovered from her garage sale purchase. The one marked *Hymns (30 min).*

She unwound a short length of the tape from the reel and let the smooth ribbon run between her fingers. She wondered if the burning man had ever listened to this tape, and somehow she knew he had. Sitting alone in his garage with beer in hand, the recorder spinning out the collective voice of the choir. Ellen pulled the tape taut on the reel and a small piece broke free, giving way with a brittle snap.

She looked once more at the businessman to make certain he still slumbered. For Ellen had a sudden, strong urge to *eat* the tape.

CHAPTER 10

Peter sat with the children around the old farm table in the little office turned kitchenette at the rear of the church. Two of the room's walls were lined with built-in bookcases—floor to ceiling in height and overstuffed with books.

Fallow insisted he sit at the head of the table. "You are our guest, after all!"

The man had removed his coat, revealing a threadbare wool sweater underneath. Whatever care he took to ensure the children were dressed in decent clothes didn't apply to him.

"Ah, pancakes! My favorite," the grizzled gent said as he poured another dollop of batter onto the electric griddle.

"Mine too!" shouted Jo.

"I don't like pancakes," Huck said, sulking.

"Yes, you do."

"No, I don't, Jo. I don't."

"You do, you'll see."

"I wish pancakes never were."

"You'll like these, believe me, Huck," said Fallow as he deftly flipped the cakes. "They're special."

"They are?"

"You betcha. These are *midnight* pancakes." Fallow winked at Peter. "Pancakes taste a whole heck of a lot better at midnight."

"I want one," Huck said, holding up his plate.

"You said you didn't want any," Jo said.

"I never!"

Fallow turned back to the table and proceeded to dish two pancakes onto Peter's plate.

"Really, I couldn't—"

"You can and you will," Fallow said, waving him off. "These jokers can wait their turn. Like I said, you're our guest."

Willa, who had been assisting the old man by mixing the batter, sat next to Peter and set a plastic bottle of syrup before him. He nodded in thanks and poured a brown S across the short stack.

"Let me introduce my brood, Peter. You've met Willa."

Peter nodded. Willa had something to do with why he was here, at least that's what the others thought. He scribbled her name down in his head so he wouldn't forget. *Willa.*

Fallow pointed at the lanky kid at the far end of the table who was doing his best not to be a part of the discussion. "And that ray of sunshine is our Dodger. Dodge for short."

"Dodger?" Peter said. "Like…from Dickens?"

"We have a literate man, here, children. Yes, from Dickens. He's our Dodger, though not so artful, eh Dodge?" The man laughed, and the boy blushed, hating the attention. Fallow set pancakes on the two youngest children's plates. "And these two ragamuffins are Huck and Jo. Huck from Twain, of course, and Jo—"

"From *Little Women,*" Jo said, digging into her food.

The skinny boy wiggled in his seat for attention.

"Down there is my Curly."

"Curly? From Steinbeck?" Peter asked.

"More like the Three Stooges."

Curly crooned with laughter, and dug his hand into the old dog's matted coat with unrestrained glee, causing it to whimper.

"Ease up on that dog, boy, or I'll find him a new home," Fallow warned. His words brought a sudden chill to the room Peter was eager to dispel.

"What's his name?"

"We should call him Harry 'cause he's so hairy," Jo said.

"No, we should call him Jerry," Huck countered.

Curly squirmed, making it clear he had no interest in either of their suggestions.

"Oh, he's just a stray that came in from the cold. Like you, Peter. We're suckers for strays around here." Fallow winked again and set two heaping plates of pancakes on the table before seating himself.

"Is this a…" Peter didn't want to presume, but he had to know. "An orphanage?"

"Hardly," said Fallow, filling up his own plate. "We're a family here, aren't we, kids?" The children murmured their acknowledgment. "Each kid gets a new name and a fresh start. Plenary guardianship—nothing temporary around here, no sir."

"And…" Peter continued, ignoring his meal. "You live here? In this church?"

Fallow nodded. "Yes, we do. The Church of the Harvest. Or so it used to be called before the congregation scattered to the winds. We just bunk here. I split up the meeting rooms. One for the boys, one for the gals. Snug as bugs, that's us." He leaned in conspiratorially. "Saves us a fortune in taxes. I'm a certified minister of the Universal Life Church. Answered an ad in *Rolling Stone*. Just have to pretend to have services every so often, but I've got that covered in case anyone comes snooping about. Added benefit? I can legally marry folks in the great State of Illinois. So, if you ever need to get hitched—"

"No, no. I'm already…"

That same blankness came to the fore, and Peter was staring into an empty room where memories once lived. The world was full of holes drawing him toward their hungry depths. He caught his breath and gripped the table.

"Give him some water." Fallow nodded to Willa, who filled a glass and handed it to Peter. Peter gulped it down, coughing out as much as he drank. Fallow slapped him on the back. "Easy, cowboy."

"I…I don't know what I'm doing here. I don't…I don't know anything," Peter said, speaking the only truth he knew at the moment.

"That's okay."

"No, it's not."

Fallow leaned back in his seat and smoothed his beard. After chewing at the sides of his mustache for a bit, he turned to the table.

"Well? Anyone wanna give it a shot?" His words were vague, but his tone was knowing, and the children responded to it as if Fallow had spoken volumes.

"Not me!" shouted Huck.

"Nope!" said Jo.

Curly turned away, opting to scratch his old dog's ears instead.

Fallow looked to Willa. "I think," she said slowly, "I think maybe…Dodge?"

"What do you say, Dodge?" Fallow stared down the boy, insisting he return his gaze.

"Why me?"

"Because we all pull our weight in this family. You know that."

Dodge let out an exasperated breath and rose from the table. "Fine." He shoved his chair back in place, startling Curly's dog.

"What's going on?" Peter asked as the whole crew got up around him and followed Dodge out of the room. "Where are you going?"

Fallow didn't answer, instead beckoning Peter back into the main room of the church. Peter rose and followed, the last to leave save for Curly, who brought up the rear, his grey mutt trailing after.

When they were all gathered in the main room, the group formed a semicircle around the reluctant Dodge. The wind whistled through cracks in the walls, and Peter could swear the church shifted perceptibly under the force of the storm.

Dodge removed first his sweater, then his shirt. He stood with his back to the group, his backbone standing out in sharp relief. He paused, and then bent down as if in genuflection.

"What's he doing?" Peter asked, feeling suddenly lightheaded.

"Trying to help you," Willa said. She took Peter's arm and steadied him.

Another wave of unease rolled over Peter as he watched the boy's body distort, turning angular, his shoulder blades shifting to unnatural positions. Pressure began to build in

Peter's ears and he was suddenly nauseous, the very sight of Dodge's contortions causing his gullet to rise.

The boy's flesh split, exposing his backbone, and Dodge let loose a rapid chuffing sound as if he were working through great pain.

Of course, he's in pain! Just look at him.

"Stop it!" Peter cried. "How in God's name is this supposed to help?"

"Wait," was all Fallow said in reply.

Young Jo shrieked. And well she should, for working its way out of Dodge's back were a pair of thin, black pincers.

Something's crawling out of him, Peter realized, his mind threatening to revolt.

A horrible, chitinous head emerged from the boy's ravaged back and stared across the room at him with bulbous eyes. Peter felt his teeth vibrate in his head as the creature's thoughts burrowed into his mind.

I see nothing. The voice of the mad thing was like rock grinding on rock. *He is a void.*

Peter screamed.

"Calm yourself," Fallow said, and even at his words, the warped vision before him slipped back into place. There was no creature, the boy's back was not breached. The proof was standing before him—Dodge was standing before him. The boy even gave him a shy wave as if in apology before retrieving his discarded clothes.

But the damage to Peter's sanity had been done, and he laughed as if laughing could save him from this place. And when Fallow approached him, put his hands on him, Peter shoved him aside and made a dash for the door. Warning voices entreated him to stop, but escape was the only thing on his untethered mind.

I want to go home! To her! I want to go...

He threw open the door and stepped into the waiting arms of the storm.

CHAPTER 11

"Make up your damn mind," mumbled the sleeping businessman slumped next to Ellen, his head thumping against the window each time the bus hit a bump. "Make up…make…"

Ellen examined the short bit of tape—shiny on one side, matte on the other—and wondered what magnetic sounds it might contain. The piano? The choir? Or maybe the voice calling out, *Ellen! Blind Rock! Ellen!*

The urge to eat the thing she held between her fingers was not a new one. It was not, as her limited research on the subject had turned up, pica. Pica was a mental disorder where people developed an appetite for non-food substances such as stones or hair or glass. No, her need to taste the tape had less to do with the thing itself and more to do with what she might draw from it. She'd done the same with one of her father's gloves after he'd gone missing, chewing on the fingertips in order to catch glimpses of him driving the car or carrying books to his office.

Sounds like pica to me.

She waved the thought away. She had no patience for such brain chatter at the moment.

The bus slowed as it passed through the tiny town of Preemption half an hour south of Davenport. The town's main street *was* the highway, and old brick buildings lined either side of the road—a boarded up bank, a barber shop complete with a barber smoking on the sidewalk, an old general store left to rot.

Ellen rolled the tape between her fingers into a ball. The tape kept wanting to expand, but Ellen held it tight.

Swallow it down and be done with it.

Ellen obeyed.

With one last glance at the sleeping businessman, she popped the ball of tape into her mouth.

It tastes like smoke.

The tape unfurled and lay flat on her tongue. Ellen ran her tongue against the roof of her mouth, wetting the strip of tape, hoping it might offer up some of its secrets. Like a communion wafer, she supposed. Her family wasn't religious, but Aunt Tuffy certainly was. Tuffy was a devout Lutheran who had slipped her a wafer one Sunday when she'd secreted Ellen to church.

"I know Rita never had you baptized, but I'm sure the good Lord won't mind."

But aside from her memory of her aunt, putting the tape into her mouth brought Ellen no insight. Instead, it made her feel profoundly silly.

Yup. Definitely pica.

She was about to extract the strip of tape when it suddenly dissolved on her tongue, filling her mouth with a bitterness that made her gag. She was about to spit the acrid wad onto the floor when she thought twice. She'd asked for a peek, and perhaps the distasteful flavor was the price.

The world outside the bus went instantly black. She could still feel the road bumping along beneath her, but all points of reference beyond the windows were gone. Snuffed out.

Ellen tried to spit and found her mouth had gone dry. She looked frantically about the bus to see if any of the other passengers were aware of the shift that had taken place. But the other passengers were gone. In their place sat withered, skeletal remains. Seat after seat of desiccated corpses where riders of the Greyhound from Davenport to Maple City once sat. Bared teeth and cavernous eye sockets, mouths agape in wonder and fear.

Slowly turning to her left, Ellen saw the businessman had also been replaced. Instead of the portly man with gin breath, she now sat next to a jawless woman with dead leaves tangled in her matted hair. The woman did not move but simply sat rigid in her seat, bones quaking with every jostle of the bus.

Ice began hitting the windshield, and the temperature inside the bus dropped like a falling elevator. A flurry of snow replaced the darkness, and Ellen felt the bus rise from the pavement, first on two wheels, then on none.

No more! No more, no more, no more!

The bus tilted left, then right. The jawless woman's body leaned toward her, and Ellen scrambled into the aisle, slipping on the ice now covering the floor. She held onto armrests on both sides as she stared forward at the bus's front windshield. The wipers lay dormant, and with no one in the driver's seat, the Greyhound was hurtling blind into the oncoming storm.

* * *

Peter stumbled, righted himself and forged ahead, the wild, wintry blow whipping about him.

"Peter! Come back inside!" cried a voice that grew fainter with every step.

Come back? No way in hell. Better to disappear into the storm than go back and endure the horror he'd just witnessed. Better to disappear along with his last remaining memories, erase himself from existence and find peace.

But was peace what was awaiting him? What if there was nothing but madness? Cold and frozen, locking him into an eternal scream?

He pressed on, the snow rising to his calves and the ice biting his face, hoping against hope he'd happen upon a road, hitch a ride, extract himself from this place.

His foot hit something hard beneath the snow's surface, throwing him off balance. Peter twisted as he fell, landing on his side. Pain shot up his shoulder, causing him to cry out. He looked back at the now-exposed headstone that had tripped him up. Its top half was missing, and it stuck up from the snow like a broken tooth.

Through gusts of white, he could still see the glow of the church door and people silhouetted there. Not a single one was venturing outside, and a moment later, Peter understood why.

A lone voice not far off sounded a single note, a mournful *ahhh* riding the wind. It was followed by another, and another. Soon, the air was filled with a chorus of voices swirling through the snow, rushing toward him, and Peter suddenly wished he were back inside the church.

* * *

The floor beneath Ellen's feet gave way, dissolving like the tape on her tongue. At first, she thought she'd fall through, tumbling down into the tempest. But she didn't. Even as the rest of the bus and its decayed passengers faded about her, she didn't fall. Instead, she rode the squall, twisting and turning in the darkness.

Ellen became aware of the earth below, a snow-covered expanse stretching on for miles. She urged herself lower, and the storm obeyed. Down she crept, descending slowly, watchful her speed not send her plummeting to the ground.

A dark spot stood out in the snow, and she steered toward it, circling. As she drew closer, she saw it was a man. A man crawling in the snow.

Struggling against the force of the wind, Ellen reached out her hand.

* * *

Pure white surrounded Peter, disorienting him. Fingers of ice raked his cheek, frozen breath howled in his ear. He was trapped, cut off, consumed. Faces appeared about him. Angry faces formed by snow and dispelled by gusts. The spirits in the storm aimed to have him, to devour him, and Peter had not the strength to fight back.

"Hold on."

The voice from the shed. It asked for the impossible. He was being eaten alive by the storm.

The air was suddenly alive with a furious blackness and the beating of wings. Sharp cries intermingled with the choir's lament. Talons dug into Peter's chest and yanked him back from oblivion. He was being whisked across the snow, banking off half-buried headstones and rocks, leaving the heart of the storm behind.

When he finally struck the cement steps leading into the church, he looked up dazed. Twin black eyes stared down at him, replaced seconds later by those of the girl, Willa, her bird once more perched upon her shoulder.

"Let's get him inside," said Fallow, as he grabbed Peter by the collar and dragged him from the snow.

* * *

"Excuse me, I've got to get by."

The voice jolted Ellen back to the bus.

A college-aged girl wearing a fleece top and pajama bottoms stood before Ellen in the aisle, staring at her with unmasked annoyance. The girl nodded toward the back of the bus, indicating the bathroom was her intended goal.

Ellen's stomach rebelled, and she turned and raced for the bathroom herself.

CHAPTER 12

"What you need is a good night's sleep." Fallow and Dodge helped Peter into the cramped bedroom near the front of the church, which consisted of a cot similar to the one in the shed, a dresser, a mirror and a wall of empty hooks where parishioners' coats once hung. The former cloakroom was windowless, and a fluorescent halo on the ceiling cast the room in a sickly, green glow. "Beats a night in the shed, I can assure you."

Peter was too weak to argue. Even his mind, which had been spinning, was beginning to shut down, and he was grateful when he felt the stiff cot beneath him.

"Don't nod off just yet," Fallow said. "You and I've got to have a few words first." He motioned for Dodge to leave them be, and the boy joined the rest of the children hovering at the door. "Shoo!" he said, and the kids scattered.

"Something…in the snow," Peter whispered.

"You found that out the hard way, my friend," Fallow said, removing Peter's wet shoes and soaked socks.

"What's out there?"

"Bad news." Fallow leaned so close, his beard tickled Peter's cheek. "These children are my world, you hear me? I'd do anything to protect them. They're special, each and every one of them. Something you'd know, if you hadn't gone off half-cocked. Some folks call them an affront to nature, but I call them family."

Fallow placed a quilt over Peter and actually tucked him in as one would a child.

"They cause worry for both the living and the dead. That's where I come in. I'm their guardian. I stand between them and those who would do them harm. Like those bastards out there in the cold."

"Why…" Peter was fading fast. "Why keep me…"

"You mean why don't I cast you out?" Fallow chuckled. "Well…I may not be as special as my brood, but I can still spot someone with tricks up his sleeve."

The man rolled up Peter's shirt sleeve, revealing the pale skin of his forearm. Fallow gave Peter's arm a swift tap, and something dark squirmed beneath the surface—black worms burrowing into flesh.

"Poor man," Fallow said. "You're all mixed up, aren't you?"

Fallow rose, flicked off the light and shooed the children—who had returned—back into the church's main room.

"Tomorrow in the daylight, we'll chat again. Until then, rest."

Peter lay there for a few minutes, balanced on sleep's fine edge. Rest? How could he rest after what he'd experienced?

A shadow flitted into the room. It danced about the ceiling like a wisp of smoke, slowly curling downward until it lit upon his chest.

Out of the smoke stepped the bird. The girl's crow. It picked its way across the quilt and came to rest on Peter's chest. It stared into his eyes, its head jerkily searching his face.

It remained on watch until Peter succumbed to sleep. And then it flitted off, eager to find comfort in Willa's embrace.

CHAPTER 13

Ellen pressed a button and the toilet flushed, secreting away the slip of tape and a half-digested box of Red Hots.

Someone pounded on the door, and Ellen suspected the girl in the pajama bottoms was not going to be happy with her. She took a handful of water from the faucet and swished out her mouth, but the bitter flavor remained. She'd need a mint to rid herself of the taste of the tape, but she knew there was nothing that could rid her mind of the swirling nightmare she'd just endured. If this is where the road was heading, she wanted no part of it.

She unlatched the door and found the driver, not the girl, awaiting her.

"Maple City. Your stop, right?"

"Yes, sir."

The man winced at the scent wafting from the bathroom. "Are your people here to meet you?"

"Should be," she lied.

"I'm going to have to—"

Ellen interrupted him with a guttural belch—a real one, not one manufactured to get him to back up, though back up he did.

"Get your stuff," the driver said, grimacing.

Ellen followed the driver down the aisle, retrieved her backpack where it sat perched next to the businessman, who was now wide awake and slipping a flask back into his coat pocket.

"How much longer 'til Macomb?" the chubby man asked.

"Twenty minutes, once we get started." The driver was growing impatient. The man wanted to *get on with it.*

Ellen trotted down the stairs and mounted the sidewalk. The bus's door swung shut with a hiss, and the Greyhound pulled quickly away.

I want Mom.

She could always say she accidentally took the wrong bus, that she had run to the restroom, gotten the gates mixed up and ended up in Maple City instead of…

But even as she let the scenario play out in her head, she knew it was a non-starter. Ellen was *not* a stupid girl, nor was she prone to absentmindedness. She'd had her bouts of distraction, that was true, but her mother wouldn't believe for a second her daughter was capable of getting on the wrong bus.

No. It was time to come clean. Because what was the alternative? With every step of this misbegotten adventure, she was moving closer to a life filled with jawless nightmares and ghostly rides through the sky. Closer to madness.

Ellen looked about. The driver had let her off at the small town's square. A circle of park benches surrounded a war monument. The soldier atop the monument faced south, one hand raised to shield his eyes, sword in the other.

Looking beyond the circle, she saw the center of town divided itself up into four quarters. One held the town's local radio station, WRMP; another hosted Midwest Savings and Loan. The third was home to the Donut Haus, a windowless bar with a Budweiser sign hanging out front, and a packing and shipping supply store.

Ellen slipped on her backpack and crossed the street, carefully dodging potholes in her chunky shoes, and headed for quadrant four.

She passed a hobby shop and the old City Hall before pausing in front of the brick façade of the building on her radar.

Maple City Library
Built by Warren County Under the Leadership
of the Maple City Women's League
October 8, 1981

Ellen swung open the power-assisted door, and the scent of fresh paint hit her nose. The old Maple City Library was getting a sprucing up. The sign taped to the checkout desk confirmed this.

Early Closing for Construction.
Check Out by 2:00. Pardon Our Mess!

Early closing? That didn't matter to Ellen. By 2:00, her runaway status would be confirmed, and her mother would be on the road heading east, cursing her only daughter. Ellen would be grounded for life, but at least she'd be safe.

It was a small but comfortable library. Being a faculty brat, she had become used to the large university library with its seeming endless collections. This place felt much more homey, with local art hanging on the walls and a section of leather chairs and a sofa where a group of elderly people sat chatting over their newspapers.

The main room had high ceilings from which hung lazily-spinning fans. A split staircase at the far back led up to what appeared to be office space and down to a lower level. To storage, perhaps. Off to the left of the main desk was another room altogether, the children's library, and Ellen supposed the doorway had been cut into a pre-existing building next door as it appeared one had to step down into the kids' room.

Stop dawdling. Call Mom. Get this over with.

Ellen stepped up to the checkout desk. A tall, dour woman with tight curls just this side of purple put down her pencil and raised her eyebrows.

"Yes?"

"I'd like to use the phone."

"The phones are for library staff. Are you a patron?"

"Yes."

"May I see your card?"

Ellen shrugged off her backpack and pulled out the little leather wallet she'd gotten in her last Christmas stocking. Not the most festive gift but one she appreciated for its practicality. She removed both her Iowa City Public Library card and the one her father had procured for her, emblazoned with the University of Iowa Hawkeye.

The librarian examined the cards, then handed them back.

"You don't have a Maple City library card?"

"No," Ellen said, and then, thinking quickly, "not yet."

The woman squinted. "Are you a Warren County resident?"

"We just got here." It wasn't a lie—she and the rest of the passengers *had* just gotten there. Let the woman assume whatever she wanted.

"Proof of residency and another form of ID," the librarian said. "School ID is fine."

Ellen eyed the phone on the table behind the woman. One of its lines was busy, but three others were just sitting idly by. Why did this woman have to make it so difficult?

"May I have an application?" Ellen asked, rounding out the deception, but to what end? She had no proof of residency, no ID. Better to leave and track down another phone. Surely an old town like this still had payphones peppered about downtown.

"Hold on, I'll get one," said the librarian with a snort that let Ellen know she was *not* a kid person. Not in the least.

The woman disappeared into the back office, and as Ellen turned, she heard a *psst!* come from the attached room. She looked and saw a young man with frazzled hair in wrinkled khaki pants and an untucked short-sleeve shirt beckoning for her to enter the children's section.

"Come on," the young man whispered. "You can use my phone."

Ellen paused, but the guy kept urging her in, going so far as to lift the receiver from its cradle and mime talking into it.

She looked back to where the older librarian stood in the doorway to the office scolding a younger employee. The woman held what Ellen could only imagine was her application.

Turning away from the exit, she stepped through the doorway, down into the children's room where the young man with the wrinkled pants stood waiting.

"All yours. Mrs. Flynt may rule the roost out there, but the kids' library is all mine."

Ellen nodded and set her backpack on the guy's small desk, which was littered with cartoons scribbled on 3x5 cards.

"Excuse the mess," he said and whisked the cartoons into a drawer. "Who you calling?"

"My mom."

"That a local call?"

Ellen fished the phone card from her pack and held it up.

"Iowa."

"Ah, then you're going to want to press 9 first to get an outside line." He motioned for Ellen to put away her card. "Save your minutes. Warren County can afford it."

"Thanks," Ellen said, thrown by the contrast in demeanors of the two librarians.

"Name's Eli. And you?"

"Ellen."

"Hey! We're both E-L's! Eli, Ellen."

"Yeah," said Ellen, eager to get on with her call. Eager to spill the beans and be done with it.

"No one calls me Eli, though. Not since high school. Ever since I started college, folks just call me Riggs."

"I gotta make this call, Riggs."

"Sure, sure! Have at it." He turned away from her, scooping up a pile of phone messages from his in-box, whistling as he leafed through them.

Ellen held the phone close as she began to dial. *319-482...*

"That's funny," Riggs said, holding one of the phone messages closer. "Ellen, right? What's your last name?"

Ellen sighed. "Gooding."

Riggs shook his head. "Ah. Never mind."

Why wouldn't the guy leave her alone? It was hard enough anticipating the fury she'd invoke in her mother once she spilled the beans, but having this man-Muppet yammering on made her crazy.

"But my dad's name was Marx."

The children's librarian quirked his head. "Now, isn't that interesting."

Ellen was about to punch in the last four digits of Rita's cell phone when Riggs held up the message for her to see.

Ellen's eyes went wide.

For: Ellen Marx
Time: 10:55 am
Remarks: Don't stop now, Spooky

CHAPTER 14

Ellen held the slip of paper tight, reading and rereading the message.

Don't stop now, Spooky

Riggs shook his head, his shaggy mane bouncing. "That's weird, right? I mean…that's weird. Do you mind?"

He reached out for the message, and Ellen felt suddenly possessive of it. She felt a strong urge to put the note in her mouth, to lock it away safe behind her teeth, but recalling the reaction she'd had with the snippet of audiotape, thought better of it. She glanced down at the note one more time, memorizing it, photographing it and stuffing it back in her brain before handing it over.

"You didn't write that, did you?" Ellen asked, already knowing the answer.

"No, you couldn't read my chicken scratches if you tried. Old Scorch is always snapping at me that she can't read my messages."

"Scorch?"

Riggs laughed. "It's what I call Mrs. Flynt out there. She's usually somber enough, but if you get on her bad side, *Boom!* She goes off. Scorched earth, you know?"

"I get it. It's funny."

"You know what else is funny?" Riggs said, thumbing the message. "This is *her* handwriting."

"You sure?"

"See for yourself." He pulled a couple of other messages from the pile and held them up for Ellen to examine. The handwriting was the same on the lot of them—precise with sharp peaks to the M's, N's and R's.

"May I have my message back?"

"Sure," Riggs said, producing it with a flourish.

Ellen puzzled over the slip of paper long enough for the young librarian to grow restless. "Look, why don't I go ask her if she got a call or someone stopped by."

"Okay."

"Then I gotta get back to shelving books."

"Fine."

"Great." Riggs clapped his hands and headed for the main library.

"You're helping me," Ellen called, a bit louder than she had anticipated. "Why?"

Riggs grinned. "Because you and your little note just made my boring, fucking day interesting." His eyes went wide. "Shit, sorry about the F-bomb, kid."

He slipped out of the room, leaving Ellen alone with Roald Dahl, Dr. Suess and Judy Blume. She glanced at the clock on the wall. 11:05. Mrs. Flynt, the librarian, had written the message at 10:55. Ellen hadn't even set foot in the library by that point. But still, the old woman had already been busy penning the note.

Ellen stared at the name staring back at her. *Ellen Marx.* She'd always felt more like an Ellen Marx than an Ellen

Gooding. Even though she had spent the majority of her life under the same roof as her mother, Ellen had always felt a closer kinship with her father. Her parents' relationship was complicated, and Ellen had no interest in trying to make sense of it. She cared more about the end result and what that meant for her. And what it meant was that she was a Gooding who dreamed of being a Marx.

Stuffing the memo into her pocket, her attention turned to a 3x5 card sticking out of the desk drawer. Ellen retrieved it. The drawing was a crude stick figure with an enormous nose flanked by two smaller, smiling stick figures. Both smaller figures held tin cans connected by a string that ran up one of the man's nostrils and out the other. For being simple stick figures, the cartoon characters had a lively sense of mirth that temporarily distracted Ellen. Below the cartoon was scribbled, *Damn Kids, Use The Phone!*

"Ah! You found one of my Library Cartoons." Riggs was back. He plucked the 3x5 card out of her hand.

"Excuse me?"

"I like to scribble funny ideas that come to me. Then when Old Warhead isn't looking—"

"Warhead?"

"Sorry. Scorch. Mrs. Flynt. I have a lot of time on my hands here. Anyway, I find an old book no one is *ever* going to check out—something like *Graveyard Nurse*—and I stick the cartoon inside."

"Why?"

"Why not?"

Ellen wrinkled her brow. This Riggs reminded her of a dog she used to know named Clipper—a big, dumb Lab that used to trot around campus. Clipper chased his own tail.

"What did you find out?" Ellen asked.

"Oh. Scorch says she didn't write it, but I know she did. She's all foggy because of her medication."

"What's wrong with her?"

Riggs shifted nervously. "I'm not sure. She spends a lot of time in the bathroom. Think she might be pretty sick."

"And you still call her names?" Ellen asked.

"Yeah, but…just to myself."

Ellen stared for a moment at the phone on the desk. Time to choose—call Mom and fess up or press on.

"Where's your local history collection?"

Riggs was busy chuckling over the cartoon, so Ellen asked again.

"Local history?" Riggs looked puzzled. "In the basement. Why?"

Ellen slipped on her backpack. "Because I have some research to do."

* * *

Riggs stood just outside the children's library room, hand raised like a crossing guard.

"Not yet."

The young man had informed Ellen that, due to the painting and renovation the library board had ordered, all of the special collections were off-limits to anyone without permission. Being both a child and sans library card, the chances were next to zip she'd be able to get her hands on the recorded interview that had taken her two buses and half a dozen lies to reach.

The woman Riggs called Scorch was holding things up. Ellen could hear the elderly librarian trying to stifle a coughing fit, each cluster of hacks punctuated with an *Oh, dear* or *Dear, God*. And what was that scent in the air? Ellen chalked it up to her imagination, but it was still tough to dismiss the touch of decay in the air. For a second, she was reminded of her mother's new friend—the postman. How she could almost taste his cologne on her tongue. Rancid and meaty. Like the dead cat she'd found behind the apartment complex one hot June day, its belly gaping open, alive with…

Stop it, she snapped at her chattering brain. *Stay on task.*

Riggs's fingers wiggled nervously. Again Ellen was reminded of the dog, Clipper, and his anxious dance when his owner was about to throw a stick.

"Go!" Riggs whispered.

Ellen scurried into the main room, dashed past the checkout desk and the group of newspaper readers, dodged around the carrels of computers and slammed headlong into a wooden crate. She fell back on her rump and stared dazed at the large box standing before her. *Book Donations.*

Get moving!

She did. Ellen scrambled to her feet and raced for the stairs to the basement. She took them two at a time, leaving the handwritten *Entrance By Permission Only* sign fluttering in her wake.

CHAPTER 15

He was trapped.

Peter raged against the suffocating closeness of the tiny room's walls.

I'm in a cage.

No, he wasn't.

Yes, I'm in a fucking cage!

He reached out to the wall on his left and felt its surface give way—spongy and warm.

I'm in a throat.

The wall's surface undulated beneath his touch.

I'm being swallowed!

No.

His fingertips identified the texture. Foam. Rolling in small hills and valleys. A soft egg carton pattern. Up, down, up, down.

Frantically he ran his hands along all four walls, one after the other. The foam was all about him. Why had the walls been cushioned so? As if to protect what they contained?

Me. I'm what's contained. I'm what's trapped.

He was suddenly aware of pressure about his ears, and when he reached up, he found twin shells clamped to either side of his head.

Not shells. Headphones.

The dim glow of a screen faded up before him. A rectangle of relief in this dark, dark place. He peered at the screen, hoping for illumination, but found only screens within screens within screens—never-ending boxes containing indecipherable waves of…what? Seismic activity? Heartbeats? What?

The light from the screen drew his attention to an object suspended before him, and he grappled with its meaning.

Mac? Mote. Mite? Mic!

He swatted aside the pop screen and grabbed the microphone, its burnished metal freezing to the touch, and pressed it to his lips.

"Help me!" he whispered. "Help me!"

His voice crackled in his ears, delayed by its trip down the wire, into the computer and back to his head.

"Help me! Help me-ee-ee-ee…"

His plea devolved into digital gibberish, piercing his eardrums like twin icepicks.

Peter tore off the headphones and reached for the doorknob. It hadn't occurred to him the room even had a door, but his hand knew. Knew by instinct.

Locked.

He gripped the doorknob with both hands, wrenching it clockwise, counterclockwise, back and forth. The lock held firm. He pounded on the door, face pressed up against the vertical glass window set in its center.

"Get me out of here!"

Somewhere outside the booth, a good stretch away, the darkness gave birth to a pulsating light. Distant and electric and wholly unnatural, the light stole his attention.

"Peter…"

The voice was barely audible. The voice was below him.

That light. So familiar.

"Peter!"

He looked down at the discarded headphones on the floor between his feet. Peter reached down and lifted them to his face. He grabbed one housing in each hand and twisted until twin mesh mouths stared up at him. A voice rose from within their twin speakers—*her* voice.

"Peter, come home!"

A burst of lightning beyond the window startled him, and the headphones loosed a terrible feedback squeal. He threw the headphones aside and turned back to the window, much to the begging woman's protest.

A building sat some fifty yards away. Above it, and silhouetted against an angry sky, was a neon sign flashing contradictory messages to the heavens.

Intermission Motor Lodge! Crossroads Motel! Intermission Motor Lodge! Crossroads Motel! Vacancy, NO Vacancy, Vacancy, NO—

Before the sign could shift again, a thicket of black tendrils rose from the ground, blotting out its neon schizophrenia.

The window cracked as a razor-sharp talon pierced the glass. The ceiling groaned as something of immense weight pressed down, down, down. The four walls lurched inward, buckling under tremendous strain.

It's crushing me.

"Peter!"

Yellow teeth—hungry and insistent—gnashed at the broken glass, the gums holding them ripping and shredding as the window gave way.

It's eating me!

"Peter!"

He broke the surface of consciousness and gasped for breath.

"Easy, easy."

The voice was low and calming, and when Peter opened his eyes, he found the bearded man standing over him. The old fellow who had put him to sleep the night before. There was concern in the man's eyes, the sort of look a father might have for a toddler on the verge of tumbling out of his crib.

"That must have been some whopper of a nightmare."

"I…"

"You're okay."

He was in the church. In the cloakroom turned bedroom. Not in the booth. Not being crushed.

"Fal…"

"Fallow," the man finished for him with a chuckle. "That's right. Papa Fallow. Good to know I made an impression."

The old man held out a steaming mug of coffee. Peter grabbed it and downed a scalding mouthful. It was awful coffee—cheap and metallic—but it helped him swallow his fear, swallow the nightmare.

"Damn. You'd make a fine commercial for Maxwell House, you know that. Good to the last—"

Peter choked on his next greedy sip, interrupting Fallow's musing with a coughing spray of coffee.

"Or not."

"Sorry."

"No problem."

Fallow pulled up a stool. He sat with a *whump* and scooted closer to the cot. He had changed since last night. Gone was the bulky coat, bulky sweater and the illusion of size those heavy items lent. Instead, he sported a faded Burlington Bee's t-shirt layered over long underwear. A sloppily-knitted cap kept his white hair from splaying in riot. The man would be right at home on any commune.

"Was it about a girl?"

Peter didn't track. "Huh?"

"Your dream. About a girl?"

"Oh. Sort of."

Fallow snapped his fingers and grinned, and Peter noticed the old boy had a couple of finger joints missing on both hands.

"Nothing in this world can stir the ole psyche quite like a woman. What's her name?"

"I…"

"You don't know."

"No."

Fallow leaned back and tugged at his beard.

"Staring at my digits, eh?"

"No, I…"

Fallow displayed both hands proudly and wiggled his fingers—or what was left of them. Peter counted three fingers missing their last joint, one missing two.

"Well, you get to be as old as I am you're bound to leave bits and pieces behind. Saves on nail trimming, though."

Peter nodded, not knowing how to respond.

"You, sir, seem to be similarly snipped."

"Excuse me?"

Fallow poked him in the chest with a stubby forefinger. "Snipped. Bereft. You know what I mean."

"You mean…pieces missing?"

"See? The man catches on quick. All those fingerprints you always thought would keep you anchored—who you are, where you come from, the name of the gal who's got you tossing and turning at night—when those basics go missing, it's hard to function in the day-to-day, know what I mean?"

"I do," Peter said, nodding. But there was no day-to-day for him. Hell, the first thing he could remember was waking up in the shed not ten hours ago.

In the booth.

No, in the shed.

Fallow tapped Peter's forehead. "You having a little convo in there? Anything you'd like to share with the group?"

The twitter of children's laugher came from the open door, and Fallow bellowed, "Get in here, you lot."

Huck and Jo tumbled into the room, tripping each other up as they scrambled to be the first to Fallow's side.

"Stop pushing!" Jo squealed.

"You're the pusher, pusher!" Huck countered.

The two grabbed hold of Fallow's arms, flanking him, using his body for cover as they peered shyly at the man on the cot.

Suddenly, a ball of hair and paws and saliva bowled Peter over onto his back. A wet tongue lapped his face top to bottom before Fallow could extract the dog.

"Curly! I told you to keep that dog tied up."

The boy with the crutches stood in the doorway, waving the makeshift rope leash as evidence of his innocence.

"Toss me that." Fallow was stern.

Curly chucked the rope a few feet into the room, and the little ones raced to deliver it to the old man.

The dog certainly looked sprier than he did last night. He tried to squirm out of Fallow's arms as the old man slipped the rope about his neck.

"Funny how he's off-leash. This dog sleep in your bed last night?"

Curly fidgeted, suddenly quite interested in the ceiling.

"You know better than that, Curly," Fallow said. He rose and walked the dog back to the boy. "Go find a place for him in the storage room. There are cushions in there. He'll be fine."

Curly nodded and led the dog out of the room just as Dodge was entering. The teen was obviously bursting with news.

"What is it?" Fallow asked.

"There are men outside. With a truck." Dodge rubbed his mouth in a gesture Peter recognized as a smoker's instinct to take a puff when nervous.

"Time to make a buck!" Fallow said, a massive smile stretching across his face, out-Kringling old Kringle himself. "Hey, Peter! Ready to earn your keep?"

CHAPTER 16

Peter approached the church door with profound trepidation. The last time he'd crossed its threshold, he'd tumbled headlong into the arms of a waiting horde.

What greeted him instead was a brilliant, white landscape that forced him to shield his eyes, causing him to reconsider whether or not the storm, the ice and the grasping things within had simply been another nightmare.

"Beautiful day!" Fallow bellowed. "Beautiful."

The man was once more bundled up against the cold in layers that seemed to add fifty or more pounds to his frame. The loaner coat Peter wore was just as substantial, and he imagined he struck a much more imposing figure than usual.

"You all right, Peter?"

Peter nodded, realizing he had managed to take only two steps out of the church.

"Like I said, it's a beautiful day. The sun is out, the shadows have been dispelled." Fallow offered up a sympathetic smile. "There's nothing for you to fear out here, my friend."

"I have so many questions."

"Lay one on me."

Peter descended the cement steps until his shoes were inches shy of touching snow. "There were...*things* in the storm."

"Is that a question?"

"Were they real?"

Fallow considered this. "Yes. And no."

"Come again?"

The man approached Peter and grabbed his shoulders with so much force, Peter thought Fallow meant to throw him to the ground.

"You and me. We're real. Right?"

"Yes."

"We're flesh and blood."

"Okay."

Fallow stared deep into Peter's eyes.

"Those folks in the snow. They have no business being here. They're as insubstantial as my breath." To illustrate his point, Fallow exhaled, releasing a cloud of vapor that curled upward and disappeared in the blue of the sky. "You understand?"

"You're saying that they're—"

"Of no consequence. The only reason I deign to speak of them at all is because they won't leave my kids alone. They *yearn* for them. Their youth, their light. But I won't let them in. No, sir. Nothing, not even the wind, can get past me."

Two men in grey coveralls awaited them next to a truck with the words Department of Public Works stenciled on its door.

"Gentlemen!" Fallow boomed as he led Peter and Dodge up to the workers. "How are you both this fine morning?"

The larger of the two, a man with a bulky frame and a voice to match Fallow's, boomed back. "Can't complain."

"I can," said the second man. This fellow was muscular but rail thin, and there was a nastiness to the man's tone that instantly set Peter's teeth on edge. "Colder than a witch's tit out. Couldn't have waited for a warmer day?"

"You'll have to forgive Albert," the first man said. "He got up on the wrong side of the bed ten years ago and has been making the same mistake ever since."

"Har-dee-har-har," the skinny man sneered.

Peter couldn't help but notice the nametags sewn to the men's coveralls. The large man's read *Big Bear*, the skinny man's, *Albert*.

Big Bear and Albert. Sounds like a bad TV show.

The skinny man suddenly shot him a look, and for a moment, Peter thought he had perhaps spoken aloud. It was only when he heard Willa's voice behind him that he realized he was not the focus of Albert's gaze.

"Should I make some more coffee?" Willa asked.

"Gentlemen?" Fallow asked, addressing the workers.

"Seeing as Albert forgot to fill our thermos this morning, that would be greatly appreciated," Big Bear said. "Thank you, miss."

Albert didn't answer. He was still staring at Willa.

"Yes, Willa. A fresh pot sounds in order," Fallow said. "Well then! Let's show you what we've got."

What Fallow had was a pile of loose copper pipe stacked up along the rear of the church. The pile was about knee-high and covered in snow and ice.

"Oh, hell no," Albert hissed. "It's frozen solid! We ain't never gonna get that into the truck."

"Never say never," Big Bear said. "Get me the propane torch."

After a few minutes of ice melting, the copper pipes fell free.

"Peter!" Fallow ordered. "First load's yours."

Peter obeyed, grabbing up an armload of warm pipe and walking it to the truck's payload. The copper was heavy and unwieldy, and he felt like a tightrope walker trying to keep his balance. After a few trips and more than a few curses, the men had loaded all the pipe in the truck.

Big Bear pulled a receipt book from the glove compartment and scribbled as he spoke. "You take this to Fred Donnelly at City Hall. He'll make sure you get paid."

"Thank you kindly," Fallow said, pocketing the slip of paper.

Willa returned with the pot of coffee, and Albert beat his companion to the thermos. His eyes never left the girl.

"You sure warmed up this cold day," the skinny man said.

Willa remained silent.

The meeting ended with thank-yous all around. As the truck drove off, the copper pipe clattering in the back, Peter could see Albert adjusting his rearview mirror to catch one last glimpse of Willa.

* * *

Back in the kitchen, Fallow eased himself into a chair at the farm table.

"That old copper's been lying around for years," Fallow said. "Feels good to swap it out for some cold cash."

"I didn't like that man," Willa said, refilling the Mr. Coffee.

"Which one?" Fallow asked.

"The skinny one," Peter said, answering for her.

Fallow waved them off. "The world's full of odd birds. You're too insulated to know that, Willa. We've got to get you out in the world a bit more."

Huck and Jo slipped into the seats on either side of Peter, growing more used to him with each passing minute.

"Where's Dodge?" Fallow asked the children.

"Outside," Huck said.

"What's he doing out there?"

Jo imitated puffing on a cigarette, confirming Peter's suspicion.

"If I catch that boy smoking, so help me—"

"He's probably embarrassed," Willa said. "I don't think he wanted to be seen like that. In front of…you know." She nodded toward Peter.

"Embarrassed?" Fallow was incredulous. "About last night? The boy's got a gift. Hell, you've *all* got gifts. No reason to hide them in the dark."

"That…thing," Peter said, finally working up his nerve. "That came out of his back…"

"All in good time, my friend." Fallow clapped his hands, causing Peter to jump. "Huck! Jo! Why don't you show our guest a little trick?"

This request was met with giggles. The twins, for twins they had to be with their duplicate smiles, raised their tiny hands and fluttered their fingers as if imitating falling rain. No rain appeared, but butterflies sure did.

"Aw, isn't that the cutest thing?" Fallow crooned.

The butterflies were miniature things and there were dozens of them. They flitted about in front of Peter's face for a few brief moments and then faded away, leaving the drifting scent of cinnamon rolls.

"Reminds you of summer, doesn't it?"

Fallow was waiting for a response, so Peter nodded. "Just like summer."

Huck and Jo took this as high praise and giggled even louder.

"Willa!" the old man said, rising. "Would you be kind enough to chauffeur us into town? We've got some cash to collect, and it'd be good for you to put in some time behind the wheel."

The prospect caught Willa unaware, and she flashed a disarmed smile. "You mean it?"

"You have your permit?"

"In my trunk."

"Go get it."

Willa rushed out of the room. Fallow rose and took up the carafe, filling his mug and raising it in a toast.

"To the open road!"

CHAPTER 17

Two doors greeted Ellen at the bottom of the stairs, along with a musty, damp odor. One door was bare, the other had a brass sign that read *Mr. Pullen*. Neither gave any indication the local history section was housed within.

Ellen reached for the *Mr. Pullen* door and froze.

The lady or the tiger?

The thought commanded her to stop.

No!

Her brain wanted to waltz her about in endless loops. To puzzle over the short story that had so vexed her in English class. The one that didn't have a clear and proper ending. To keep her from pressing forward.

What was behind the door the man chose? The lady or the tiger? The lady or the tiger? The lady or the...

She quickly glanced back up the stairs. Riggs had one foot on the top step, waving her on, mouthing *Scorch!*

I haven't got time for this!

But it was too late. Her brain was determined to trip her up. Such occasions were rare, but they did rear their ugly heads from time to time. When she was nervous, when she was stressed. Her mind flitted back to third grade. She was rendered immobile at the water fountain with a line of kids waiting behind her—her thumb pressed down on the button, the water burbling unsipped down the drain. It had taken the gentle nudging of Mrs. Orton, the kindergarten teacher, to end her fugue. It had taken…

Shut up.

It had taken someone else to break the spell.

I said, shut up!

Ellen steeled herself. She could do this. She didn't need anyone. She wasn't a third-grader anymore. She could choose to move forward. To *act*.

"C'mon, kid. Inside, inside!"

Riggs's whispered urgency gave her the push she needed. She grabbed the doorknob, turned it and scurried into the dark.

Riggs slipped into the room and quickly shut the door behind him.

"Shit. Where's the light switch? Shit."

Ellen stood stock still, hands clasping the straps of her backpack. Because the room was *alive*. No, not the room—whatever the room contained. She felt the presence of people coming and going, voices rising and falling. Whispers, snatches of songs, spirited debates. The collective chatter of a hidden community. It was as thick as the mildew in the air.

"Got it!"

The lights flickered on, and the room fell silent.

As Ellen's eyes adjusted, she found herself in the middle of a windowless room with a tile floor, a low ceiling, and very little room to maneuver. The place was packed—shelves overstuffed with books, binders and stacks of papers bound by rubber bands. Plastic bins crowded the floor in a rush-hour sprawl, each sporting a hand-scrawled label indicating its contents. In short, it was a mess.

"Sheesh," said Riggs, sucking on his teeth. "Guess I know what they'll have me doing this summer."

"This is the research section?" Ellen asked, trying to make sense of the clutter. "Local history?"

"Yeah, it is. Although it looks like history's a bit of jumble at the moment. The guy who used to curate it kicked the bucket a few years ago after they let him go. Budget cuts, you know?" He picked up an oversized book with a frayed binding and opened it. The cover came off in his hand.

"How am I supposed to find anything in here?"

"What are you looking for?"

Ellen paused, unsure whether or not to give voice to her object of interest, as if speaking it aloud might shatter the tenuous threads that had led her from Iowa City to this dank room. But the prospect of searching blindly through this den of dissonant documents made her head spin.

"Blind Rock Interview: Pat Porter. I think it's in RealMedia Format."

"Ah!" Riggs crowed. "*That* I can help you with."

He picked his way further into the room, catching his hip on the edge of a desk piled high with boxes of slide carousels, knocking the ancient phone's handset off its cradle, igniting a scolding red button. He quickly replaced the handset, pirouetted around the desk and hopped over an over-stuffed cardboard box, crushing a second with his next hop.

"Damn."

Reaching a tall, freestanding bookcase, he plucked a plastic shoebox from a shelf, along with some sort of device in a black leather case. As he returned to the desk, doing lethal damage to the crushed cardboard box, Ellen recognized the object he had in his hands. It was a cassette player.

"RealMedia is just for the samples they stick on the web. These are the tapes they source 'em from. Would you mind?"

"Huh?"

Riggs nodded toward the boxes of slides covering the desk. Ellen wriggled off her backpack and made quick work clearing a spot for Riggs to set up the player. As the tousle-haired librarian searched for an extension cord, Ellen sorted through the cassettes.

Like the rest of the room, there was no rhyme or reason to the order of the tapes, although each was clearly labeled. Ellen got a hit—whether or not it was a *real* hit or just a flash of imagination, she wasn't sure—of Mr. Pullen, namesake of this room, sitting at this very desk, carefully organizing and cataloging each tape. If he saw the state of the place today, no doubt he'd be less than happy.

"Pat Porter is a history buff. He's always in and out of here. We're friendly. You think something on that tape of his is connected to that memo, huh?"

"Maybe."

"Ooo! Spooky indeed."

Ellen extracted a Trans-Siberian Orchestra cassette from the mix and set it aside. "Is this all of them?"

"All the tapes? Pretty sure."

Ellen's heart sank as she examined the last cassette. "It's not here."

"Seriously?"

Riggs did his own inventory, to no avail. "Damn. I don't know where it'd be, then." He looked out over the sea of historic detritus surrounding them. "Somewhere out there, I guess."

The phone rang, and Ellen jumped.

"Oh, no." Riggs answered the call. "You've got Riggs."

His face fell, and he looked to Ellen. He didn't have to say anything. She knew. They'd been caught.

"No, no, no," Riggs stammered. "I'm just looking for staples. I've got a lot of paperwork I've got to organize and…no…yes, but…look, Mrs. Flynt…"

Ellen picked up her backpack and put it on. This is where the road ended. It was time to pack up and head out.

"No! I'll be right there," Riggs said, slamming down the phone. He turned to Ellen, shaking his head. "I can buy you fifteen minutes, tops. Then she's coming down here to check and see if I've been smoking reefer."

"Smoking reefer?"

"Her words." He headed for the exit. "Check those tapes again. I could swear it was in there. If not…" He left her hanging and disappeared.

With a sigh, Ellen flipped through the cassettes one last time. *Prime Beef Festival Interviews: Various, Maple City's Bicentennial Interview with Mayor White.* There were eighteen in all—none of them the Pat Porter interview. None of them of any use.

She was about to head on out when she considered the tape player. It was smaller, more compact than her garage sale reel-to-reel, and a heck of a lot more modern, but a relic in 2003 nonetheless. It had a counter with an analog readout. She pressed its button, and the counter slipped back to 0-0-0.

Her finger wandered to the controls, pressing and depressing pause, pressing eject…

The little door on top opened, revealing the business end of a cassette.

Gingerly, Ellen slid the tape from the player and held it to the light, reading the label written in Mr. Pullen's even hand.

Blind Rock Interview: Pat Porter

CHAPTER 18

"The Massacre at Blind Rock remains, to this day, one of the least understood chapters in Maple City history. In 1894, the Church of the Harvest community was thriving. By 1895, they no longer existed. Mr. Porter, would you mind? Just speak right into the microphone..."

"Thank you, Mr. Pullen. You're correct—The Blind Rock Massacre has, on the whole, faded from collective memory. The only reason any history exists at all comes from word of mouth, you know? Families passing the story down from generation to generation. Like that. You won't find anything about it in any of your books. It's a dirty, little secret, you know? Something folks want kept swept under the rug.

"The Porters go way back to Maple City's founding, back to the 1830s. My people came here as blacksmiths, carpenters and cooks—folks who did real work. Not a lot of lawyers or politicians in my family.

"The way I heard it told from my great-grandfather, Otto Porter, was that in the mid-1840s, just after Maple City became Maple City, officially founded, you know, it started to draw more and more folks. Population growth. And with that growth, you got all kinds. Some stayed, some left. Mormons passed through on their way to Nauvoo. You ever been? Pretty sure there were some Sauk, some Meskwaki still about, maybe a few *other native tribes. Anyway, there was plenty of open land for everybody, and everybody came.*

"One group, the group I'm going to tell you about, settled on the outskirts of town in 1894. The Church of the Harvest, they called themselves. The land they settled was rotten. For farming, you know? Peppered with rocks that would ruin a plow. Crops shriveled there, and livestock got sick. One family went completely blind—probably due to fouled well water—which is one story about how it got its name. Blind Rock. Not sure I believe that. A lot of myth builds up around places. Like Cripple Creek in Colorado, you know? Used to go out there every summer. Some say it got its name due to a cow breaking its leg in the creek, some say it was a horse, some say it was...well, you get the picture. Sometimes history is out of focus. Anyhow, the land gave folks a bad feeling. Like something awful happened there at one time. Or would, down the road. Anyway, it suited those Church of the Harvest folks just fine as its reputation kept the townspeople away.

"See, they didn't venture into town much. Didn't mingle. They kept their people and their ways to themselves. That didn't sit right with folks. They started making up stories—about weird doings out on the prairie. Started calling them Blinders behind their backs. And whenever one of the Blind Rock people did come into town, folks wouldn't leave them be. Mocked them and harassed them. Ignorance, you know? And fear. There was a lot of fear back in those days.

"Anyway, one night in 1895, a bunch of the town's big names, prominent families got old Maple City riled up. A city councilman's child had gone missing. They found a short

message written on the boy's bedroom wall in blood. 'BR.' Well, of course folks took that to mean Blind Rock, and so…

"…with all the rumors and…

"…witchcraft and the like, you know? And what do folks tend to do to witches?

"…tools and weapons. None of my people, you understand? The Porters wouldn't truck with that sort of nonsense. But the rest…

"…men, women and children…

"…burned and…

"…Blind Rock…that's why you won't hear any of this from folks around here. They…because it was their…Blinders, you know? To them, the massacre never…be happy to…out of mind, and…and…"

CHAPTER 19

"I'm a tape recorder killer," Ellen confessed to the empty room as Pat Porter's voice devolved.

She punched the Eject button, and the cassette popped up, revealing its tape disappearing into the player's works. The missing sections of the story? The player had gobbled them up.

"You are not supposed to be in here."

Mrs. Flynt, old Scorch herself, stood in the doorway, pointing accusatorially. Ellen was busted, good and busted, but she found such occasions still required some response.

"I was looking for the restroom," Ellen offered without conviction. Because it was obvious the librarian wanted her gone. Not just from the research room but from the library itself.

Riggs hung back behind the woman, powerless. He was mouthing something, probably asking if she'd found the tape or urging her to stay quiet or some other such thing that wouldn't change the fact she was on her way out the door.

"Restrooms are for patrons. And you're not a patron." Old Scorch wasn't messing around.

"Yet," Ellen countered feebly and headed for the door. The librarian stepped aside, letting her pass. Yup, the woman was sick, all right. The woman was dying. She could smell it on her.

Riggs tried again to catch her attention, but Ellen ignored him, instead mounting the stairs two at a time. She heard the door close below her, felt the woman ascending the stairs, caught another whiff of the woman's impending death.

"You come back with your mother next time," the woman said, ushering her toward the exit.

"What if my mom is dead?" Ellen sassed. It wouldn't help her cause, but it felt good.

"Then bring your father."

And with that, Ellen was outside the library looking in with the woman's words still ringing in her head.

Then bring your father.

Not fair for her to say that. Just another reminder. The mention of her father had caused her heart to leap, expecting to find him rounding the corner, arms upraised, calling out to her, "Spooky! There you are." Not fair at all.

Ellen turned back to the town square where the bus had deposited her. No bus, no way home. Just the statue with its weapon upraised, ready to do battle.

To kill men, women and children? To massacre The Church of the Harvest?

"Hey, wait up!"

Riggs—Clipper the dog in human form—bounded after her.

"Did you find it?"

"The tape?"

"Of course, the Pat Porter tape!"

"Yes."

Riggs let loose a silent cheer, hands in the air. "Great. Did it solve your mystery? Did it explain why memos for you are showing up on my desk before I even laid eyes on you?"

"Aren't you working?"

"No, I took my lunch break."

"It's early for lunch."

"We're closing early, so this is pretty much my midday."

"That doesn't make sense."

Riggs mimed pulling out his hair. "Tell me! What was on the tape."

"I didn't get the whole story," Ellen said. "There were parts missing."

"Aw, man!"

The shaggy guy puzzled a moment, pacing like a character on TV.

"People really do that?" Ellen asked, brow wrinkled.

"Do what?"

"Pace?"

"Sure, they do. Hold on, hold on…"

"Yes?"

Riggs pulled a TracFone from his pocket and waved it triumphantly. "This is your lucky day, little miss. It just so happens that *I* have the man's number."

CHAPTER 20

An engine coughed in the distance, strained and finally roared to life. A moment later, a vehicle lurched around the corner of the church, Willa behind the wheel. Peter had expected a car or a pickup truck. But this?

"That there is a 1948 Dodge two-window school bus," Fallow crowed, answering Peter's wide-eyed expression. "Looks like an armadillo, doesn't she?"

She did at that. The thing was all metal, and it slipped and slid in the freshly fallen snow. It was half the length of a normal school bus and squat at that. Decades of Midwestern winters had stripped it of its original yellow, replaced by decades of patchwork paint jobs. The girl behind the wheel was as wide-eyed as Peter, and she gripped the wheel tight as the bus careened down the icy dirt drive.

"Let's see if she remembers to downshift instead of braking," Fallow said, eagerly awaiting the outcome.

Willa hit the brakes, the bus stalled and came to a stuttering halt.

"Guess not. Come on, Peter. Last one aboard is a rotten egg!"

Willa proved a far more accomplished driver on the country road leading into town than she did maneuvering about the church grounds. Once her passengers were settled in their ratty, leather-covered seats, she revved the engine back to life and circled past the mounds of snow with protruding headstones, swerved left and made a run for the straightaway.

"How's she feel?" Fallow asked over the roar of the engine.

"Like a rusty, old bus," Willa said as she shifted gears.

"Where are we going?" Peter asked, clinging to the seat in front of him as the bus swerved on ice.

"Into town." Fallow scraped ice from his window with the nails of two fingers. "Gotta collect on that copper, and I figure a trip into Maple City might help jog your memory."

Peter didn't know about that. He feared it would take more than a jog to shift his thoughts back into place. Every time he tried to look back into the past, a warning buzz lit up his brain, announcing *Access Denied! Access Denied!* Best to stick to the present moment. Best to keep talking.

"Thank you," Peter called up to the front. And when Willa didn't answer, he said, louder, "Thank you, Willa!"

"For what?" the girl asked, startled by his loud voice in the small bus, missing a beat and bouncing over a snowdrift.

"For saving me last night. For pulling me back in."

"That wasn't me."

"Thank your friend, then."

No reply.

"Your feathered friend."

"I heard you."

Fallow leaned in. "The kids are touchy about their talents."

"And just what talents might those be, exactly?" Peter asked, growing less comfortable with the lack of answers.

"Sit back and enjoy the ride, my friend."

The cold air had roused Peter enough to stir his ire—with the vagaries surrounding his present state, with the slippery explanations offered by this man, this shock-haired keeper of children.

"I will *not* sit back. I'm tired of being kept in the dark." Peter was shaking by this point. He tried to stop, but the words just kept on coming. "Explain, or I'm jumping off this bus, I swear to God."

The old man nodded, and instead of more evasion, he rose and pounded on the ceiling.

"Willa. Pull over."

* * *

The town was close enough Peter could see the AM antenna reaching upward, a lofty water tower standing like one of H.G. Wells's tripods against the sky.

Willa stood in an open field, looking for all the world like she'd rather be anywhere else. Fallow tromped about in the snow, making a swooping, footprint circle in the snow about her.

"What are you doing?" Peter asked.

"Explaining. You see, circles help my dear Willa. Don't know why, but they do. Don't they, girl?"

Willa remained tight-lipped and pulled her coat tight about her.

Peter hung back at the road by the bus, the sun melting the calf-deep snow, dampening his pant legs. "We don't have to do this now."

"Oh, yes we do!" Fallow bellowed. "Do you trust us, Peter? I don't think you do. But I think we can fix that. Time to let you into our little circle, so to speak. Share some family secrets." Completing the last of the circle in the snow, Fallow turned to Willa. "Well, Willa? What shall we show our new friend?"

Peter was on tenterhooks. He had no idea what was about to happen. But the girl…she seemed as bored as if Fallow had just asked her to recite the Pledge of Allegiance.

"Guess I could call a few things."

Fallow threw back his head and laughed. "Call a few things! Isn't that rich? As if it were as easy as falling off a log."

The man scooped up a handful of snow, pressed it hard in his hands and threw it before Peter could react. The snowball struck him squarely in the chest and exploded, ice ricocheting into his face.

"Peter! Wake up! You're gonna wanna see this."

Willa looked at Peter and shrugged, and he was suddenly reminded of another reluctant child being made to perform. To sing a song at Christmas. A little boy. What was his name? What the hell was his name?

The girl's face went slack.

The circle of compacted snow went black, as if suddenly infused with ink. From above, the girl would be a small point at the center of a great O in the snow.

The circle began to spin, dark snow turning to slush, turning to icy water until a rushing, obsidian moat formed about the girl. Flowing counterclockwise—containing her.

Up from the inky swirl, ribbons of black rose, screaming streamers cutting wounds in the bright winter landscape. And from those wounds, figures arose. Dancing and writhing, eager for escape. Hoofed and horned, all teeth and nails—things so filled with riot they threatened to unseat the mind. They were kin to the creatures in his nightmares. They *were* his nightmares.

And the spectacle caused the blood to sing in his veins, thrumming with the collective heartbeat of the rising throng. He felt the black worms twist in his arms, in his head and recognized them for what they were. An infestation. Something *not* him. Something *not* Peter.

Whatever the girl was summoning from the circle was inside him as well. Yearning to answer her call and be free.

He dropped to his knees. "No more!"

Fallow bent down until they were nose to nose. There was fire in the man's eyes, and he seemed quite insistent Peter pick up what he was laying down.

"You get it now, Peter? That's us. Laid bare," the man said, his mustache quivering. "Can't explain any better. You wanted to understand her talent? *That*, my friend, is her talent. All those shades you're so afraid of out in the snow? They're afraid of *her.*"

The monstrosities were gone. All that was left was a tall girl in a field, hopping from foot to foot, eager to get back in the warm bus.

"So, I'll ask again. Do you trust us?"

Peter nodded, for to not agree seemed incredibly risky, given Fallow's mercurial nature.

"Great!"

Fallow helped him to his feet. When they were back inside the bus and seated across from each other, Peter asked, "And where do you fit into all of this?"

The man smiled.

"I'm their dad. Maybe not by blood or by logic. But…yeah, to them…I'm Dad."

Willa plopped behind the wheel, but before she turned the ignition, Peter caught her glancing back at him in the rearview mirror. And what was it those dark eyes were searching for? Approval? Applause?

"Can we get going?"

"Yes, Willa," Fallow said.

The engine coughed and Willa coaxed it to life. She steered the bus back onto the road, the snow surrendering to slush beneath its wheels in the bright morning sun. Maple City lay ahead, ready to jog Peter's memory, if Papa Fallow was worth his salt. The prairie receded in the distance as civilization blossomed ahead.

To them…I'm Dad, Fallow had said.

The words rolled about in Peter's mind, and as they did, a painful new hole ripped opened inside.

I'm Dad.

CHAPTER 21

"Yes?"

The woman's voice was barely audible, and Riggs had to bump the volume.

"Hello!" Riggs shouted into his phone, over-compensating for the woman's whispered greeting. "Is Mr. Porter there?"

"Who's calling."

"This is Riggs. I mean, Eli…Eli Riggs."

"Hello, Eli."

"Mr. Porter and I chatted last week about me maybe coming to work for him. Part-time."

"I see."

Riggs fidgeted. Ellen wished he would just get on with it and cut to the chase. People *never* cut to the chase. This was an opinion she shared with her father.

"Oh, just cut to the chase!" her father would beg students who called him for extensions on their papers, a bump in their grade or a recommendation they should have asked for two weeks ago. She liked the phrase and loved the sentiment. Cut to the chase, Riggs.

"Well," said the voice on the other end of the line, "Patrick isn't here right now."

Riggs mimed shooting himself in the head. "Great. Can I leave a message?"

The woman answered with a coughing fit that threatened to go on and on and on.

"Let me find a pen…"

"Thank you. My number is 309…"

"Haven't found one, yet."

Ellen snatched the phone out of Riggs's hand. "Do you know where he is?"

"Who is this?"

"I'm Eli's…sister. Where is Mr. Porter?"

It was a bold move, but Ellen didn't have all day. With every tick of the clock, the hour drew closer when she would have to board the bus to Aunt Tuffy's, and her investigation would cease. Time to get on with it. Time to cut to the chase.

"He took the car downtown, I believe. Trying to move things along at Pizza Carl's. Oh! I found a pen."

"Thanks." Ellen hung up on the woman and tossed the phone to Riggs. "Where's Pizza Carl's?"

* * *

The wiry man in the stained apron was pissed.

"Three weeks, Porter! That's what I told you yesterday *and* the day before that. Why do you gotta come down here and bust my balls?"

Ellen and Riggs stood in the open doorway of Pizza Carl's, unsure whether to enter or leave the two red-faced men inside to their heated argument. Ellen opted for the former. She stepped into the oven-hot room and took a seat at one of the many empty tables. Riggs slunk into the room and sat across from her, putting his attention on the menu rather than risk making eye contact with either of the shouting men.

"No, Carl. We agreed you'd be *out* in three weeks. Not starting to pack, you know? Not hiring the movers. *Out.*"

"Bullshit!"

Pat Porter stood his ground as Pizza Carl loosed a string of expletives that fascinated Ellen. Sure, there were the usual F and S-words she'd heard her mom utter hundreds of times, but Carl seemed to have dozens more at his disposal.

Riggs leaned in. "Maybe we should come back."

"No."

Pat held up his hands. "Look, I'm not going to waste your time or mine. I'm going send Steve Erikson over here in a couple of days…"

"You keep that bastard away from me!"

"I'm sending my lawyer, and if he sees you've made some progress on the move, fine. If not…well, then you'll be seeing a lot more of Mr. Erikson."

"Rat bastard!"

Pat glanced over to where Ellen and Riggs sat—Riggs wishing he were under the table, Ellen wishing she had popcorn. "You've got some customers."

And like that, the man was heading for the door. In a second, he'd be gone.

"Mr. Porter!" Ellen called.

The man stopped. "Yes?"

Ellen had no follow up. How do you transition from *Mr. Porter!* to *Tell me more about the Blind Rock Massacre?*

"Hey, Mr. P," Riggs said, grinning nervously and waving. "You got a sec?"

"Not particularly, Eli."

"Just a sec?"

The man checked his watch, sighed and approached. His outfit was J.C. Penny from top to bottom. "What do you need?"

"I was wondering if you'd given any more thought to my coming onboard? For the summer? I've been practicing all my cocktails, pouring through my Mr. Boston, pardon the pun…"

"If you hadn't noticed, Eli, this place is still a pizza joint."

"I can see that."

"I won't be hiring for the bar until fall at the earliest."

"But, in case you need someone to run errands for you, help with the transition and this and that…?"

Ellen grabbed hold of the reins. "I listened to your interview about the Blind Rock Massacre. Very interesting, very informative. I'm writing a paper, and I'd very much like to hear more about it. The tape was old, and I didn't get the whole story, and I'd really like to…"

"Slow your jets, dear," Pat said. "Glad you enjoyed it, but now's not a good time."

"When's a good time?"

Pat peered down at her. "Do I know you?"

"I'm a big fan of local history. It would mean a lot to me."

Mr. Porter checked his watch for a second time. He pulled a business card from his wallet and held it out. "Come by my house tomorrow morn, and you can ask me anything you want."

"Tomorrow?" Ellen balked. "I'd really like to talk to you today…"

"7:30 tomorrow morning. Best I can do."

Ellen took the card, and the man headed for the door. He paused for a moment and looked back. "Blind Rock, you say? Funny."

"Why's that funny?" Ellen asked.

"I was toying around with new names for this place the other day, and Blind Rock kept popping into my head. What do you think, Carl? Blind Rock Tavern a good name for my bar?"

"Bastard!" Carl shouted.

"You have a good day too."

And then Pat Porter was gone.

"We did it!" Riggs said, slapping the table. "I am *so* back on his radar. And you! You've got a meeting. Wins all around!"

Ellen shifted into full meltdown. "I can't meet him tomorrow! I won't even be here. I…"

Visions of her mother calling Aunt Tuffy elbowed their way into her head. *What do you mean she wasn't on the bus? Where the hell is she? Where the hell is my daughter?*

Ellen was starting to hyperventilate when the disgruntled proprietor suddenly appeared at the table, pen and pad in hand. "What'll you have?"

"Oh, we weren't…" Riggs redirected as Pizza Carl nailed him with a wicked stare. "Two slices?"

"Drinks?"

Riggs deferred to Ellen.

"Water, please."

"Make that two," Riggs added.

Pizza Carl mumbled under his breath and headed back to the kitchen.

Ellen grabbed the red pepper shaker and shook a healthy dose onto her awaiting tongue. The burn was instant and necessary.

"You are one weird kid."

Ellen tossed Riggs a nasty look. "And you're hanging out with an eleven-year-old."

"Well, when you put it like that."

Pizza Carl plopped two plates of oily slices on the table, along with a pitcher of warm water and two red, plastic tumblers.

"No wonder he's going out of business," Riggs said as he bit into his slice. "Sheesh, it's not even hot. You not eating? Can I have your slice?"

Ellen was definitely *not* eating. Instead, she was staring at her plate. The piece of pizza was half-eaten, nibbled away in tiny bites. Something had already snacked on her meal.

The table grew warm under her hands, and the air was suddenly thick and meaty. Ellen glanced up at Riggs, but he was underwater. At least, that's what it looked like. The guy was opening and closing his mouth at turtle's pace, but no sound came out.

It struck Ellen as crazy, but she could swear she heard time *slow*, felt the space between seconds grow. And this deceleration made her sick to her stomach.

A small shadow darted around the front counter, catching Ellen's eye. Whatever it was had immunity to the shift. It also had something in its teeth.

That's not a...

But it was. The rat reappeared from behind the row of gumball dispensers. It stopped in the middle of the room when it caught Ellen staring. It sat up on its hind legs, offering a better view of the prize it held clamped between its jaws.

An ear. A purple human ear.

Ellen screamed, and the force of it released a belch from her suddenly-soured stomach. The rat didn't startle—instead, it clutched the severed ear with its tiny paws and sank its incisors into the putrid meat, causing Ellen to scream again.

More hungry rats poured from behind the counter. Each had something juicy in its teeth—a toe, a tongue, a strip of scalp. They swarmed the floor, fighting over noses and lips.

Ellen grabbed Riggs's arm, and found that Riggs was gone. In his place sat a hollow-eyed man, a greasy rodent clinging to his hair, burrowing into the space where an eye once lived. A single bloody tear trailed down his ravaged cheek.

The corpse's shriveled lips parted, releasing the stench of something long dead.

"Bli-i-ind Rock..." it croaked.

Ellen howled. She grabbed her tumbler of water and chucked it at the dead man.

"Are you nuts?"

The man was gone. The rat was gone. Riggs was back, and Riggs was wet.

Pizza Carl was out from behind the counter like a shot. "What's going on here?" He eyed Riggs suspiciously. "This guy bothering you?"

"No, I..." Ellen stammered. She jumped to her feet, toppling her chair, and made a beeline for the door. "Sorry!"

Riggs called after her, but all Ellen could hear was the hungry sound of teeth on bone.

CHAPTER 22

Ellen had made it halfway down the block by the time Riggs caught up to her.

"You mind telling me why you chucked your drink at me?"

"I said I was sorry."

"You're upset. I can see that. Don't know why—don't need to know. Think I'll just mosey back to the library. You have a good one, kid."

"I need to pay," Ellen said, suddenly realizing she'd dined and dashed. "I have to go back and pay."

"Don't worry about it. I took care of the man."

Ellen ripped off her backpack and unzipped the main pocket, searching for the money—her *birthday* money.

"I can pay!"

Riggs whistled loudly, and Ellen winced. "I paid for it. It's done. You're welcome." He stared down at her, hair still dripping. "You need to call your mom."

"No."

"Cuz you're getting a little—"

"I said, no!"

Riggs zipped his lip and instead stared up at the marquee of the Rivoli Theater. Where movie titles once blazed, the sign simply said, *Space Available.*

"You know, I used to see movies here every weekend when I was your age. James Bond was my favorite. Mr. Voss who owned this place never booked any movie above PG. But sometimes, an R-rated horror flick would make its way past him, and…damn! You haven't heard screams until you've heard a bunch of ten-year-olds watching Freddy Krueger in the front row." Riggs looked back at Ellen, whose breathing had resumed a semi-normal pace. "Back there, you sounded just like one of those kids."

"I'm fine."

"Sure you are."

As they made their way down Main Street, heading back toward the town square, Ellen reached into her pocket and gripped the folded memo, trying to draw strength from her father's words.

Don't stop now, Spooky

Why not? Where are you leading me?

Don't stop now, Spooky

Throw me a bone, will you?

Don't—

"Stop!"

Brakes screeched, and Ellen leaped out of the path of the oncoming van. The driver laid on his horn as he sped off.

"You are in another world," Riggs said, ushering her across the street.

Ellen couldn't agree more.

As they approached the library, Ellen held out her hand.

"Phone."

"Now you're coming to your senses."

Ellen waved Riggs away and punched in her aunt's number.

"Hello, Gooding residence," Aunt Tuffy said.

Ellen decided to kill two birds with one stone. First, she made it known that she would *not* be arriving this evening after all. Second, there was no need for Tuffy to call Mom because Mom was "like that" at the moment. It was shorthand she and her aunt employed to describe a brewing Rita storm. If Tuffy pampered Ellen with gifts, Mom would get "like that," if a waiter brought the wrong appetizer, Rita would most definitely get "like that."

"Understood," was all Tuffy said. If Rita was "like that," she'd leave her the hell alone.

"See you tomorrow," Ellen concluded.

"Done?" Riggs asked.

Ellen shooed him away. "One more call."

But there wasn't one more call. Only her mother's voice asking her to leave a message. When the beep came, Ellen panicked and hung up. No worries—plenty of time to call back. It was probably better to let her story marinate a bit before trying it out on Mom.

She handed Riggs back his phone.

"Can you get me back inside?"

"Where? The library? Not a chance. You're on Scorch's naughty list. Not gonna happen."

"Last favor," Ellen said, pressing hard. "Please?"

"What do you need? I could bring it out to you."

"I need to use the restroom."

"We could go back to Pizza Carl's. He's got a bathroom—"

"I need a *women's* room. I'm getting my period."

Ellen was decidedly *not* getting her period. She had yet to pass through that door, but the guy in front of her didn't know that. And Ellen had found the mere mention of the word could often work to her advantage.

"You…"

"I need a clean restroom. You'll distract her?"

Riggs clucked his tongue, and for a moment, Ellen feared she'd tapped the last of the guy's goodwill.

"Last favor?"

"I swear."

* * *

Ellen hunkered down behind the squat book deposit box, a position that afforded her a clear view of the front desk through the glass door.

Mrs. Flynt looked up from her paperwork—sending out overdue notices, no doubt—as Riggs approached. Ellen watched as the guy launched into an animated monologue. She'd offered Riggs a few suggestions for the diversion, but in the end he'd simply said, "Leave it to me."

Whatever he was up to was working. Old Scorch's temperature was rising. She held up a warning finger and came out from behind the front desk. Riggs gestured toward the children's room, and Mrs. Flynt marched past him and through the door, leaving her post.

Riggs didn't even look back—he just gave a little wave. Her signal to make a run for it. Ellen didn't waste a second.

She zipped in through the front door, crossed the main room at a good clip and disappeared into the stacks. Ellen paused a moment to calm herself, staring at the car maintenance books shelved in front of her. She doubted she had much time. Riggs may have bought her a few minutes, but Mrs. Flynt would soon see through whatever lie he was spinning and be back on guard shortly. She had one shot, and she'd better take it now.

Ellen zigzagged through the stacks until she was deep in the heart of the library. Until she could see the book donation box she'd slammed into on her last sprint through the main room.

Don't be full. Don't be full.

She closed her eyes, prayed for luck and walked briskly from the cover of the stacks.

"When you make up your mind to do something, it's best to plow straight ahead," her father had advised her after she'd had a heated argument with Mom about taking swimming lessons. Ellen had zero interest in sharing an oversized bathtub with a bunch of rowdy kids. She wanted to spend her summer exactly where she was now—nestled inside an air-conditioned library. She'd been wavering, considering buckling to her mother's demands.

"When you decide on something, Ellen, decide and be done with it."

Ellen had decided. She was going to hide in the box.

She crossed the distance from stacks to box, glanced around once—no eyes on her—lifted the donation box's lid and climbed inside. Thankfully, the box was only half filled, and once she was safely inside, she squirmed off her backpack and went about rearranging the books, pulling them out from underneath, dragging them up and over herself, creating the world's heaviest and most literate blanket.

The library was closing at 2:00. She could endure being ensconced for a few hours.

And then what?

Once the librarians and patrons were gone, she'd get to one of the *for patrons only* phones, call Mom and find some excuse for not putting Aunt Tuffy on the line. She'd find some quiet corner where she could wait out the night, allowing her to make her morning appointment with Mr. Porter. To get the rest of the story…

Even as she played out her next moves, Ellen knew it was a *child's* plan, lacking in substance and vulnerable to a million things that might go wrong. Like when she'd made up her mind to walk from Iowa City to Denver to rescue a German Shepherd she'd read about with wheels for back legs and who needed a home. But it was the only plan she had.

Ellen nudged aside a thick almanac biting into her hip when she heard Riggs's voice whispering her name. He passed by a number of times before giving up, assuring her she was doing a bang-up job of hide-and-seek.

She allowed herself the luxury of a deep breath, relishing the decidedly bookish scent of her hiding place. She took another, breathing in fiction and memoirs and discarded magazines. The mingled scents quieted her yammering mind, shut out visions of the dead eager to commune. Blocked out the whole world.

And then, in a turn of events that would surprise and alarm her later, she found herself drifting to sleep.

CHAPTER 23

Maple City was depressed, as was most of the Midwest. The farm crisis had taken a toll, both economic and emotional. Fallow gave Peter the rundown as Willa steered them down Main Street. Half a dozen farmers in the community dead by their own hand, bowed under mounting debt and dwindling crops.

"When the farmers lose money, they don't shop in town. When shops veer into the red, the whole town bleeds."

Peter stared out the window at the once bustling burg. Stanton's Footwear, Dean's Appliances, Maple City Furniture—all shuttered. The only bright spot on the block was the Rivoli Theater. The movie theater boasted *Rocky II* and *Moonraker.* The letters, stark black on white, hurt Peter's head, as if their very presence were an affront to his sanity. A question, a suddenly very important question, leaped to the fore.

"What year is it?"

Fallow burst out laughing. "Well, shit. I was hoping this trip would help wake up that old grey matter of yours. Guess I was wrong."

"Tell me."

"1979," Willa said. She was staring at him again in the rearview mirror. And was that pity in her gaze? Peter thought it was.

"Last year of the decade, Peter. Let's hope the next brings this town a bit more luck." Fallow snapped his fingers at Willa. "Here we are! City Hall. Home of all paper-pushers."

The girl parked with more than a bit of verbal guidance by Fallow. A large sign greeted them, announcing the empty lot next to City Hall would soon be a construction sight. *Future Home of the Maple City Library*. A Pink Floyd fan had defaced the sign, covering it with *The Wall* stickers and scrawling *We Don't Need No Education* for emphasis.

Fallow strode to the entrance to the building and held open the door for Willa and Peter. "Entrez vous!"

The lobby was sad and sterile, a shell of what must at one time have been rather impressive. The place was solidly built if not well maintained. An ornate check-in desk sat unattended. Cardboard panels lay tacked over the original signage, indicating room assignments.

"Public Works, City Clerk…" Fallow mumbled, reading off the handwritten sign. "Here we go. Room 106."

Fallow motioned for Peter to take a seat on one of the hard benches lining the lobby walls.

"Shouldn't take me too long, God willing."

Then, without so much as a backwards glance, Fallow set off down one of the dark hallways snaking away from the lobby into the belly of City Hall and disappeared.

Peter sat and removed Fallow's coat, which had become overkill in the furnace-blasted lobby. Willa stood across from him, leaning against the wall next to the outline of a long-gone water fountain, a capped water pipe poking from a hole highlighting its absence.

Peter realized this was the first time he'd been alone with Willa. He thought to break the ice with small talk, but the girl beat him to the punch.

"You look familiar."

"I do?"

"Not really." Willa struggled to make sense. "Something *about* you is familiar. Not you. Something—"

"Something about me."

"Yes."

They let the conversation die out, both hard-pressed to keep it going. A muffled shout from down the hallway where they'd last seen Fallow solved that.

"He's...quite a man, your father."

"He's not my father. He's my guardian."

"Oh, well I—"

"He makes us call him Papa, but that's just like a first name."

"I see."

"Like Peter is a first name."

"Okay."

Peter was fine with letting Willa steer the conversation. The way she looked at him, he could tell there was more, so much more she had to say. But instead, she turned her attention back to him.

"You don't know where your people are?"

"No," he admitted. "I don't even know if I have people."

"You do."

"How can you be so sure?"

The girl took a step toward him. With her dark, flowing hair and serious eyes, she looked unlike any of the pasty people he'd seen walking the streets of Maple City. No, Willa was from *away*, of that he was certain.

"When you tumbled into the world, you were calling out to someone."

Peter sat at attention. It was the first time anyone had spoken of his curious arrival at the church, and he didn't want to miss a detail.

"What did I say?"

"Hann…something."

"You mean Han? Like…Solo?"

Willa shook her head. "That's all I could make out. You were broken. All you wanted was Hann…or whoever."

Peter decided to leap in with both feet. "Where did you bring me from?"

"I don't know. I never know."

"What?"

Willa's hand flailed. "I…I just reach and pull something out. Like a rabbit out of a hat. I don't know how I do it. I've always been able to do it."

Peter rose, startling the girl. "Where do you *think* I came from."

"I don't know!" Willa shouted.

Her cry broke the spell, and she turned away, wouldn't look at him even though he remained standing, eager to continue the conversation. Eager to get to the bottom of it.

When it became clear Willa was done talking, Peter walked to the far side of the lobby and sat apart from her, giving them both space. He'd revisit their conversation later, when he could. For now, the girl was a closed book.

He was still staring at his shoes when he heard the man approach, heard the foul and familiar tone as he addressed Willa.

"Someone tell the good Lord above that one of his angels is missing!"

Peter looked up, on red alert.

The skinny man in the coveralls stood precariously close to Willa. "Hello, angel."

Albert. His name is Albert.

"Leave the poor girl be," a voice said. Peter turned to find Big Bear standing at the exit, frowning.

"I'm just having a little fun, Bill."

"Doesn't look like fun to her. I'm heading over to the fairgrounds to clean up the mess those high school kids left us. You coming?"

"In a sec."

The big man shook his head and pushed open the door.

Peter's could suddenly hear his heart pounding in his ears, and when the skinny man turned to look at him, all the air left the room.

"What you starin' at?"

Without warning, a screaming shockwave passed through Peter's body, and he fell to the floor, the impact robbing him of his breath.

The lobby was gone. He was in a basement, crouched in the dirt.

A man's voice came from above, spitting cruelly.

"Serves you right, you little shit."

Peter gasped for air. "Daddy..."

"I warned you, didn't I? I need my shuteye. Didn't I warn you?"

"Don't." It was all Peter could do to form the word.

The man leered down at him. "Be quiet, I told you. You know I told you. Don't listen. Just like your mama. You don't never listen."

"No!"

Peter's voice echoed in the lobby. He was back.

The man across the room turned away from Willa, his face a younger version of the sneering vision he'd just seen.

"You got a problem, buddy?" the man in the coveralls asked.

Peter couldn't answer. He was petrified. After searching and searching for memories, *any* memories, one had exploded from the ether and pierced his soul. Fallow had hoped the trip into town would jog his memory—his memory was good and fucking jogged.

He squeezed his eyes tight, at once willing the scene away and coaxing it forward. A snippet from his past, searing though it may be, had shot across his path. And like a child reaching for the inviting glow of a red-hot stovetop, Peter grasped for the memory once more.

"Thinkin' maybe it's time..."

"Daddy."

"Time for you to go. Let me sleep. Leave me be."

The man took a step down the stairs.

Peter's hand went to his head and came away wet. "I'm hurt!"

"Yeah," the man said. "Time."

As he gave the belt another snap, the man's grey lips pulled back in a skeletal grin.

"Time to see your mama."

Too much. The scene threatened to swallow him whole.

Peter struck the ground with his fists and felt his knuckles crack against the unforgiving tile floor. He leaped to his feet, bloodied hands up, ready to do battle, but he was alone in the cavernous room.

The man in the coveralls was gone. And so was Willa.

CHAPTER 24

Ellen's eyes snapped open. Where was she? She was being smothered. She was trapped. A coffin? Was she in a coffin?

She sat bolt upright, tossing off the weight encumbering her and shoved hard on the lid.

A midnight-dark room awaited her.

I'm in the library. I'm in the library.

The mantra calmed her racing heart. Ellen gripped the sides of the donation box and lifted herself out.

It's night. Why is it night?

The only lights in the place came from exit signs and a stray reading lamp, left on by the newspaper rack. She rushed over to the lone lamp and held up the watch attached to her pack.

11:02.

Ellen had once found a box in the closet her father kept at her mom's apartment. Inside were wonders—comic books that weren't quite comics. Instead of ridiculous superheroes, the kind her classmates drooled over, these contained stories that lit up her young mind. *Frankenstein, War of the Worlds* and the one that would haunt her dreams, *Rip Van Winkle*. The idea someone could fall asleep and awaken years later was horrific to her.

And yet, what had she done? She'd gone and Rip Van Winkled her way to 11:02 at night.

Mom!

Even more frightening than the prospect of losing half a day was losing the opportunity to cover her bases with Rita. Abandoning the pool of light, Ellen picked her way to the front desk. She hadn't noticed a single security camera while casing the library. Heck, the Maple City Library hadn't even shelled out for magnetic security sensors at the front desk. The folks in this town were on the honor system.

She slipped behind the desk and was instantly on edge. This was Mrs. Flynt's domain—this was Scorch's lair. She shook off her nerves and reached for the phone. The line lit up, she pressed 9 and dialed her mom.

As before, there was no answer. That was either good luck or bad news. Rita was either locking lips with the postman or filing a police report.

Returning the phone to its cradle, she looked out at the dark room. The Night Library, as she dubbed it. She wasn't afraid, and this surprised her. The prospect of Rita's finding her out, now *that* terrified her, but standing alone in this place, even after the visions she'd had? Nothing.

It was because Dad was close. She could feel it. He might not be as tangible as the rats or the busload of dead folk, but he was near. The message in her pocket, the money in her backpack, the birthday card—how could she be frightened when Dad was close at hand?

With an entire night to kill, Ellen decided a second visit to the history collection was in order. The Porter interview might be toast, but perhaps there might be some other useful information she'd overlooked.

She walked to the stairs, relishing having the whole place to herself.

When I grow up, I won't have a living room or a dining room or a guest bedroom. I'll turn them all into libraries.

She descended the stairs, eager to dive into the clutter of boxes and stacks of old books. As she sifted through the mess, she realized she and her mother had something in common— the love of poking around in other people's things, looking for treasures.

After an hour or so, Ellen had to concede she had come up short. In all the piles of photos and documents and notebooks she examined, there was not a single Blind Rock reference to be had. The only thing of any use in that regard was the tape. And it remained tangled up inside the player.

Sitting at the table, she did what she had wanted to before old Scorch had arrived on the scene. Taking a pencil, she tried to extract the tape from the machine's works, careful not to damage it.

A TV commercial popped into her head, and she found it next to impossible to rid herself of it.

Take out wrenched ankle. Ha-ha-HA! Take out wrenched ankle. Ha-ha-HA!

She had never played the game Operation. Never would. Games were for bored brains, and hers never was.

Take out wrenched ankle. Ha-ha...

"What do you think you're doing?"

The voice surprised Ellen, causing her hand to jerk, ripping the tape. She backed quickly away from the table, ready to bolt.

Behind the chair where she had just been sitting, a pale mist moved back and forth, back and forth. If Ellen didn't know better, she would say there was another person in the room, and that person was agitatedly pacing to and fro.

"You've ruined it!"

Ellen adjusted her focus, like she did when taking the vision test at school. The more she focused, the better she could see the man in the wool jacket with patches on the elbows. He was upset, and desperately trying to repair the damage Ellen had done. Unfortunately for him, his hands passed through the tape player.

"All that time. All that work!"

Mr. Pullen. It's got to be...

The spirit wasn't particularly frightening. She'd seen his kind before. But there was something different about this encounter. Something she couldn't quite put her finger on.

That was, until Mr. Pullen put his finger on the tape player. With a swift tap of a button, he ejected the cassette.

I'm helping him do that.

Ellen was astounded. It seemed the more she concentrated on the distraught librarian, the more access he had to the world. The *living* world.

She let her concentration wane, testing her theory. Once more, the tape player eluded Mr. Pullen's grasp.

"Stop that, you naughty girl!"

Ellen grinned. She was still marveling at her discovery when a loud crash echoed from above. Something big had fallen in the main room of the library.

CHAPTER 25

Peter dashed out of City Hall, looking left and right. No Willa. Just the empty church bus and a cluster of pigeons.

"Willa!"

His voice was thin, his vocal cords clenched against the vision he'd experienced. The pigeons remained unstartled.

"Willa!" he shouted again, louder this time, and this time the sky rats took flight.

He was about to head back inside and track down Fallow when he heard a muffled cry. Whirling about, he caught a glimpse of movement, partially obscured by the sign announcing the new library's construction. He rushed toward the empty lot, ducking around the sign and found the man in grey and the girl standing ankle-deep in the snow. Willa's back was against the wall as she did her best to retreat from his advances.

The girl's eyes met Peter's, and in their connection, her demeanor shifted dramatically. She placed her hand on the man's shoulder and threw back her head.

Peter heard whispers fill the air, and felt the blood go hot in his veins.

Willa was doing her trick.

And whatever was inside him was responding.

* * *

Ellen raced up the stairs. She heard Mr. Pullen raise one last complaint before his voice faded away.

Good. Not a big fan of the librarians in this place, living or dead.

A book flew past her, striking the reading lamp, sending it crashing to the floor where it cast long shadows into the room.

Enough. No more.

But there was more. A hell of a lot more.

The shelving unit containing rows and rows of audiobooks spun about and teetered on edge before spilling its CDs. Then the stack fell to the ground, shattering into pieces.

The red exit signs about the library flickered on and off, on and off, adding an emergency strobe to the chaos.

Ellen shouted into the empty yet roiling room.

"Dad! If this is you, cut it out!"

A portrait of a board member long dead toppled off the wall and impaled itself on the Illinois flag.

No. Definitely not *Dad.*

* * *

The man in the coveralls tried to take a step back.

"What's that noise?" the man asked, wincing.

Peter was wondering the same thing, until he realized it was coming from his mouth. A gargled cry that had been building up in his throat burst forth, and in it was rage. At the man, yes, but at himself as well. A part of him, the part drawn to the surface by Willa's whispered song, was rebelling, yearning to break free.

The blank spots, the spaces where his inventory of memories should be—the lack of Peter was congealing and eager for...

Escape!

The world turned negative to Peter's eye. The snow was suddenly tar black, the sky a churning umber. The man in the coveralls was red, blood red, and the darkness rising up within him wanted the man redder still.

Peter leaped for the man, reaching out with not hands but claws, his vision drilling into the man's head, seeing his frightened skull within.

The darkness within him cried out—a foreign voice, and yet familiar.

I am Whisper. I am Mr. Tell!

"No!" Willa cried.

With a swirl of beak and feather and talon, he bit down on the man's nose.

* * *

Faint figures appeared—they were so dim Ellen at first waved them off as shadows cast by the toppled lamp. But when one reached out for the other, grasping the other by the neck, Ellen took cover beneath Mrs. Flynt's desk.

Hunkered beneath, she could only imagine what was happening above. Something heavy fell, glass shattered, wood strained and splintered. And above it all, a gust of air whistled past, riding on great wings.

Ellen grabbed her ankles and rocked against the cacophony.

A lone voice rose above the din, and although Ellen couldn't be certain, she thought she heard it cry, *"No!"*

Then all was silent.

Daring to open her eyes, Ellen saw the first black feather float gently to the floor before her. Followed by another. And another.

CHAPTER 26

Fallow pulled Peter off the man with the bloodied nose.

"Are you crazy?" Albert shouted. "You broke my nose, you bastard!"

"Get out of here before I call the cops," Fallow roared. The man in the coveralls didn't have to be told twice. He scurried away, leaving a trail of blood in the snow.

Fallow turned Peter roughly about. "I leave you alone for five minutes…"

"What did I do?"

"Just about tore that man's nose clean off, that's what you did, Peter." Fallow sounded more impressed than angry.

Willa turned to Peter. "You're not whole. Neither is Whisper. You're still…mixed."

"I can see that," Peter said, trying to adopt Fallow's seeming lack of concern. But Willa was not having it. She stepped close, getting in his face.

"You've got some of him inside you. Stuff that doesn't belong to you."

"Easy, Willa," Fallow cautioned.

"You're a thief!"

A winter wind whipped across the vacant lot, stirring up snow.

"Easy, I said!" Fallow barked. The snow squall settled. "Let's go before we draw a crowd."

* * *

Peter was silent on the ride back to the church. Fallow attempted to press him into conversation, prattling on about the paltry sum the pencil-pushers at City Hall offered for the copper and where they could stuff their goddamned check. As if today were like any other.

Willa remained silent as well, though her words still rang loud and clear in his ears.

You've got some of him inside you. Stuff that doesn't belong to you.

It was true. It was there, just beneath his skin. An oozing blackness filling in the holes of his soul, masking the absence of…him.

You're a thief!

As they approached the church, the two little ones rushed outside, waving their hands frantically.

"What's the matter now?" Fallow sighed.

Peter accompanied the old fellow off the bus. He turned back to Willa, but she had already swung the bus door closed and hit the gas. The armadillo on wheels kicked up ice as she steered it back to its home behind the church.

"Curly's crying!" Jo said.

"He's crying and he won't stop," Huck added.

"I already said that."

"No, you didn't."

They followed the distraught children into the church and found Curly sitting in a pew, holding the empty rope leash.

Dodge was attempting to comfort the boy, but Curly shrugged him off.

"What's wrong?" Fallow asked.

"It's the dog," Dodge said, putting his hand on Curly's shoulder, only to have it shrugged off again.

"Gimme a moment," Fallow said to Peter. He approached the boy and knelt before him. The man took Curly's hands in his and leaned in until their heads were pressed against each other. The contact gave the boy permission to truly let go, and he howled in anguish. Fallow whispered to him, and the boy nodded, comforted by the old man's words. Fallow slowly drew the rope out of Curly's grip and handed it to Dodge.

"Take this away," was all he said.

Peter watched as Fallow soothed the boy, speaking low, ruffling his hair. He watched until he felt out of place, awkward in the privacy of the moment. He turned and exited the church, leaving Jo and Huck to continue gawking at Curly's grief.

Stepping into the bright winter sunlight, he held his hands up high, looking for any trace of darkness beneath his palms and found none. Whatever had risen in him had settled back for the time being. Hiding? Lying in wait?

A sharp crack caught his attention, and he turned in the direction of the retort. Willa was standing in the field behind the church, arm pulled back, winding up. She let something loose and another crack echoed across the plain.

She's afraid of you.

Peter picked his way through the snow toward the girl.

She thinks you're a thief.

He raised a hand in greeting. "Don't mind me."

"I don't," Willa replied, bending to pick a stone from beneath the snow. She rose quickly and whipped the stone across the surface of a small, frozen pond. It hit the surface—*crack*—and continued skipping across the ice until it disappeared in the drifts beyond.

Peter likewise bent and searched the snow. He wrenched a piece of limestone from the earth and skipped it across the pond. The stone hit an outcropping of ice and skittered off sideways.

"Thank you."

Peter wasn't expecting the girl to speak, but he was glad she did.

"For stopping that man from—"

"You're welcome." It was hard enough for the girl to thank him—no need for her to relive the vileness imposed upon her. There would be enough vileness awaiting her in the years to come. Such was the sad truth for women and girls.

Willa retrieved another stone and chucked it across the pond.

"Good one," Peter said as the rock joined its brethren in the snowy white drifts.

Willa picked up another cold shard. "Sometimes I drop myself into a stone."

Peter didn't reply, waiting to see where the girl was going with this.

She held the stone close to her chest. "I concentrate and pour all of my joy and anger and sadness into it. Let it soak it up like a sponge. And then…"

In a move that would impress any pitcher, Willa flicked the stone across the ice. The pond responded with a resounding crack as breaks in the ice spread out from the point of impact.

At first, Peter thought the stone had split, shattering with the force of Willa's throw. But when a dozen stones broke off in multiple directions, skimming across the frozen pond, he realized he was wrong. The stone hadn't split—somehow, under Willa's watchful eye, one stone had become many.

"That's some trick," Peter said.

"It's no trick," the girl replied. She regarded him for a moment, seemed about to speak, then thought better of it. She left him there by the pond, and traipsed back to the church. A dark, curious figure against a sea of white.

* * *

That night, after a simple meal of spaghetti and canned vegetable medley, the kids opted to go their own ways. Young Huck and Jo were the first to disappear to their respective rooms followed by a sulking Dodge, then Willa. By nightfall, Curly was nodding off at the kitchen table, one of his crutches lying unnoticed on the floor. Fallow sat contentedly, a hand on Curly's arm.

"Coffee?" the old man asked, raising his mug.

"No thanks."

"Don't know what you're missing."

Gentle warbling drifted through the air—the little ones were singing. Huck and Jo's song brought a smile to the old man's face.

"Day is dying in the west; heaven is touching earth with rest..."

Peter half-expected Fallow to take the opportunity to chat, to at least remark on the incident in the vacant lot, at least mention the man in the coveralls with the bloodied nose. Instead, Fallow rocked back in his chair, its legs creaking under his weight and hummed along with the little ones' song.

"Wait and worship while the night sets the evening lamps alight..."

Peter left him there, retiring to his makeshift bedroom in the cloakroom. He kicked off his shoes, still damp from the snow, and flopped down on the cot.

The night wind had risen, and riding its waves, the laments of the lost.

They have no business being here.

Fallow's words came back to him as the church walls groaned beneath the press of a snowy gust.

They're of no consequence.

"I know how they feel," Peter said to the empty room. A profound sense of loneliness rose in his gut, washing over him, leaving him as mournful as poor Curly. The boy had lost his dog; Peter had lost so much more. He had lost *everything.*

The door to the room creaked. Its hinges were misaligned, and the latch didn't catch, and so when it swung open a hair, Peter hardly noticed.

But when the mist entered the room, he noticed—noticed and sat up.

No, it wasn't mist. It was smoke. And it settled in a small cloud about his feet. Peter felt a slight press of weight as the blackness searched out a form and solidified. The first aspect to gel were the eyes, shining and corvid.

It was Willa's bird. The one she called Whisper. It was her Mr. Tell.

The creature filled out, birthing wings and sprouting feathers. It snuck up his legs before it was fully formed, each hop on more substantial legs.

Its eyes held him in place. As intense as its mistress's, the crow's eyes locked on his, insistent without threat. And as it reached his chest, Peter felt the same, familiar thrum that came when Willa incanted her secret words, his blood turning to music in his veins.

The crow glanced down at his left arm, free from the confines of the wool blanket. Exposed. The room was dark, but Peter sensed the black swirling beneath his skin. With a clean jerk, the bird sank its beak in his arm. There was no pain, just an uncomfortable twisting of sinew. The crow lifted its head, drawing black tendrils from his arm that squirmed like terrified worms.

The creature gulped them down and dove back for more. Peter felt a sucking, as if poison were being siphoned from his chest. A quick catch, then a gush.

He's taking back what's his...

The bird fed and fed, and Peter felt darkness drain from him. Returning to its owner. And when Whisper had had his fill, he stood up straight and locked eyes once more.

Did the room just get colder?

The winged thing steadily crept up his chest and bent its beak to his face. With the closeness came doubt. Did it mean to comfort him as Fallow had Curly? Or was it going to pluck his eyes out?

Its head twisted as if something invisible had taken hold, eager to snap its neck. The movement pained the bird, but it did little to fight against it. It stood solemnly still as its neck contorted and its beak snapped.

All went still, and the crow gave a short, slight cough, producing something small from its throat. It was a stone, a round polished thing. Blood red.

The bird worked the stone forward with a series of chatters and bent closer still. Peter felt the tip of its smooth beak part his lips.

It means to feed me...

And then the stone was on his tongue. It was cold and arrived on the bird's steaming breath.

"Yours," the bird rasped.

Without a second thought, spurred on by instinct, Peter swallowed the stone, feeling it draw an icy line down his throat.

His task complete, the bird vanished—dissipating into the cold, night air.

Peter felt the stone disappear into his core and awaited its effect. For the bloodstone was an offering, was it not? A reward for protecting Willa? Surely, there must be an effect...

Fruit-sweet breath warmed his lips and pressed down hard.

Hann...

He remembered that kiss.

Hann...

It lit up his very soul.

Hannah!

CHAPTER 27

"**E**llen!"

Ellen practically peed herself. The letter opener she'd found in Mrs. Flynt's desk was still clasped in her hand. She sat up and found herself perched atop the library's front desk. She vaguely remembered crawling up here, fearing that if she fell asleep, rats might scurry from the shadows and feast on her toes.

"What the hell, kid?"

Riggs stood staring in disbelief.

Panic gripped Ellen's chest and she fought back a shriek. The ruined library, her trespass—she was about to feel holy hell rain down.

Instead, Riggs chuckled.

"So, you hid out, eh? I had a feeling. You were so keen to stick around and then…*poof!* You were gone. Mind getting off the desk?"

Ellen's eyes zipped about the room. The library was as it had been before the night rampage. No impaled portrait, no literary carnage. The only thing out of place was the jar of pens she'd upended when Riggs called her name.

"Down," Riggs repeated.

Ellen obeyed. She hopped to the floor and almost toppled over, so weak with fear were her legs.

"What time is it?"

"Thirty minutes 'til Scorch and counting. I was hoping I could get in, get you out with her being none the wiser." He flipped a loose key in the air and caught it with a flourish. "Not supposed to have a master, but they sure do come in handy sometimes."

"But what time is it?"

Riggs glanced up at the clock above Ellen's head. "7:15."

"Mr. Porter!"

"Huh?"

Ellen grabbed hold of Riggs's dress shirt so hard three of his buttons popped loose.

"Come on."

"Come on, what?" Riggs said, grumpily retrieving the wayward buttons.

"I'm supposed to meet Mr. Porter at 7:30."

"Good luck. He lives halfway across town."

Ellen stomped her foot. The guy wasn't helping. It was already 7:15, she hadn't yet spun her web of lies around Mom and the guy wasn't helping! "You're an adult. You have a car, right?"

"Keep dreaming, kid."

"You can drive me."

"Not a chance. Now, we gotta get outta here before…."

Ellen heard the assisted door hum as it swung open. Standing in the doorway was Mrs. Flynt, sack lunch in her hand and a livid expression on her face.

"Mr. Riggs!"

"Double shit."

Ellen braced against the full brunt of the coming barrage and was surprised when the elderly librarian directed her heat at Riggs.

"How did you get in here? You don't have opening privileges."

"I…I…" Riggs stammered.

"And what are you doing here *alone* with this minor?"

"Excuse me?" The insinuation in Mrs. Flynt's voice made Riggs bristle. It also caused him to pull his shirt together in front, for its loss of buttons had exposed his pale belly.

Mrs. Flynt swooped past them, heading for her desk. "This is highly inappropriate. I'm calling Don Whittaker. I think you two need to have a chat."

"No, no, no," Riggs cried, frantically waving Mrs. Flynt away from the phone. "You don't have to—"

"Sheila?" Mrs. Flynt asked, speaking into the phone. "Is Don there? This is Alice Flynt over at the library. We have a situation here." She lowered her voice for effect. "It involves a child."

Ellen was about to ask Riggs what bug had crawled up the old woman's behind when Riggs grabbed her by the hand and rushed toward the exit.

"Fucking Scorch."

"Slow down!" Ellen cried, but Riggs wasn't listening. He was too busy getting them the hell out of there.

They burst through the door into the square, and Riggs veered right, quickstepping it down the alley between the library and City Hall.

"What are you doing?" Ellen asked, a bit louder this time, planting her feet and causing Riggs to slow.

When he turned back, he was red-faced and sweating. "She's calling Don Whittaker."

"Who's Don—"

"He's a board member *and* an ex-Chief of Police. Last thing I want is him thinking I'm some sort of perv."

"How's running away going to help?"

Riggs threw up his hands. "I have no fucking idea."

Ellen glanced back up the alley to see if they were being pursued, but of course they were not. Scorch was still back at the library tattling on Riggs. The poor guy was distraught—the guy needed a plan.

Ellen took charge. "Where's your car?"

Riggs nodded toward the end of the alley. "Over by Maple City Dairy."

"Come on."

Not pausing to look back, Ellen trotted down the alley, her backpack bouncing with each brisk step. Soon, she heard the nervous flap of Riggs's shoes on pavement and knew she had him where she wanted him.

"It's right over there," Riggs said, pulling his keys from his pocket. The blue Jeep Liberty with one wheel up on the curb sitting in front of the ice cream shop gave a short bleep of its horn.

"Shotgun," Ellen said, taking a rare stab at humor.

"What?"

"Oh, just get in and drive."

* * *

Riggs couldn't stop kicking himself.

"This is stupid. What am I doing? I should go back. I didn't do anything. This is stupid."

Riggs had said Pat Porter's house was halfway across town, and so when he steered out toward the *edge* of town, leaving the house and elm-lined streets behind and veered onto the highway that curved toward the prairie, Ellen grew worried. She pulled Mr. Porter's card from her pocket and read off his home address rather loudly.

"I know where he lives." Riggs was short with her. He had every right to be, Ellen supposed. He was upset with himself and probably her as well, but the fact remained she had a 7:30 meeting. Emotions were messy things—they got in the way. Best to let 'em slide.

She checked her watch. "Because it's 7:27."

"So?" Riggs was over her.

Still she pressed him. "I'm risking a lot just being here, you know?"

"You're singing to the choir, jailbait."

"What's jail—"

"Forget it."

Ellen fumed. Why did everything have to be so confusing when it should be simple? She had the means to get to Pat Porter's house on time, and she was determined to plow through whatever nastiness the other side had to throw at her—she got her determinedness from *both* Mom and Dad. Why then was this guy making things so difficult?

The Jeep suddenly lurched right onto the shoulder, and Riggs hit the brakes. They slid on loose gravel, and for a second Ellen thought they were heading for the shallow ravine lining the highway. But after a couple of feet, Riggs gained control of the vehicle and brought it to a halt.

"What's wrong?" Ellen asked.

Riggs looked back over his shoulder. "I think I hit something."

They hopped out of the Jeep, Riggs warning Ellen back onto the grass as a convoy of semis rumbled past. He knelt to examine a small bundle of orange fur. It wasn't moving.

"It's dead, but I didn't do it."

Ellen stepped closer. The fox was most certainly dead, had been for quite some time, by the looks of it. Its eyes stared blankly at the world it had left behind, reminding her of Reynard the Fox from the play—just the same hollow *nothingness* of the actor's tattered mask.

Ellen looked away.

"I'm going to drop you off at Pat's house, and then I'm driving back to the library." When Ellen started to speak, he held up a hand. "I gotta go clear this up."

"But what do I do after—"

"Pat's a good guy. He'll make sure you get back to your mom." He paused. "I'm sorry."

"For what?"

"For not acting like an adult."

Ellen considered this. "If you acted like an adult, I wouldn't be able to hear the rest of the story. So, apology not accepted."

"You're a weird kid, kid."

"I know."

After letting a truck full of squealing hogs whoosh past, the heady scent of manure swirling in its wake, Ellen and Riggs walked back to the Jeep and took off.

Ellen glanced back at the dead fox as they merged onto the highway. She felt a tug of sorrow as she spotted the animal's disembodied essence step from a tangle of bittersweet and approach the corpse. The ghost fox bent its head and sniffed its own remains in curious wonder.

CHAPTER 28

Peter lay sprawled on the sofa, wrapped in an afghan. The TV was on—PBS was busy trying to coax donations out of their viewers in exchange for public television-inspired gifts. The New York Philharmonic would return shortly, they promised, but first…how about this lovely tote bag?

It was a lazy evening in Manhattan. Even the rush and honk of traffic was taking the night off. Peter stretched and made himself more comfortable on the sofa, his toes gripping the afghan.

The mingled scents of curried chicken wafted from the kitchen—onions, garlic and ginger. And from down the hallway, the bleats and blats of a videogame.

This is perfect. I could live in this moment forever.

This thought was followed closely by another.

Where is everyone?

He kicked off the afghan and rose. The old floorboards creaked beneath his bare feet as he walked to the kitchen. He leaned through the doorway and found the curry unattended. He recognized the scent of spices about to burn and zipped over to the stove and stirred. Too late. The mix had already turned to tar.

He turned off the burner and set the pan aside.

"Hon? Where'd you go?"

The only answer came in the form of the shriek of a smoke detector. Peter slipped into the hallway and strained on tiptoe to twist the detector from the ceiling. Once he had, he held it in his hands, still complaining until he deprived it of its battery.

"False alarm. It's just the curry."

No reply.

The sounds of the videogame were quite heated, and Peter went to the bedroom door to peek in on the action. There was no one in the room except the CGI witches and warlocks doing battle on the TV screen. The game's controller lay untouched on the bed.

He walked over to the bed, noting its odd construction, its steel arm rails. A hospital bed. An *empty* hospital bed.

"Peter?"

Peter's heart leaped and he spun about.

A woman stood in the doorway. She was about his age, maybe younger, and dressed in sweats and an oversized football jersey. Perfect attire for this lazy day. And oh, how he longed for her, yearned to throw his arms around her and smell her hair and feel her hands on his back. The curry was ruined, but no matter. They'd order from Tandoori Chef. Chicken tikka masala for him, saag paneer for her.

Peter jerked, migraine-sharp lightning flashing through his head. Something was off, out of sync. The picture before him was marred. What was it?

Her face! What's wrong with her face?

Instead of nose, eyes and mouth, the woman's face was a swirl. Like stirred coffee creamer. The features wanted to form, he could feel that, and yet the swirl remained.

"You've come home."

173

No. This isn't right. This isn't—

A dry, croaking sound drew his eyes back to the bed, and what he saw there broke him. A frail boy with a swirling face—like mother, like son—lay tangled in bed sheets, tubes piercing his arms, his legs, his swollen stomach. Jet black liquid poured into his body from a chandelier of IV bags. Inside each bag, drowning in liquid, was a crow squirming and biting to be free.

This isn't right!

He felt the woman's arms wrapped around his middle, and when he turned into her embrace, he caught the slightest hint of her true face. Then, in the space of a heartbeat, it was gone—melted into a whirling mass.

"I missed you."

She leaned in and her face engulfed his. The world was suddenly all white rush and roar.

Hannah!

"Dude, what's your problem?"

It was Dodge who had spoken up. The boy was glaring at him beneath his bangs, seeming ready to jump up from the table and take care of business should it prove necessary.

He was in the kitchen standing before the farm table, the kids, all five of them, staring up at him. Peter realized his hands were full—in one he held a large, cold can of generic orange juice, in the other, a church key can opener.

"Where were you?" Willa asked.

"I…" The vision was already fading, save for the woman and his need to be with her. "I don't know."

"I want juice," Jo said, ready to move on.

"I want more," Huck shouted.

Peter fumbled, still not quite in the room. "Let's see, I was…"

"Making breakfast," Dodge finished for him. "Do you want me to do it?" he added with a huff.

"No, that's okay." Making breakfast? Not curry? "Where's your father?"

"Papa's in his office," Willa answered. "Remember? He said to start without him."

Had Fallow said that? It didn't sound familiar.

Come on, Peter. Snap out of it.

"Right. His office," he stammered, feigning recognition.

He set the can on the table and held it fast while he fitted the church key to its metal rim. In his haste, the can opener slipped when he applied pressure, and its sharp, metal point dug into the meat of his thumb.

"Damn it!"

"Language!" Huck and Jo cried in unison.

Peter brought his hand to his mouth and sucked on the wound. It smarted like heck. This gesture brought universal dismay to the table.

"Disgusting!" Dodge said.

"That's going to get infected," Willa warned.

"Gross!" the youngsters chimed in.

He drew back his hand, chastised by the chorus of displeasure he'd elicited. "Sorry. Do you have a first aid kit?"

A small, warm hand circled Peter's, and he looked down to find Curly eyeballing him cautiously. The boy's mouth was quirked to the side, working hard.

"Quiet," Curly said, and although it came out more like *kite*, Peter understood. He stayed still as the boy closed his eyes.

Curly's hand, which had at first felt slightly fevered, grew cold. The boy began to pant—silently at first, then with rising, rhythmic chuffs, expelling puffs of vapor like the little engine that could.

The ragged gash Peter had opened up on his hand drew closed. The wound stung even more as it mended, causing Peter pull back. But Curly held tight.

"Stop," the boy said, or so Peter interpreted.

A moment later, the work was done and Curly sat back, beaming. Huck and Jo applauded.

"Good trick!" Jo said.

"Great trick!" Huck sang.

"What trick is that?" echoed a voice from outside the kitchen. Papa Fallow entered, dressed in worn work clothes, and surveyed the scene suspiciously. "Well? Anyone going to tell me?"

The twins responded by pointing at Curly, whose self-satisfied grin quickly faded.

Fallow's demeanor suggested diversion was the best tactic, and Peter was quick to change the subject.

"Hungry? I was just making breakfast," Peter said, owning the task.

Fallow didn't answer. He just looked around the table at the downturned faces and wagged a stump finger at them. Peter noted the man's hands were dusted black. Charcoal perhaps? Fallow then turned and walked out of the room without saying a word.

"I guess not," Peter said, breaking the silence. Dodge was the only one to laugh.

* * *

After making a semi-successful meal of scrambled eggs and beans—with the requisite jokes from the little ones about beans and toots—Peter shooed the kids out of the kitchen and set about doing the dishes. The old man sensed a secret, a little conspiracy amongst his crew, and Peter didn't want to give any reason for suspicion by spending more time alone with them. He would have been fine fessing up about the wondrous healing the boy had gifted him, but he'd taken his cues from the kids, and the kids were definitely eager to remain silent.

Besides, he liked doing the dishes. Not that he *always* had, he thought. But he had learned to like it after being taught a few tricks of the trade by Hannah...

The return of her name sunk a deep shaft in his heart and brought back the memory of the woman's embrace and her swirling face. Peter dropped the pan into the soap-filled sink, shattering a juice glass.

"Careful or you'll cut yourself again." It was Willa. She'd been watching him. For how long, Peter had no idea.

"Butterfingers," Peter said by way of explanation and pulled the stopper from the drain. "Don't worry, I won't go poking my hand around in the suds."

"Why'd you drop the pan?"

"Because you startled me, that's why."

"You dropped it before you knew I was here.

Touché.

Peter turned to her, wiping his hands clean with a frayed dish towel. "I had a visitor last night."

"Did you?"

"Did you send him?"

Willa shook her head. "I call him. I don't send him."

"I suppose it was his idea then."

"What do you mean?"

Peter held up his arm and unrolled his sleeve. There was a slight impression—not quite a divot—in the flesh of his forearm where the bird had drawn its meal. "He took back some of himself. And gave me some of myself in return."

Willa glanced about nervously. Peter had the sudden impression his revelation came as quite a shock to the girl.

"He didn't tell me," Willa whispered. "He always tells me."

"Tells you what?"

"Everything. He's my little whisperer. My Mr. Tell."

Peter gingerly picked the two pieces of the broken juice glass from the sink. "Will you ask him where I came from?"

Willa snorted. "I already know where you came from, silly. I plucked you out of the circle. Same as everything I draw forth."

The phrase struck Peter. *Draw forth.* A phrase more archaic than he imagined most teenagers employing. It was Fallow's phrase—he was certain of it. Fallow explaining the girl's talent to her.

"Would you introduce us?"

The girl found this tremendously funny. "You want to meet him?"

"I do."

"My bird."

"Yes. Although we both know he's no bird. Don't we?"

Willa kicked at a warped floor tile, and it flapped back down. Kick, flap, kick, flap.

"Let me talk to him."

Don't you mean *commune* with him, Peter thought but didn't ask. Best to not give Willa any reason to back out.

"Thank you."

"Don't thank me yet," she said as she gave the warped tile one last kick and ducked out of the room.

Peter turned back to the broken pieces of glass. He fitted them together to make sure he hadn't missed any stray shards and found he hadn't. The glass had split into two clean pieces.

Split, Peter thought. *Just like me.*

CHAPTER 29

Ellen rapped on the dashboard with her fingers, urging Riggs on. Her anxiety earned her a rebuke.

"Cut it out, kid."

"It's after 7:30. Mr. Porter said—"

"We're here." Riggs pulled the Jeep to the curb in front of a ranch house with a well-manicured lawn. A ceramic garden gnome standing in a bed of geraniums bid them welcome.

"Are you really going to just leave me here?"

"That's the plan."

"That's *your* plan, not mine."

Riggs simply shrugged. "It's 7:34."

Darn it!

Ellen swung open her door and left it open as she stepped out of the Jeep, forcing Riggs to lean over in order to close it.

"It's been a slice," Riggs said with a wave. He pulled away from the curb and headed off down the street, leaving an ever-so-slight trickle of oil in his wake.

It's been a slice. Pizza slice. Pizza Carl. Pizza rat. Rat teeth...

"Shut up," she commanded her brain. It didn't listen. The inner prattle continued until she reached the front stoop and pressed the doorbell.

Rat teeth, buck teeth, tooth decay...

A perfunctory chime sounded, followed by a man's voice. "Be there in a minute."

Ellen waited, growing more nervous with each second that ticked by. She stared off across the front lawn and spotted a second, smaller gnome hidden in the same patch of flowers where its larger brethren stood.

Mom knows you're missing.

Shut up.

She's worried.

I'm not listening.

You are in so much trouble.

The door swung open, silencing her tattling mind. Pat Porter appeared, a maroon track suit having replaced his J.C. Penny duds.

"Right," the man said with a sigh. "Right. You're…"

"I'm Ellen. You said to meet you here at 7:30. I know I'm a little bit late, but it's not my fault. My ride—"

"Come on in."

Pat stepped back and ushered her in.

"I like your gnomes," Ellen offered.

She was suddenly aware of a sour smell permeating the house, like cheese left in the sun. Mr. Porter had done his best to mask the odor with overlapping pine scents—candles, sprays, no doubt a little incense—to lackluster effect. The stench was in sharp contrast to the immaculate, if definitely Midwestern, interior design. Paintings of farm life decorated the walls along with the grille from an International Harvester tractor. Americana-themed pillows adorned every chair, and sheet music for *I'm A Yankee Doodle Dandy* sat open on an upright piano's music rack, ready to be played.

"Thanks. They're my sister's."

"They're cool," Ellen added, unsure how to shift gears.

Mr. Porter helped her. "Shall we sit?"

"Yes, please."

Pat sat on the sofa, and Ellen opted for the pink chair nearest the piano, setting aside a pillow that read, *America is Blessed! Psalms 33:12.*

"I can give you fifteen minutes," Pat said, all business. "You said this was for a school paper?"

"It's for a paper, yes," Ellen lied.

"Aren't you going to take notes?"

"I've got a mind like a steel trap." It was another of her father's phrases, and it pleased her to use it, but it set her brain off on yet another tangent.

Steel trap. Mouse trap. Rat trap. Rat...

She resisted the urge to shush herself aloud, electing instead to pinch her right thigh. It worked.

A pained moan from the other room cut into their conversation, and Mr. Porter pinched his nose hard. "So, you listened to my interview."

"I did." Ellen was perched on the edge of her seat. How could people keep such uncomfortable furniture around? "And I was very interested in—"

Another moan, louder this time. The man in the track suit smiled sadly. "My sister's not well this morning."

Ellen recalled the woman with the thin voice who had answered Pat's phone. Ellen had hung up on the poor woman once she had the info she needed. Too late to do anything about that now.

"Sorry. I won't keep you. I just wanted to know what happened to all the people at Blind Rock."

"What happened to them?"

"Yes. The recording was messed up at the end."

Pat frowned. "That's a real shame. Tim Pullen put a lot of effort into those interviews, God rest his soul. He took real pride in—"

"Mr. Porter." Ellen was so close, but this man was pulling her off task. Time to get to the meat of the story. "I know you're busy, so let's cut to the chase. What happened at Blind Rock? To all the people."

"They were slaughtered, of course." Pat cracked his knuckles and looked at the ceiling, as if he could see the history he was narrating playing itself out above his head. "Back in 1895."

"By who?"

"Heck, the whole town. A councilman's boy went missing and folks started pointing fingers. Mainly, they fingered the Blinders who kept to themselves out on the prairie, you know? Because of the message written in blood on the boy's bedroom wall."

Another cry from the other room—another wince from Pat.

"And so the town went out and killed them?" Ellen asked, recalling one of the final tidbits she was able to glean before the recorder ate the tape. "Because they murdered the boy?"

Pat held up a finger. "There's a hole in your story, dear."

Before the man could elucidate, someone rapped on the wall of the closed bedroom. Mr. Porter rose.

"I'm sorry. I've got to get my sister up. She likes to sit and look out at her flowers in the morning." Ellen *really* wanted the man to continue, but he was already at the bedroom door. "Then we'll finish up."

Pat ducked into the bedroom, and a mumbled conversation followed. Ellen heard the clink of a chain, the ratchet of some device and the gentle cry of a woman at the end of the effort.

Pat returned, sweat on his brow, pushing a woman in a wheelchair. The woman was dressed in a pastel robe and head scarf, and she was thinner than Ellen thought humanly possible.

"Miriam, we have a visitor. This is Ellen."

Ellen shivered as Pat's wan sister turned her way because she'd finally recognized the scent beneath all that pine spray. It was human decay.

His sister? She looks old enough to be his mother.

Miriam Porter smiled weakly and nodded. Her skin was yellow and there were deep, blue circles under her eyes. The woman held her head up by sheer force of will.

"Hello, Ellen."

"Shall I put you over by the window?" Pat asked.

"That would be nice."

Before Mr. Porter could move, the doorbell sang its tune.

It was Miriam who responded. "My, Patrick. We haven't had this much company in ages."

Pat offered Ellen an apologetic shake of the head and answered the door.

It was Riggs.

"Eli, if you're here to pick up your friend, we're not quite finished—"

"Oh, I can wait," Riggs blurted out, slipping past Pat and finding a seat of his own. The guy looked as nervous as if he were on the menu.

Ellen mouthed *What's wrong?* But Riggs wouldn't even look at her. Instead he stared down at his tapping feet.

Pat positioned his sister's wheelchair so she could gaze out at the yard as well as enjoy the company of their guests, should she wish to do so.

"Where was I?" he asked.

"You said there's a hole. In the story," Ellen prodded.

"Right," Pat answered, getting back on track. "Like I said, the town was riled up about the missing boy. Did I say riled up? Heck, they were *fired* up. They headed for the prairie determined to spill blood. And spill blood they did. But later that night, when those men rode back into town—"

Riggs leaned to glance out the window. The springs in his chair shifted, releasing a low twang. Realizing he was suddenly the center of attention, he smiled broadly—a painful, fake smile—and motioned to Pat. "Please, continue."

What the hell is wrong with him?

Pat resumed his story. "When those men returned to the councilman's house, they found the boy hiding out in the cellar, too scared to come upstairs."

"Wait. The boy wasn't dead?"

"The boy had written the message himself. In rat's blood." It was Miriam who spoke, her voice quavering. Her bruised eyes locked on Ellen. "He had recently read *The Adventures of*

Tom Sawyer, you see, and had a desire to watch his own funeral, just like the boys in the story."

"My sister's the real history buff," Pat said, rising and joining his sister at the window. "I got all my stories from her."

Ellen shifted in her seat, trying to shake off the image of the rat at Pizza Carl's with the ear in its teeth. "So, you're telling me that the Blind Rock Massacre—"

"Was caused by a young boy's prank," Miriam said.

"They killed all those people because of a prank?"

"They didn't just kill them, dear. They obliterated them. You know what obliterate means?"

She did. Obliterate, lay waste, wipe out, destroy.

"They painted the prairie with the families' remains."

Pat squeezed his sister's shoulders. "I don't think the child needs to know all the grisly—" His phone buzzed in his pocket. He pulled it out, checked the number. "Gimme a sec, I gotta take this." He retreated into the kitchen, leaving Ellen and Riggs with the wasting woman in the chair.

Ellen was prepared to press on with more questions, but Miriam Porter had had enough excitement for one day. She rested her chin on her chest with a deep sigh.

Riggs leaned in and whispered, "We gotta go."

"Why do we have to?" Ellen asked, annoyed.

Glancing back at Miriam to make certain she was no longer awake, he mouthed, "Police."

Ellen wasn't quite sure she caught this and repeated his explanation. Riggs shushed her emphatically.

"A patrol car. Circling the neighborhood. Maybe I'm just being paranoid, but…I parked on the side of a house a couple doors down. I need you to tell them, explain to them that

Scorch got her wires crossed. That I never laid a finger on you. That…"

The guy was spinning out of control.

"Okay, okay. Call the library. I'll tell them I hid out. That it's all my fault. That there's nothing funny going on, okay? But I have to hear the rest of the—"

Miriam lifted her head and let out a short gurgle. Her chest heaved slightly and her stocking feet curled stiffly.

"Are you okay?" Ellen asked. The pale woman was looking about the room, a confused look on her face. "Should we get your brother?"

The sickly woman's gaze landed on Ellen and she pressed her hands together in wonder, as if suddenly surprised by a welcome visitor.

"Oh, my," Miriam said, her voice oddly huskier than before. "You didn't stop, did you?"

"Excuse me?" Ellen asked.

The woman smiled, and color as vibrant as the flowers in her garden rushed to her cheeks. She held out a trembling hand.

"Good for you, Spooky."

CHAPTER 30

Hours passed like years. Peter spent the time leafing through Fallow's books and discovered the man had quite an eclectic taste—art history, Sartre, home gardening. When his vision grew bleary, he took a late afternoon hike around the church grounds. He tromped past the snow-covered cemetery with its jutting headstones, before walking laps around the frozen pond.

Peter hadn't seen Willa all day, not even a chance meeting in the kitchen. He was beginning to think she was avoiding him. That meeting her dark friend was a no-go.

He thought of the woman from his vision—Hannah, his swirl-faced girl—walking with him, and it comforted him. She was the only familiar part of these past few days, the only person who had any semblance of *home*. Willa's feathered companion had placed the memory of her on his tongue, and he wanted more. Needed more.

It's chilly out.

It is.

You should have brought a cap, Peter.

I know.

You're such a stubborn man.

I know, I know.

The comfortable rhythm was there, but the woman to whom the other half of the conversation belonged wasn't. He was alone, wandering in circles in the snow—a stranger even to himself.

Peter was about to head back toward the bus hugging the side of the church when a spot of dark crimson in the snow caught his eye.

He picked his way over uneven ground, his leg diving knee-deep at one point, until he reached the glint of red peering up through the ice. It was a bloodstone the size of a fist. Peter knelt and brushed aside the snow. There was a second companion to the red stone. And another, and another. The snow rose in humps forming a large circle.

Circles help my dear Willa. Don't know why, but they do.

Peter couldn't argue with Fallow, there. The circle the old man had stomped into the field had allowed the girl to bring forth monstrosities. But Fallow's had been freshly made—this circle of stone looked and felt as if it had been here for oh so long. He placed his hand on the red keystone and was certain it had felt the chill of countless winters.

"Leave your hand on it too long, and you'll go blind."

Peter whirled about. Willa had snuck up on him, leaving barely a trace of her movements in the snow.

Willa laughed. "I'm just fooling."

"Ah. Good one."

"I thought so."

A melody drifted to them across the plain, and before Peter could ask its origin, Willa pointed back at the church.

"Papa likes to play music in his office. Up there."

From what Peter could judge, the girl was pointing at the steeple.

"His office is up there?"

Willa nodded. "It's his private place. No kids allowed. I checked it out once when he went into town, though."

"Anything interesting?

"Not unless you're into bad artwork and old books."

The girl kicked snow from one of the protruding stones.

"They used to call this place Blind Rock, you know. At least that's what Papa says. He says something in the water made people sick. But I don't think that's the real story."

"What's your theory?" Peter asked.

Willa bent and dug into the snow and ice with her bare hands until the black dirt beneath revealed itself. She laid her palm on the frozen earth.

"I think it's a place of secrets. Like a blind spot. You know the phrase 'out of sight, out of mind'? I think this place is like that—the land likes being left alone. Likes staying in a blind spot. Anyway, that's what I think. Does that make any sense?"

"I suppose," Peter said, thinking of his own blind spots. Like the blank, secret face of the woman named Hannah.

The girl rose and brushed the snow from her hands.

"He'll talk to you," she said, matter-of-factly, as if they were negotiating a business deal.

"Oh. Good," Peter said, both frightened and relieved at the chance to get some answers out of Willa's familiar. For that is what the bird was, wasn't it? A spirit that visited her from the ether?

It visited me as well. With the gift of memories.

"But no questions."

"Excuse me?"

Willa faced him. Gone was her casual demeanor. Now, she was dead serious.

"He'll speak. You listen."

"But how am I supposed to—"

"Take it or leave it."

Peter didn't like the prospect of being muzzled. The whole point of reaching out to the girl's companion was to ask what needed to be asked.

"Do I have any other choice?"

Willa shrugged.

"Well, then. Let's do this."

"Step into the circle," the girl said.

Peter complied, although he was starting to feel iffy about the whole endeavor. He'd seen what the girl could do, what she could draw forth, as she put it. He wondered what being in the middle of all that mind-bending chaos would do to his sanity.

"All set."

The girl standing outside the circle didn't acknowledge him. She simply tilted her head and the bird was there, perched nervously on her right shoulder, nestled against her wool scarf. Or had it been there the whole time? Listening unseen?

Willa wasted no time. She closed her eyes and whispered low, and Peter knew he wouldn't recognize the words even if he could hear them.

The crow stretched its wings out wide, and as it did so, alarm rose in Peter's breast. The thing meant to grab him, to snatch him up. To whisk him from this snowy field and rip him apart mid-flight, feasting on his innards like it would a terrified mouse.

But, no. The bird remained perched as it beat its wings. And with each muscled flap, it grew less substantial, like black ink dissolving in water.

Peter tried to speak and found that he could not, that the girl's mention of *no questions* was not a request but a warning. Cautioning him of what was to come.

For Peter was dissolving as well.

Like a jet of smoke, Willa's familiar shot forward and engulfed him. Whirling him about.

I am Whisper!

Peter fought against the dark curtain being drawn between him and the world, but Willa's companion was insistent.

I am Mr. Tell!

The girl, the church, the circle of stones—all faded from view.

And you are known to me...

The last thing Peter sensed before he succumbed to the darkness was the sharp scrabble of claws and the taste of soot.

CHAPTER 31

Ellen gasped.

"It almost hurts to look at you," said Miriam who was no longer Miriam.

Ellen dared not reply, lest speaking might shatter the odd thing taking place in the Porters' living room. One wrong word, and she might scare him away.

Him. Dad. For somehow it *was* Dad.

"What's she talking about?" Riggs asked. His question earned him a sock to the stomach.

"Shush!" Ellen whispered. "Don't move. Don't say a word."

Riggs obeyed. Good dog.

"You got the card?"

"Right on my birthday."

"And the cash?"

Ellen pulled a few bills from her pocket. "I still have a lot of it."

This is crazy...

The woman's face relaxed into another smile. "Good. It's all that boy had to spare. I felt bad taking it from him, but where else was I going to get three hundred dollars?"

"I don't know what you're talking about," Ellen said stubbornly, but she knew. It was the young postman's money she held in her hands. Her mother's new friend, Bo. And was it also his hand that wrote her birthday message? It was certainly his hand that delivered it.

The woman coughed, and for a moment Miriam was back. And the scent of her breath unlocked tumblers in Ellen's mind. She thought of Bo and his slaughterhouse cologne. She thought of Mrs. Flynt's funereal fragrance. All three—the postman, the librarian and the woman in the chair—had smelled of death. Bo and his cigarettes, Scorch and her medication, Miriam and her death rattle cough—the clock was ticking for each and every one of them. And before the Grim Reaper rang their bell, her father had stepped in.

"You've been talking to me this whole time," Ellen said. "Through them. Through her."

"Guilty."

Riggs made as if to interject and received a second slug to the stomach. Ellen struck him harder than she had expected, because a dreadful realization had just crept into her life. Her mother was right. Dad was dead. Dad was *dead.*

"It's okay."

"No, it's not!" Ellen cried. And it wasn't. If her father was really dead, nothing was going to be right ever again.

"It was an accident, pure and simple. I was driving too fast and the Plymouth—"

"No!"

The woman in the chair beckoned, but Ellen refused to go to her.

A muffled shout echoed from the other room, causing Riggs to stiffen. "Oh, shit. Pat knows."

"Blind Rock," her father said in Miriam's voice. "You need to go to Blind—"

"Eli?" Pat's voice echoed from the other room. "We need to talk."

Ellen grabbed the thin shoulders and squeezed. "Why? Why do I have to?"

"Please, dear. You're hurting me."

Realizing she was shaking the woman, Ellen stepped back. Her father was gone. Miriam was back. And she hadn't even had a chance to say goodbye.

"Come back!"

Riggs was about to bolt for the door when the woman reached out and grabbed his arm. Miriam seemed as surprised by this move as Riggs. And she was doubly flustered when another's voice pried open her mouth.

"Give her your keys!"

Riggs didn't bat an eye. He dug out his keys and held them out to Ellen.

"What the hell?" Pat Porter stepped into the room, catching its three occupants in an unusual pose—his sister clutching Riggs, Riggs handing his keys to Ellen, all three staring at him with alternating guilt and alarm.

"I just got off the phone with Don Whittaker. You have anything you'd like to tell me?"

Riggs looked to Ellen. "Go."

Ellen went. She scooped up her backpack as she made a dash for the door. She could hear Mr. Porter calling after her, could hear Riggs's preemptive explanations, but no matter. Ellen was out the door and leaping over flowerbeds and garden gnomes, keys in hand.

CHAPTER 32

The engine roared to life as Ellen turned on the ignition. The radio followed suit.

"Up next, 'Crazy Like a Fox' by Motörhead!"

She switched off the music and grabbed the steering wheel.

Now what?

The Jeep had been easy enough to find—it was right where Riggs had told her it was. Wedged a bit too close to this house with the awful yellow siding.

Now, here she was—an eleven-year-old kid sitting behind the wheel of someone else's car, four years shy of her first driving lesson and no destination in mind. Forget Spooky. She was nuts.

The radio crackled back to life, Motörhead putting the pedal to the metal.

You make me crazy, crazy like a fox!
You've been doin' it all the time
You know I love you, love you lots
Crazy like a—

A rush of static flushed the song from the airwaves, followed by a voice that caused Ellen to stomp down on the gas.

Foot on the brake, Spooky.

Definitely *not* Motörhead. Definitely Dad.

"Okay. It's on the brake."

Now, ease the gear—it's on your right, honey—ease it to D. D means drive.

Ellen obeyed, hand on the gear, gear to D, ready for the next step.

Both hands on the wheel, and…

Ellen didn't need any more instruction. Compared to navigating the ins and outs of the supernatural world, driving was a cinch. She pressed down on the gas with her chunky shoe, and the Jeep leaped into the street.

Easy!

Ellen slammed on the brakes, and the Jeep skidded hard. The smell of burnt rubber hit her nose.

"Where are we going, Dad?"

Motörhead did their best to stage a comeback, but her father was having none of it.

Blind Rock.

As if there could be any doubt.

"Left or right?"

Left.

Left, it was.

Ellen hit the gas, coming dangerously close to sideswiping a parked motorcycle and having less luck when it came to a row of recycling bins. With an explosion of aluminum cans and bottles, Ellen zipped away from Pat Porter's neighborhood, ears pealed for her father's next instruction.

At the next turn, the Jeep swung wide, mounting the curb before crashing back, jostling Ellen wildly enough for her to realize she hadn't taken the time put on her seatbelt. She slowed to a stop in the middle of the road and rectified this situation.

Straight ahead and then left onto the highway for a stretch. You ready for the highway, Spooky?

"Not one bit."

A car with a spotlight pulled out from one of the side streets. It moved slowly, like a shark in shallow water. Blue and white. Prowling for Riggs.

The police car wasn't approaching but receding. A lucky break. Surely her father would tell her to back it up. R...R was for reverse, right?

Pull forward. Slowly.

"You gotta be kidding me."

Pull forward.

The phrase caught in her Ferris wheel mind and began to spin—slowly at first, then faster and faster.

Pull forward, forward pass, pass out, out smart, out fox...

"Please, stop," she begged her brain. The prowler up ahead had come to a stop. Had they noticed the blue Jeep sitting like a turtle in the middle of the road?

Middle of the road, middle of the day, day dream, nightmare...

Ellen felt the gentle brush of skin on skin, and her hand moved of its own accord, throwing the Jeep into drive. Bracing lest a ghostly foot take charge of the gas, she pressed the pedal ever so slowly, just like working the pedal on Aunt Tuffy's old sewing machine the time the woman had tried to teach her some "womanly skills."

The Jeep rolled forward slower than a float in a parade, and—to Ellen's mind—just as obvious.

Ellen had a vision of Mom on Route 67 heading east to Maple City. Mom and Tuffy had spoken, and her lie was out. Ellen knew this as surely as she knew she would never drive again after today. Being behind the wheel put her on the spot like nothing she had ever experienced. And she was certain that when Rita finally put *her* on the spot, the experience would be epic.

The Jeep was just half a block behind the police cruiser when the cruiser's flashing lights ignited. Ellen was about to hit the brakes when the vehicle's loudspeaker broke into song. It was Motörhead. As the Jeep rolled slowly past the cruiser, she caught a glimpse of the officer frantically trying to the cut the noise.

You know I love you, love you lots
Crazy like a fox!

"Love you too," Ellen said. "Now, let's get out of here."

The Jeep serpentined past the cruiser, crept to the stop sign and escaped left onto the highway.

* * *

Ellen found it much easier driving on the open road, save for the occasional rush of a passing semi. Truckloads of goods apparently so late, they were worth risking running her and the Jeep off the road.

Stay in the right lane for five minutes. You've got this, Spooky.

Houses grew more spaced apart as she drove, the odd business or two popped up. Soon, she was passing the high school football field and outdoor community pool—landmarks of the edge of town. She held the Jeep steady as a tandem Walmart tractor-trailer whooshed by, and then...she was free and clear, sailing down the highway into the prairie, flanked on either side by sunbaked soybeans.

"I'm sorry, Dad. I'm so sorry you're dead."

Once again, Ellen felt tremors of sorrow, and she feared she might lose what tentative control she had over the vehicle. The stretch to keep her foot on the gas was already causing a cramp, and the arrival of fresh tears threatened to cloud her view.

Do you mind?

The nerves in her arms lit up when her father spoke. He was ready to step forward, should she allow it, and she was all too happy to oblige.

Ellen took her hands off the wheel. Not her physical hands—those remained—but her true hands. The ones she took with her on her journeys into the shadowed night, into dreams that always felt a tad more real than the real world itself.

She curled up in the driver's seat even as her body remained alert—steady eyes on the road, firm grip on the wheel. Her physical self even adjusted the rearview mirror. Something she never would have thought to do.

Do you remember when we had our talk? After you told me about the dead boy who joined us on our stroll?

"Treat," Ellen said. "His name was Treat."

She was back home on the sofa. Her mother was out getting Chinese food because she refused to tip the delivery people, and besides, it was right down the block. Dad sat with her, a funny look on his face. It took him all of ten minutes to finally speak.

"How did you know that boy's name?"

Ellen was busy punching the keys on his old typewriter, amazed at the connection between force of punch to darkness of type.

Ellen, Ellen, Ellen, Ellen...

She was determined to fill the blank page with her name.

"Ellen, how did you know that boy's name?"

"I don't know."

"I think you do."

She looked up from the typewriter. "He told me."

"You mean you read it. In the newspaper—"

"No!" Ellen said, bristling at being led. "He...told...me. Just like he told me he was doing bad in school, and that his grandpa just died and he didn't have any friends. Hey! Part of this ribbon is red. How do you make the words red?"

Suddenly, all she could see was red. She felt her hands abandon her as well as consciousness. When the fugue state had passed, she was back once more on the sofa next to Dad, her fingers poised in midair above the typewriter keyboard.

"Oh, Spooky..."

They both stared at the page tucked into the typewriter's feed. A few black lines of her name were followed by a single red paragraph. Ellen's father rolled the page up so they both could get a good look.

> Treat held out his wallet, but when it came time to relinquish his hold, he hesitated. The wallet contained his student ID, his credit cards and the only photo of him and Grandpa Barnes. That hesitation was all the man needed to plunge his knife into Treat's belly and twist.

"How did you do that?" her father asked.

"I dunno."

"Ellen…"

"Look. I made it red!"

The Jeep hit a bump in the road, tossing Ellen about, and she woke with a start. At first, she had no idea where she was. Where was the typewriter? Where was Dad? Why was the world moving so fast?

Another jolt, much more violent than the first, yanked Ellen into the present. She was behind the wheel of Riggs's Jeep. And she was skidding off a gravel road toward a ditch.

"No-no-no-no-no!" she cried.

The Jeep left the road, becoming airborne for a moment before the grille struck the far side of the shallow ravine. Ellen lurched forward, her seatbelt biting into her chest. Despite the belt's keeping her from flying out of the vehicle, her head hit the dash upon impact as all forward momentum was suddenly thwarted. Pain shot across her brow as the Jeep continued tumbling to its left, finally sliding to a stop on its passenger side.

The force of the impact stalled the engine and it died sputtering complaints.

"Why didn't you wake me up?" Ellen asked, wincing at the pain in her ribs. The radio, like the rest of the Jeep, was kaput.

Unbuckling her belt, Ellen grabbed her backpack, which was now lying on the cracked passenger side window. The door on her side was heavy, never intended to be opened upwards like a hatch. Ellen managed to hold it open long enough to shove out her pack and wriggle after it, dropping to the ground below. She gingerly touched her forehead. A knot was already rising, but there was no blood, thank goodness.

The field had a nasty lingering odor, and Ellen got a mental flash of squealing swine. Great. The soybeans had been recently manured.

After retrieving her backpack and brushing off the dirt— manure— she turned to survey the damage.

Riggs is going to kill me.

She was facing the oily underbelly, growing oilier as severed lines spilled their dark liquid. The Jeep was wedged in the ditch like a giant blue June bug. A *dead* June bug.

Glancing about, Ellen found she was in the middle of nowhere. The brown gravel road she'd been driving snaked off through green fields stretching to the horizon. Only the rise of buildings in the distance gave her a point of reference. She was well outside Maple City—alone on the prairie.

A twisted tree a couple of hundred yards to Ellen's left caught her attention, and when she shielded her eyes from the blazing sun, she spotted a large pile of debris scattered in the field.

No use staying here. Go take a look.

Ellen wasn't sure whether the voice in her head was her own or her father's. Either way, she had nothing to gain by hanging around Riggs's smashed-up ride. She put on her pack and tromped off across the field, aware her black sweatshirt would soon have her dripping with sweat yet stubbornly resolved to endure it.

After ten minutes in the hot sun, Ellen reached the point where the soybeans stopped. They ended in a ragged line, the outermost plants withered and brown, replaced by barren, black soil.

Ahead, sitting in the midst of this sterile stretch, were the remains of a building, its wooden planks bleached white under the Illinois sun.

As Ellen approached, the first thing she noticed was the charred, crumbling skeleton of a steeple.

Careful, Spooky.

This time it was most certainly Dad who spoke. And Ellen planned to heed his advice.

She walked gingerly toward the pile of debris as if, with every next step, the earth might open up beneath her feet and swallow her whole.

CHAPTER 33

For a moment, Peter was certain he was dead. There was no sound, no light, no *him*—nothing.

If I'm dead, whose thoughts are these?

Good point.

Like electricity returning after an outage, the world flickered back into view. As it did so, Peter struggled to make sense of what he saw.

He stood in the middle of a barren landscape. Black snow stretched for miles in all directions. The sky was acid trip red. And the air was hot and burnt and smelled of overcooked meat.

This is how it sees the world...

Such a place, if one remained too long, would consume all hope. Peter didn't believe in Hell, but he couldn't ignore his eyes. If this was not *the* Hell, it was certainly *a* Hell.

Something rose up before him, birthed from the pitch black ice. The figure was all wings and legs and arms, each feature fighting for control in a painful struggle for continuity. It loosed mournful howls and angry curses as it twisted and broke, formed and broke again.

Finally, the tortured mass compromised on an unfinished mix of man and bird. It bore a human face with glistening black eyes. Instead of teeth, talons lined its mouth. And it dragged a single, useless and blistered wing behind. It was a monstrosity whose very sight brought agony.

Us. Alone.

Peter couldn't deny that. It appeared that he and the bird creature shivering before him had this hellscape all to themselves.

Like before. Whisper and Peeeee…

His name hung unfinished on the thing's tongue, and he could see the act of communicating was torture. Bloody spittle accompanied each movement of its jaw.

…eeeeter.

Its chest heaved and snapped with effort, as if living itself was a task that cost it dearly. Peter wanted to run, wanted to flee this place of madness, but he had asked for this, hadn't he? This parley. And the thing meant to have its say.

Never wanted. Only for her. Always for her.

The scarlet sky flashed with black streaks. Peter caught a glimpse of Willa spinning about the clouds, sketched in black lightning, the bird caught in orbit around her. With each dark artery streaking through the sky, the picture grew and changed. The bird in midair, the bird on her arm, the bird no longer a bird but a swirling shadow that now danced as frantically as the girl herself. Talons gripping air, dark leathery wings beating away black stars.

Whisper's memories filled the skies, scribbled in obsidian streaks—a child's scrawls in the stratosphere. Willa as a child stepping into the circle, Willa delighting as the bird emerges from thin air, taking wing about her. Willa as a woman, a baby clutched in her arms.

Thunder rolled across the land, and with it, Willa's voice.

"Shadow, I draw you forth—you dare not resist. This is your charge. I give my last blood to bind you. You must obey. This is your charge."

The creature placed a hand on its distended belly, nails digging past feathers and into flesh.

You-me. Me-you. Mixed together. No more. Time to part.

Peter wanted to scream, *tried* to scream. But the crimson skies above had the monopoly on screams. He tried to turn away from the vision of Willa wrapped up in the arms of a lightning-scribbled man. That face! Even in its crude depiction, the man stood out in the clouds, black veins of lightning sketching his particulars. Grim eyes, cruel mouth and a patch on his chest that read *AlbuuR*.

The creature was a child, and the man was his monster. A man named *AlbuuR*.

Albert. The man from the alleyway. Albert Carver. The one who attacked the girl, meaning to have her. Would he have his way? Claim her in the end? It seemed to Peter the creature's memory ran forward and back, his entire history linked to the girl. And somehow, to him.

Peter was so caught up in the shadow play that he hadn't noticed the liquid streaming from his nose. He wiped at it and his hand came away black. The droplets rose, drawn to Whisper. The flow continued—dark ropes flowing from him to the creature, which welcomed the effluence home.

I take back me.

With a single swift movement, Whisper ripped a gash in his belly, dumping glistening offal onto the ground. He wept and shrieked and cried out for the girl even as his insides poured thick and steaming on to the black ice.

Amidst this putrid gush, stones like ruby yolks dropped to the growing pile of Whisper's innards. Dipping a stray wing into the mix, the creature scooped up the stones like a miner panning for gold. Once it had them—half a dozen in all—it held them out to Peter.

And give back you.

Peter stared at the stones and knew at once they were kin to the stone the bird had proffered the night after his trip into town—after he had bloodied the workman's nose in protection of Willa. He looked into the creature's face, expecting to see fear or anger or some such emotion that might cause the thing to turn on a dime. Choose to turn those razor sharp digits on him. Instead, he saw something else. Could it possibly be…gratitude?

Take. It is you.

Could it be the thing was grateful for the end of things? That it was weary with sorrow and exhausted by its charge?

Take!

Peter took the stones.

And as soon as he did, a choir of howls rose from beneath the snow.

No…

There was fear in the creature's voice that sparked fear within Peter. Something was rising from the ice. More than something. *Many* things.

Dark stalks sprouted from the earth all about them. All manner of appendages broke free from the snow, rising upward, lifting unnameable beasts from below.

The first to crawl free was a charred, chitinous thing with long, stringy hair. It rose from the frozen ground, leaving chunks of hair and skin behind. It glared at Whisper, at Peter—hungry in its twisted aspect.

Sister…

Others joined it. Tortured things rife with deformity. Broken and biting and *starving*.

Eat!

Whisper's plea grabbed Peter's attention from the growing cluster of demons circled about them. He held up the first of the bloodstones and wiped it clean of gristle. He popped it into his mouth and swallowed hard. Again, his throat registered the cold streak of the stone's downward progress. And once more…

He was standing in the foyer of a dilapidated farmhouse. To call it a mess would be an understatement.

A woman stood with him, her back to him. And how he longed for her.

"Oh, my God," the woman whispered. "This place is amazing."

Peter blinked. "What?"

Hannah turned back to him and clutched his arm. Hannah! *He saw her face—every detail down to the way her hair curled disobediently about her ears.* Hannah.

"A broken place we can put back together."

The roar of a new monstrosity filled the air, and Peter shoved another two stones into his mouth.

Peter found Hannah leaning against a graffiti-covered wall. "I miss him," she said. "I miss my Michael."

"I know."

"I miss him so much!"

He held her close as her sobs shook them both. And he made the decision for her. They were moving into the house—the house of the broken bird. They were moving in and fixing everything. The house, themselves, the whole goddamn world.

A leathery wing slapped him across the face. Whisper, gutted and growling, urged him on.

Peter!

The horde was close and moving closer. They meant to feed—on him, on Whisper, on the stones in his hand. On *Hannah*. They meant to eat *Hannah*.

Four stones left—three large, one small. Already so many answers flowed through his veins. Larson, his family name was Larson. Hannah and the boy. These glimpses were handholds, but they were not enough.

He downed the third and the fourth stones together and his throat turned to ice.

Big Bear. The Intermission Motor Lodge. Pizza with the family. Mushrooms…Hannah hated *mushrooms.*

Chunks of his life lodged in his throat, and he struggled to swallow them down.

The first wave of the horde was upon them. They reached out for Whisper, and Peter wanted to yell *Fly! Break free!* but could not. A beast resembling an inside-out lion pounced—a four-legged nightmare, organs outside its body and dripping onto the snow. It opened its mouth and filled the world with teeth. It bit down on Whisper's neck.

Glowing eyes approached from all sides, pinpricks of fire locked in on the stones.

A large wing encompassed him, and he looked back to find Whisper weak and in pain. Even as the beast ate away the back of his head, Whisper drew Peter to him, meaning to protect him to the end.

I have enough, Peter thought. With what I've got, I can find her again. I've got enough.

As the shifting, snapping demons descended, claws, teeth, talons and split bones ready to shred them to pieces, Peter freed himself from Whisper's embrace and stood alone.

Two stones—one large, one small.

Peter balled them up in his fist, and the stones spawned another memory. He was a Cubs fan.

Go Cubbies!

With the joy of a man suddenly remembering cool, spring evenings playing catch, Peter wound up and pitched the stones out over the heads of the horde. Willa, stone-skipper extraordinaire, would be proud. The bloodstones rose, disappeared momentarily in the red sky, and plummeted to earth beyond the demons' reach.

A collective cry rose up, and the demons took the bait. The beast tossed Whisper aside, following the rest as they galloped across the black field of snow, eager to be first to the prize.

Peter knelt before Willa's familiar, who had slumped to the ground. Whisper was more carcass than crow, and he shrank in his misery, his small black and bleeding body collapsing into a twisted and feathered mass. Helpless, exposed and longing for home.

Please...

Peter took the woeful creature in his arms and called out to Willa from the depths of his mind. Eyes scrunched, urging their return, begging her to hurry the hell up.

He felt a tug—his call answered. And then...nothing.

211

Something's wrong.
Bloodstones acquired, the horde turned back toward him.
Something's *definitely* wrong.

CHAPTER 34

Sweat trickled down the back of Ellen's neck as she trudged around the church ruins, but she wasn't about to remove her sweatshirt. If ever she needed her good old protective black about her, now was the time.

Or was she still wearing it out of spite? The thought surprised her. Could it be she refused to remove the sweatshirt because she remembered Mom's look of disapproval when she'd worn it the first time? When she'd stuck her nose up at the cheery, bright outfits her mother had selected for her from amongst the myriad of garage sale possibilities, opting once more to drape herself in drabness?

Ellen felt a twinge of guilt. Her mom might be self-centered and a pain in the ass, but she did try. For all of her moods, she was still Mom. How must the woman feel right now? No doubt she was frantic, using all of her manic powers of persuasion to track down her wayward child.

Oh, and how Ellen would pay for sneaking away.

Quiet. No time for that.

She got back down to the task at hand, which was locating whatever Dad had in store for her.

The grounds had been picked over thoroughly. Apart from the burned tangle of wood left to decompose on its foundation in the June sun, Ellen found little other than a lone rotted-out tire and the half-buried remnants of a metal shed.

Ellen pulled a rock from the dirt and chucked it against the rusted metal. It gave an unsatisfying dull clang when the rock hit, a far cry from the gong sound she had wanted—something to waken the dead.

"Hello?" she called. She was alone in the field, and yet she knew she was *not*. Ellen Gooding was never truly alone. Treat had found her, the bus people had as well. People were always finding her. Dead people, that was. She cocked her head with a sudden realization. Funny that the living seemed to have little use for her.

The trill of a child's laughter snapped her back from her reverie. She glanced about quickly, only to discover the source of the sound was not some spirit trying to make contact, but a woodpecker hidden among the charred planks, searching for a meal. Ellen dispatched it with a clap of her hands. The startled bird took to the sky in search of a quieter place to feed.

She circled the grounds a couple more times before coming to the conclusion she had come to a dead end.

That was until she spied the stone circle.

If she had looked right instead of left, she would have missed it entirely. But there it was, making almost indiscernible arcs in the earth.

"I've dreamed of you," she said, addressing the great ring of stones. Ellen closed her eyes and forced her mind to recall her journal entry.

A split man. Bird and man. Torn apart. The circle, the girl, the spell. A conjuring. The man, the bird. Torn apart. Torn apart in the winter circle with the blood-red stone.

Ellen walked the perimeter of the stone circle.

In her dream, the great O sat in the middle of a snowy field. Here, in the stretch of dead ground, there was no bird, no man, no girl, no spells being cast. Just an abandoned collection of dull, grey rocks someone had sunk into the…

Wait a sec…

Ellen stopped before a stone unlike the others. Darker. She stood directly over it, spat and wiped the saliva back and forth on the rock's surface with the toe of her shoe. There it was— the blood-red stone.

She knelt and spat again—no need for manners alone on the prairie—and rubbed the stone clean, or at least clean-ish.

Red stone. Blood red. Bloodstone…

This time, Ellen allowed her brain to continue whirring on its own. She was too entranced by the ruby object embedded in the earth. The sun seemed to cause the stone to glow. Like the emergency button in the elevator at the university's Art Library. Ellen was alone in the elevator when it got stuck between floors, and she'd pressed the panic button, watching it glow red as she screamed at the operator trying to calm her, crying that she needed to get out, out, *out!*

Get out, get gone, gone fishing, fishing hole, hole in the ground, hole in the ground, hole in the ground…

Ellen rose, shrugged off her backpack and set it aside.

Hole in the ground, hole in the ground, hole in the ground…

And stepped into the circle.

CHAPTER 35

Peter felt the tug again, and he knew Willa was on the other end of the line trying to reel them in. But she was too late—the multitude was upon them. Their sheer numbers blotted out the sky.

He drew Whisper close, as one would a child, and bent his head.

The end.

"Whisper! To me!"

Willa's voice tore the world in half, and Peter fell through the gap. Tumbling into darkness, still clutching the bird, for Whisper was bird once more, reconstituted by the sound of the girl's voice and the hope of escape.

Home!

Gone was the black landscape with the red sky. Gone was the horde that befouled it. It vanished into the darkness like great sails ripped free in a storm, the demons tumbling, howling into oblivion.

Peter closed his eyes against the rushing nothingness. And when he landed, he landed hard. He quickly locked his arm about Whisper and rolled with the fall, doing his best not to crush the bird.

He came to rest on his back, panting with the suddenness of the landing. The sky above was dark, save for the welcome full moon. It was night. He must have been gone for hours.

Where was Willa? Surely she hadn't abandoned him. The earth beneath him was wet. Why was it wet?

Peter turned his head, and his gaze met another's. A woman in calico lay sprawled next to him in the dirt, staring back at him with dull, slightly-crossed eyes. The side of her skull was crushed, drenching her straw-colored hair crimson. A robin's egg blue ribbon lay unfurled across her cheek. It was the woman's blood that wet the ground—her blood he was lying in.

The woman's hand shot out, grabbing at him blindly.

"Where's my boy?" the woman whispered, sanguine bubbles forming on her lips. "He won't…he can't…"

Her jaw twitched as death slipped in the back door.

"Not on his own…he needs…please! Find my…" Then she was still.

The bird squirmed in Peter's arms.

Home. Now.

He wholeheartedly agreed. Whisper yearned for Willa as he longed for Hannah. Home sounded like a really good idea about now.

Peter rose to sitting and surveyed the scene. The field he was in was dark, but in the moonlight he spied others—men, women, children—scattered about like piles of discarded laundry. Some had been set ablaze, others struggled against groups of attackers, fending off the vicious blows raining down on them.

Roaming teams of men with axes, rifles and flaming torches set upon the injured and dying with such force, with such fervor, it seemed they meant to wipe the fallen from the face of the earth.

Must flee. Must go. Home!

"I hear you," Peter replied. "Home."

A man with a torch appeared from the dark, looming over them. Blood stained the angry man's shirt and hands.

"Found one!" the man called out to the shadows moving in the night.

He planted the torch in the ground and waggled a gore-stained barrel knife in Peter's face.

"You never should've come here, Blinder!"

"Please, I don't understand…"

A quick flick of the man's wrist, and Peter felt a burning line across his chin. He darted out his tongue and tasted copper.

"That's for the young'un you killed. You had this coming. All of you. Damned if you didn't. Time to pay up, Blinder. Time to bleed."

The man made his move, and Peter wasn't ready. He raised a hand to fend off the attack and felt cold steel sink into his flesh. The tip of his finger fell free, and warm blood cascaded down his palm.

The man hooted with glee. "I cut him! Cut him good. And lookee here, boys. This one's got his demon with him. Let's see if it bleeds too."

As the man reached out for Whisper, the crow loosed a single, black tendril from his chest, startling Peter. He had felt the creature go limp in his arms, had assumed he had succumbed to his injuries. Apparently Whisper had one last trick up his sleeve.

The barbed shaft caught the man in the neck, piercing his larynx. The man squealed at the impact of the sting. With the last of his strength, the crow retracted the tendril, ripping open the man's throat.

The injury was grim, but the man would live to murder them both. Peter was certain of that. But he would never be able to tell his tale. Not aloud, anyway. Not without his voice box.

Enraged and sputtering blood, the man slashed away at Whisper, ripping free ribbons of black flesh and feathers.

"Stop!" Peter begged.

The man gripped Peter's wrist in reply, meaning to let his knife feed on more fingers.

"Come! You must obey. To me, Whisper. Come!"

What came next was no tug, but a full on assault. Peter was suddenly pulled in countless directions—borne across the field, lifted into the sky, dragged beneath the earth—the only constant being his grip on the bird. Everything was rush and blood and *flee.*

Peter felt himself stretched thin and feared he would snap, splintering off in a million directions. Like one of Willa's skipping stones, breaking in two, into six, into…

"Shit."

He heard the word clear as a bell. It was not Willa who had spoken, but another. Not an incantation but a curse.

Peter trained all his attention on the word, willing himself toward it. There were only two options, really. Give in and be scattered, or grab for the voice.

Hannah. He had to get back to Hannah.

Peter reached his injured hand out into the void, and…

…he felt snow rise up beneath him.

He swooned with the sudden return, his stomach threatening to spill its contents. His hand screamed, and he thrust it into the ice, finding both pain and relief.

Home!

Peter prayed Whisper was right. He looked up. Willa stood in the exact same spot as when she had sent them into the mix, into the ether.

"Let's never do that again," he said, forcing the levity.

But Willa wasn't listening to him. In fact, she seemed wholly disinterested in his return.

He turned, following her gaze.

Standing behind him in the circle was a girl, shorter and squatter than Willa, dressed in an oversized black sweatshirt, her jaw hanging open.

"Shit," the girl said.

CHAPTER 36

Ellen gawked at the scene before her. The surrounding fields, green with growth only a moment ago, were suddenly blanketed white, and the sky had dimmed from sea blue to a dark and brooding grey.

Was this another vision? Like the dead people in the bus or the flesh-eating rats at Pizza Carl's? Ellen didn't think so. For one thing, it was *freezing* out. She was suddenly thankful for the heavy sweatshirt because the temperature had dropped fifty or more degrees.

Another strike against this being some sort of mirage was the tall girl staring at her from outside the circle.

"Who are you?" the girl asked.

Ellen sensed—no, she knew—that if the girl had reason to join her in the circle and slap her silly, she would feel the sting of those slaps. The girl was too tangible, too engaged to be anything other than flesh and blood.

She was also, most assuredly, the girl from Ellen's dream.

The girl, the snow. Only thing missing is...

A man with a bloodied hand appeared at her feet, completing the picture, his arm wrapped about a sickly, black bird.

"Let's never do that again," the man said to the tall girl. But the girl had her eyes trained on Ellen.

"Shit," Ellen said.

"Begone!" the tall girl ordered, hands working their magic. But Ellen was not about to *begone*. Nope, she was going to damn well stick around and see how this played itself out, thank you very much.

The tall girl let loose with a string of phrases foreign to Ellen's ears. The only effect the incantation had on Ellen was a sudden spark of jagged light in her periphery. The sort of electric aura that preceded the migraines she thought she'd left behind in third grade.

When the tall girl raised her hands a third time, clearly frustrated, Ellen raised her own in protest.

"Look, I don't know if you're trying to make me disappear or turn me into a newt, but could you cut it out? You're giving me a headache."

"Where do you come from?" the tall girl insisted.

"Iowa," Ellen said, determined not to be pushed around by this girl, even if she did outrank her in age.

"Why did you answer my call?"

"I already answered one of your questions," Ellen chided. "My turn. Is this 1895?"

"Are you serious?"

"Always."

The tall girl looked confused. "It's 1979."

"1979? Wait…is this Blind Rock?"

"That's *two* questions."

"I've got a situation here," Peter moaned.

Both Ellen and the tall girl looked down where he lay.

"You're hurt!" the tall girl cried, pulling the scarf from about her neck and kneeling.

Ellen wanted to look away. Blood in movies she could take—blood in real life made her woozy. She would have averted her gaze had it not been for the bird. The more she looked, the more she became convinced it was not only a bird.

"You're *both* hurt," the tall girl cried, as she lifted the crow. "Oh, Whisper. What happened to you?" The bird seemed to drip in her hands, and Ellen was reminded of a video at school about animals caught in an oil spill. The thing the girl held aloft seemed more liquid than crow.

Was this what her father had wanted to see? If so, Ellen didn't get it. Sure, the scene resembled the one in her dream, all cast members accounted for, but to what end?

"I saw you in a dream. All of you," she blurted out, hoping this might speed things along, get the conversation flowing, cut to the chase. Instead, the tall girl continued tending to her two downed patients—the man with the bloody hand and the dripping bird.

"Fine," Ellen said, ready to be rid of the whole business. The math was simple. She'd gotten here by stepping into the circle. Logic dictated if she stepped back out, she'd find herself back in the summer sun.

Sorry, Dad, but I'm outta here.

Ellen took one giant step to her right, breaking the circle's perimeter.

Nothing happened.

Zip. Zero. Nada.

Her big exit had landed with a thud.

Ellen was about to step back into the circle and have another go at it—maybe she needed to keep her eyes closed, maybe she needed to think of the soybean field—when a light appeared in the distance as the church door swung open wide. Figures appeared silhouetted until they drew nearer. At the center of the approaching group was a large bearded fellow, bundled up against the cold. Flanking him were children. A loping teen, two little tykes and one bringing up the rear on crutches, working twice as hard as the others and moving at half the speed.

The old man and the kids stopped just short of the circle.

"You folks having a party and you didn't invite us?" the bearded man boomed. There was a knowing confidence to his voice that made Ellen uncomfortable, like he was both asking a question and answering it at the same time. It was a trick her mother often employed. Perhaps that was what so unnerved her.

The two younger children played in the snow, blissfully unaware of the tension that had suddenly descended on the circle. The teen couldn't bring himself to make eye contact, and the kid on crutches had yet to catch up.

The man put his hands on his hips, surveying the scene without saying a word. That was, until his gaze landed on Ellen.

"And who might you be?" the man asked, perplexed.

"I'm Ellen." She had the distinct feeling avoiding answering directly was *not* the way to go with this guy.

"Welcome, Ellen. The more the merrier," the burly fellow said.

"He's been hurt," the tall girl said to the bearded man.

"I can see that."

The two little ones abandoned their play and focused on the wounded man and the spreading red in the snow.

"He's messy," the little girl said, transfixed by the man's injury.

"Messy," the little boy parroted.

"Yes, he is," the bearded man said, staring down upon the man and the bird.

Ellen had always been good at sensing the imminent arrival of rain or snow or bad news, and her gut told her the wind had started to shift.

"He is one messy, messy man."

CHAPTER 37

Fallow clucked his tongue. "That's a nasty cut you've got there, Petey-boy. Must smart like the dickens."

It did much more than that. The pain pounded in Peter's stump finger. The snow masked the extent of the injury, but every time he sought to withdraw his hand, the nerves lit up anew.

"It's fine," he lied.

"Papa, we need to—"

Fallow hushed Willa with a wave of his hand. He stepped across the threshold of the stone circle and bent down.

"No, it's not fine. Is it? But you got off easy. You didn't have to stick around for the rest of the slaughter, did you? For the screams and the tears." Fallow made a few imaginary cuts through the air.

The old man removed one of his woolen mittens and held out his bare hand. He wiggled his collection of stump fingers in Peter's face.

"Don't you worry about your chin. Chins mend. Nothing a thick beard won't cover," Fallow promised, stroking his own facial hair.

Peter struggled to his knees. Stray snowflakes had begun to fall as the sun eased its way toward the horizon. Huck and Jo delighted in the flakes, launching into their own impromptu song.

"Who are you?" Peter asked.

The old man grinned. "Why, I'm Papa Fallow, of course."

"Answer the question."

The old man rose. He dropped his grin and all pretense of congeniality.

"Must be nice to be free of that nightmare. Free of that fellow's hungry blade. Can you imagine what he would have done if our Willa hadn't called you back? What damage he'd do?" Fallow's nostrils flared. "Well, I can. Oh, yes, I most assuredly can."

The setting sun broke through the darkening clouds, painting Fallow's features in sharp relief. And despite those features being etched deeper by time, Peter finally recognized them as his own.

"Who are you?" Peter shouted, already knowing the answer.

"Well, my boy," Papa Fallow said. "I guess you'd say I'm the stone that got left behind."

CHAPTER 38

"*To say that you and I had different experiences that night is to put it mildly...*"

"You never should've come here, Blinder!"

"Please, I don't understand..."

A quick flick of the man's wrist, and Peter felt a burning line across his chin. He darted out his tongue and tasted copper.

"*You see, we walked the same path, you and I. Until things went sideways. Until we parted ways...*"

"Time to pay up, Blinder. Time to bleed."

The man made his move. Peter raised a hand to fend off the attack and felt cold steel sink into his flesh. The tip of his finger fell free, and warm blood cascaded down his palm.

"I cut him! Cut him good."

The man reached out for Whisper, who loosed a single, black tendril from his chest, catching the man in the neck, piercing his larynx.

Enraged and sputtering blood, the man gripped Peter's wrist, meaning to let his knife feed on more fingers.

"*It happened when she called me...us back...*"

Come! You must obey. To me, Whisper. Come!

Peter was suddenly pulled in countless directions. He felt himself stretched thin and feared he would snap, splintering off in a million directions. Like one of Willa's skipping stones, breaking apart into two, into six, into…

"Willa brought you *back. Back to safety. But* me? *You know her trick with the stones, how they split and split and split again. Well, it's not just stones she has that effect on…"*

The sensation vanished as quickly as it had appeared. Willa's voice faded. Peter suddenly realized Whisper was gone. And not only that. He felt a great emptiness inside, like a slaughtered animal emptied of its innards.

"When she brought you back, she split flesh. Yours and mine. One became two. The Peter who returned and the Peter who didn't…"

"Youu-u f-ffen ba-aa-aa!" the man with the knife gurgled as he struck again.

Another cut.

Another finger.

"One stone returned from 1895 and one got left behind…"

Another cut.

Another finger.

"You know, the name Peter means stone…"

Cut.

"Funny the things you think of when you're being hacked to bits…"

Finger.

Peter curled into a ball, howling over his mangled hands. The man with the knife leaned over him, speaking close, his breath fetid.

"Gonna let you bleed awhile. Like you bled that boy. But don't you worry. I'll circle back. And when I do, I'm gonna take them eyes of yours, Blinder."

One last slice across the scalp, and the man disappeared into the night.

Slowly, in an attempt to coddle his wounded hands, Peter dugs his elbows into the earth and tried to rise.

"Maybe I should have stayed down…"

He fell on his first attempt, landing full force on his right hand, causing him to cry out.

"But you'd left me with something. Something that demanded I get up…"

Peter planted himself again and pressed upward. His muscles quaked with the pain, but they allowed him to lurch into a crouch. With great effort, he rose.

"Something I carry with me to this day…"

He looked about the moonlit killing field and cried out.

"Hannah!"

And again.

"Hannah!"

"You may have taken her face with you, but you left me her name. I knew I wouldn't die that night. She was out there somewhere. And damned if I wasn't going to find her…"

Peter stumbled forward. There was nowhere to run—torches blazed all around. Yet, still he pressed on.

He passed a thin man lying on his back, red jelly where his eyes should be, his belly split and spilling onto the black earth. He circled around a pair of women, their arms reaching for each other even as the life drained from their eyes. The fallen were all reaching for each other, as if fearful of dying alone.

Peter squinted. Standing in the midst of this ruin was a young boy. At first, he thought the boy had been run through with a pitchfork or pike, but he soon saw the figure before him sported a single, homemade crutch. The boy was bent over, his free hand grabbing for the crutch's twin.

When Peter approached, the boy recoiled in fear, and Peter's hands screamed anew as he realized how grisly he must look. Still, he risked holding his hands up to put the child at ease.

"I won't hurt you."

"But I was going to have to be patient…"

The boy with the crutch gestured with his chin, and Peter heart sank as he realized the boy was not fearful of him but of whoever was *behind* him.

"As patient as Job…"

Peter whirled about. The man with the knife now had a club, and he struck Peter across the nose with it. A thunder crack of shattering bone and cartilage echoed in Peter's ears and all went dark.

"They buried us in a common grave. Sisters, brothers, grandmothers, sons. All the Blinders. And me, of course. The one who was left behind."

When Peter roused, it was still night. Or so he thought. But the more he tried to focus on the scene about him, the less success he had. He felt a great pressure on his chest. When he tried to take a breath, his mouth filled with dirt.

Buried! he thought. They buried me!

Peter tried to move and found he couldn't. He tried to shout and ate more earth. He rushed straight past panic and headlong into terror.

"My story would have ended right then and there if it weren't for an act of divine providence…"

That was until two small fingers brushed against the top of his mangled hand.

His ferocious air hunger instantly abated, and although he was blind and immobile, he knew whose fingers had just made contact here in the dark underneath.

It was the boy with the crutches.

"Or perhaps it was just dumb luck…"

He felt the small hand burrow closer until it gripped his own. No matter that the boy's grasp lit up raw nerves. He was not alone.

"For the next thirty-odd years, I lay in the earth…"

Peter closed his eyes, praying for his heart to stop racing.

"Teetering on the edge between life and death. Fending off the rats…"

Promising Hannah he would find her.

"Lying fallow."

No matter what the cost.

"The boy and I were not the only ones who survived that day, who were buried and left for dead. You see, the people of Blind Rock were cut from a different cloth. Like the boy, they had their secrets, their companions. And those secret 'friends' kept them this side of death."

Peter felt a tingling in his hand. The boy was sending something his way. He felt a sudden connection to those buried below, like electric signals traveling through neurons or water traveling through roots. They were connected—all of them. Feeding each other…life.

My hand touched the boy's, the boy's touched another's, the other's touched another's and so on…

He felt a cold rush pour into his body and realized something was being portioned out. A medicine. A tonic. A whispering kindness.

The offering gave Peter an extra boost of strength, and he tried to move. *Patience,* the others told him. *Rest,* was their advice.

"Rest? Never. Patience? Impossible."

He had to get up—he had to get *out.*

And so, I fed deeper…

Alarm rose from below. *Sip! Go gently! There's plenty for all.*

"Instead, I gorged. I was famished for life. I was barely Peter anymore—you had taken so much of you when you left. I needed to fill myself. Become whole. To patch myself back together again…"

The Peter left behind drew upon the others. As he did so, he felt himself expand. Ethereal creatures—the Blinders' companions—flowed into him. Sustaining him. Taking root. Soon, he was Peter in name only. He was a collection. A throng. Lying fallow.

"To satisfy my hunger…"

He was legion.

"Until it was time to rise."

CHAPTER 39

"And rise we did, Curly and I," Fallow said. "Summer of 1932. Just in time for the Great Depression. A young pastor—leader of a new congregation that had set up shop in the abandoned Blind Rock church—found us in the field, baking in the sun next to the hole whence we'd crawled. We stayed with him and his church a spell. Until the young ones grew up and moved away, the elders grew old and were buried. In the end, it was just the pastor—now going on sixty—Curly and me."

"'As God is my witness, you were dead when I found you,' the man confessed a week before he packed his bags and headed west. 'Are you Lazarus himself?'"

"'No,' I told him. 'Although I'm starting to suspect I might be Methuselah.'"

Fallow laughed and motioned Curly to his side.

"That just left the two of us, didn't it, Curly? But we made do, didn't we?"

The man held out his hand, and Curly took it, gingerly. The moment skin touched skin, Fallow exhaled, his breath crimson in the light of the setting sun.

"You see, our Curly may be unassuming, but his grip is quite special."

The boy tried to pull away, but Fallow held him fast.

"Poor kid. He's still gun-shy because of the dog." Fallow smiled down at Peter. "You remember the pooch we had when you first got here? That mangy old thing?"

Peter didn't reply. He was trying to process what he'd just heard.

Fallow shook his head. "The boy couldn't help himself. Always giving it scratches, hugging it close…"

Wisps of the old man's beard began falling from his chin. His cheeks flushed.

"He loved that mutt down into nothing. First a puppy, then nothing at all. His touch is what you might call rejuvenating. That's his special gift. That's why he's part of our little family, isn't that right, Curly?"

"Too…much," the boy managed. The boy was about to pass out.

"Don't worry. Not much further to go." Fallow's weight dropped, his clothes sagging, suddenly too large for him by a couple of sizes. The last of his facial hair sloughed off, revealing a silvery slice across the chin. With every passing second, Peter saw more and more of himself in the rapidly de-aging man.

"Excuse me," the girl, the newcomer, said clearing her throat.

Fallow waved her off. "Not now, child. Almost there."

Willa stood transfixed, her hands working themselves into fists. Peter wished she would act, bring down hellfire on this man or send him into the world of the red sky to be ripped to pieces, a feast for the hungry ones. But she remained planted in place, her jaw set in fear.

Huck and Jo cowered behind Fallow, fearful and yet clinging to him nonetheless.

Fallow let go of Curly, and the boy stumbled back into Dodge. The man held up his hand and waggled his fingers. His stumps remained.

"Thought maybe I'd get some of my digits back, but I guess that's not how it works." Fallow chuckled. "To tell you the God's honest truth, I didn't know if it'd work at all. Tell me, Peter, how do I look?"

He leaned down to Peter, and his smile was as sharp as broken glass. It was like looking at himself in a cracked mirror. Yes, the man before him did bear a striking resemblance to him, but…something was off. It wasn't in the features, for they were an exact match, save for perhaps a slight crook of the nose caused by the man with the club.

No, it was something lurking behind the eyes that differed. Something squirming inside. And as Peter watched, the man's left cheekbone rose and fell, as if a worm or some other creepy-crawly had moved beneath the skin.

Fallow saw that Peter saw, and his grin faded.

"Dodge!" the man shouted. "Look inside this man and tell me what you see."

The lanky teen made certain Curly had his crutches firmly planted before picking his way through the snow to Fallow's side.

"Here? Out in the open?" Dodge asked, looking about the group, his eyes landing on the new girl.

"Yes!" Fallow roared. When he did so, Peter noted the man's jaw muscles allowed the mouth to open slightly wider than normal. Like a snake unhinging its jaw before swallowing an egg.

With an embarrassed shudder, Dodge removed his coat, his shirt and stood bare-chested in the dimming light. At first, it seemed he wouldn't be able to coax his companion to show its face, but then he doubled over, crying out in pain. His back split as if ravaged by a ragged nail, and from the wound, the thing emerged, buzzing and chittering—all legs, spines and stalk eyes. Once more, Peter felt its voice grinding inside his head.

He is filled with a life. Boy, man, husband, father. There are hollows, yes, but he is whole. He is—

Fallow reached out and grabbed the dark-shelled creature, ripping it free from Dodge's body. Dodge shrieked and fell to the snow, an angry gash running the length of his spine. This time his injury was slow to heal, and Willa hurried to his side, scooping up snow and packing it against the wound.

"What have you done?" Willa cried.

Fallow's only answer was to hold the frantically squirming creature aloft and crack it in half, as one would a boiled lobster. Once more his jaws unhinged and, with predatory speed, he wolfed down one half and then the other of Dodge's dark, squealing creature.

"Always hated the way that thing got in my head. Glad to be rid of it." Fallow looked about at the collection of astonished faces about him. He looked at his hands, saw them covered in the creature's black blood, and for a moment he seemed surprised by his own actions as well.

His introspection quickly vanished.

"Peter," he said with a newfound coolness. "You've got some memories that belong to both of us. And I aim to have them."

In a flash, Willa stepped between Fallow and Peter. Her hands, which had been balls of pure tension, were open now, her fingers twitching as if imagining witchy retributions.

Fallow responded by retreating from the circle. He grabbed Huck and Jo by the scruffs of their necks and lifted them as easily as one would puppies, holding them aloft in warning. Once more, there was a discernable shift in his features as something writhed beneath his skin.

"Stand down, Willa, or I can't promise I won't make a snack out of the little ones."

His words were a gut punch that caused Willa to step back. She glanced down at Peter, and he saw a begging fear in her face he had no idea how to quell.

"Put them down," Peter said through bared teeth.

Fallow nodded but didn't comply.

"Took a long time to gather this little crew of mine, Peter. Not only did I have to track down the scattered bloodline fragments from the massacre, I had to find just the right ones, just the right talents. And these two?"

Huck was, by this time, bawling his head off. Jo looked pissed and was busy conjuring attack butterflies from thin air. Fallow batted them away with a puff of breath.

"Well…we both know what a fondness we have for kids, am I right?"

Peter spat. "If you ever find Hannah, she'll take one look at you and run."

"Be quiet."

"You're just a shadow of me. She'll see you for what you are."

"Quiet!"

"A monster."

Fallow shook the children at Peter like they were weapons. Peter supposed, at this point, that they were. If he pushed this nightmare version of himself any further, he might use those weapons.

"Take her," Peter said, only he wasn't addressing Fallow anymore. He spoke to the withered, black shadow before him on the snow. Whisper was little more than a wisp at this point—a swirl of black ink. He turned to Willa. "Tell him to take her."

Willa's eyes were wide. Peter didn't know if the girl would do it, if she *could* do it under the circumstances. He could see she was holding back, and if Fallow hadn't been using the little kids as human shields, she would no doubt be drawing forth assistance from the dark beyond.

Instead, she reached for Whisper.

The blackness solidified at her touch, becoming a bird once more.

"Oh, my Whisper. My Mr. Tell. I must ask another favor of you. And then I'll let you rest. I promise." The bird responded by nuzzling her hand with his beak.

Without another word of instruction, Whisper hopped over to Peter. He paused, regarding Peter with curious turns of his head.

"Let's go," Fallow said. "Time's a-wastin'."

Whisper hopped a few steps closer.

"Give me a moment to get her clearly in my head," Peter said to the bird.

He cast his line into his mind's lake and drew forth Hannah. Smiling and wearing a St. Louis Cardinals cap just to

239

screw with him. The porch of their cabin rental in Maine. Pines all around—the scent of heaven—and beyond, the Longfellow Mountains. Her leaning in. Blueberry stain on her lip.

"I'm pregnant."

The mingling of fear and excitement in her eyes. Her warm kiss.

I take.

Peter opened his eyes. Whisper had climbed the front of his coat, poised and ready to extract his love.

I take, Peter.

"Thank you," Peter said.

The bird placed its beak into Peter's mouth. He felt a knot rise in his throat as Whisper extracted the cabin, the Longfellow Mountains and Hannah's blueberry lips. The peaceful scene slipped away like smoke.

Whisper fluttered to the ground. He held a glistening orange stone in his beak, made even more vibrant by the brilliant sunset.

The bird set the stone in the snow.

Willa screamed, but it was too late.

Fallow fell upon Whisper, mouth stretched to near splitting, and swallowed him whole.

CHAPTER 40

When the man called Fallow ate the bird called Whisper, Ellen decided it was time to get the hell out of there. Whatever drama these people were involved in was too hectic for her. It was like trying to watch seven TV shows at the same time when you didn't know any of the characters' names.

And besides, the fields around them were getting rather crowded.

About the time the old Santa-looking fellow started spinning back the clock, she'd spotted the first of the watchers. The man was quite a ways away, and the first thing Ellen noticed about him was that he was dressed in old-timey clothes. The kind Pa Ingalls would wear. Or Almanzo.

He was also, most assuredly, a ghost.

The man didn't quite fill his space in the world. Bits of the landscape behind him peeked through.

Another figure appeared to her right. Then another. Standing watch as the sun beat a hasty retreat.

Hasty retreat. Tasty treat. Treat the ghost...

"Excuse me," she'd told the group, certain a gathering of ghosts might be something they'd want to know about.

"Not now, child," the old man had said, blowing her off. And so, she remained silent as the boy called Dodge pulled what looked to her like a giant cricket out of his back, as the bird produced a stone from the injured man's mouth and through the whole bird-eating spectacle.

But as the sun finally disappeared below the horizon and the spirits surrounding them began to close in, it was time to hoof it, as her dad would say.

The older kids? They were on their own. The adults? Forget about it. They were too concerned about each other to even listen to her. But the little ones, the girl and the boy who now lay sprawled and squalling in the snow, having been dropped in favor of a squab?

Those two. The little ones. I can take them.

There was only one stretch of field absent any ghosts, and it led straight to the old church. That made choosing her direction of escape a breeze.

Ellen stepped out of the circle, brushing past the tall girl, the wounded man and the rest. She unceremoniously yanked the two kids to standing and laid down the law.

"We're running to the church, you hear me? I'm older, and I can run faster than you. Unless you think you're faster than me. Do you think you're faster than me?"

The trick—one her dad's methods of getting her up and moving when she used to lie on the floor in the middle of the grocery store, refusing to move—worked. The girl and boy, startled out of crying by the challenge, piped up.

"I'm faster than you!"

"No, I'm faster!"

The newly-formed trio took off across the field. As they dashed over snow drifts and around protruding stones, Ellen called back to the older members of the group who were still facing off across the circle.

"Incoming!"

CHAPTER 41

The girl in the oversized sweatshirt stomped past Peter and yanked the two little ones to their feet.

Ellen. Her name is Ellen.

The name sparked something in Peter's mind, but when he reached for it, it was just another missing puzzle piece. Before he could figure out why the girl seemed so familiar, Fallow was scrambling for the orange stone. For Hannah.

Peter made a grab for it as well and it slipped from his fingers. But it wasn't Fallow who ended up with the stone. It was Willa.

"Incoming!" Ellen yelled. And then the girl was dashing across the field, dragging Huck and Jo behind.

Fallow rose and sniffed the air. He scanned the darkening horizon and moaned.

"They're here. Damn them, they're here!"

Peter followed his doppelganger's gaze. A crowd approached on all sides—men, women and youngsters. They raised their arms in unison, in mock greeting. There was nothing welcoming in the gesture, only the desire to grab and hold tight—to hold and smother.

As the figures closed in, Peter recognized the woman with the straw-colored hair. Her head lolled to the side, her split skull spilling forth its contents. And still she approached, arms outstretched, eager for a hug.

Peter rose, the effort causing his hand to throb. The girl, Ellen, and the little ones were already a good two hundred yards on their way toward the shelter of the church, their tracks crisscrossing each other in the snow—evidence of their chaotic escape. He turned to Willa who stood with stone in hand, transfixed by the approaching spirits with a mix of wonder and horror.

A gust of wind lifted the upper layer of snow and whipped it Peter's way, temporarily blinding him. His last venture into the fields after dark rushed to the fore, and he remembered the cries and the cold, clamoring hands that had tried to pull him back into the storm.

He had evaded them the first time he'd encountered them outside the church. He could do it again.

Liar, he told himself. *It was the bird that saved you. It was Whisper. Buddy, you're on your own.*

Peter reached out to Willa, intending to make a run for it—he had locked onto the direction of the church's steeple before ice hit his eyes—but the hand he took was not the girl's. It was the hand of something dead.

* * *

Jo sailed through snow while Huck proved more of an anchor.

"I want Papa! I want Dodge!" the boy said as he tried to dig the heels of his boots into the snow. "I want Curly! I want Dodge!"

"Your sister's beating you," Ellen said, regretting her choice to wear the chunky shoes. "Are you really going to let a girl win?"

"She's not winning!"

"Yes, I am!" Jo had really taken the competition to heart. By this point, she was dragging Ellen, who was, in turn, dragging Huck. Their path through the snow was a decidedly zigzag affair.

"Go right, go right!" Ellen called to the girl, as a man with no jaw had suddenly appeared to their left. Ellen's imagination was already running wild, but she could swear she could smell him as they passed. A mix of clay and sweat and rot.

Jo veered right, and they passed the shade with zero contact.

The church was within sprinting distance, but Huck was running out of steam.

"Stop pulling, you poop!"

The boy went down on his knees.

The man with no jaw stopped and turned.

Ellen tugged on Jo's arm, causing the girl to brake.

"Hey! You like Christmas, right?" Ellen barked at the girl. *Of course, she does. What kind of kid doesn't like Christmas?* "Let's play reindeer. I'm Dasher, you're Prancer and your brother is the sleigh. Sound good?"

Jo looked back at her with a grin, seemingly about to reply in the affirmative, when she spied the no-jawed ghost.

"That man…"

"Don't look at him."

"His face is all…"

"Don't look! Let's go! Sleigh ride!"

Ellen flipped Huck over onto his back and forced one of his mittened hands into Jo's before grabbing the other in her own. With the girl's eyes still latched onto the spirit—who had grown interested and was now approaching, upper lip curled and baring teeth—Ellen shouted out, "Here comes Santa Claus, here comes Santa Claus, right down Santa Claus Lane!"

The ferocity of her yell-singing broke Jo's concentration, and the girl joined in.

"Vixen and Blitzen and all his reindeer are pulling on the reins!" They sang as they made a renewed effort to get to the safety of the church, hauling the limp Huck behind them.

* * *

Peter squinted hard, willing his eyes to focus. When they finally obeyed, he wished they hadn't.

The nightmare gripping his hand was an elderly woman, stooped low by her injuries, which were many. White hair hung over a distorted face, and the hand that clutched his was attached to an arm so shattered, it bent in all directions like the branch of a Halloween tree.

Peter pulled back and felt the woman's cold fingers pass through his muscle and tissues, leaving a sickening ache in their wake.

It's like she's made of ice…

The full force of the rising wind hit, pelting ice obliterating Fallow and Willa from view. Peter heard Willa cry once, and then his ears were filled with hammering gusts and howling ghosts.

"Help me!" a voice called from the swirling snow. It was Dodge. Covering his face from the icy assault, Peter strained forward into the wind, toward the sound of Dodge's plea.

He soon came upon the teen wriggling back into his shirt and coat. Curly lay weeping in the snow.

"Grab his crutches!" Peter shouted as he lifted Curly and threw him over his shoulder, amazed at how light the boy was. The kid's body shook with sobs.

"You lead the way," Peter called to Dodge as he took the end of one of the crutches the teen had retrieved from the snow. "You lead, I'll follow!"

* * *

As the trio approached the church, Jo let go of her brother's hand and made a run for it, dropping the reindeer game and reverting to race mode.

"I win! I win!" she crowed, slapping the door.

"No, you never!" her brother cried, pulling free from Ellen's grip, leaving her holding his mitten. Huck rolled over and stumbled through the wind and snow until he too was at the church door. He gave it a double slap for good measure. "I win."

"You didn't win, Huck."

"Yes, I did!"

Ellen grabbed the door handle. "You both won, okay? Let's get inside." *Kids. Ugh.*

She opened the door, shoved the twins inside and slipped in behind them, but not before taking a look back down the path they'd come.

Rushing forward, following the tracks she and the kids had left in the snow, were Fallow and the tall girl. They dodged the man with no jaw and kept coming.

I never should have opened that birthday card.
Ellen slammed the door shut.

* * *

At some points, the swirling snow hid Dodge from view, even though he was only a couple feet ahead.

Anyone could have hold of the other end of that crutch...

Periodically a window would open in the white, and Dodge reappeared. Abracadabra.

"We're not going to make it to the church!" the boy cried.

"Just keep moving. We'll make it."

Dodge stopped in his tracks.

"No, we won't."

The boy pointed. A break in the storm revealed the church sitting like a boat in the middle of the eye of a hurricane. The steeple, which had always listed, bent further still.

Fallow was racing toward the building, dragging Willa behind him. And standing between Peter and the church was a growing crowd of the dead.

We're fucked.

"Come on!" Peter said, taking the lead, veering off from the church.

"Where are you going?" Dodge asked.

"The shed!"

CHAPTER 42

Ellen squatted before the two children and forced a smile. "You guys are really good at playing games. I'll bet you know all the best hiding places for hide-and-go-seek."

"No more games," Huck whined. "I want pancakes. I want Papa."

"You're a baby," his sister said.

"Am not!"

Ellen turned to the girl. No time for subtlety. "Best hiding spot. *Now.*"

Jumping at the challenge, Jo wrinkled her nose at her brother and scurried off into the heart of the church. Ellen followed, dragging the sniffling Huck along with her.

Jo ducked into the storage room and disappeared.

Ellen heard the church door opening behind her and double-stepped it to the storage room. Huck complained, but there was nothing to be done about it. They had to get into hiding.

As she pulled Huck into the tight room and closed the door, she thought for a second the girl actually *had* disappeared—there was nothing in the room but old cushions, an empty water bowl and some castoff choir robes.

"Up here!" a small voice whispered from above.

Ellen looked up. A wooden ladder attached to the wall led upward to where Jo stared down at her through a square cut into the ceiling.

"Wait for me!" Huck called, suddenly excited. Before Ellen could help him to the ladder, the boy scrambled up and disappeared through the hole.

"And stay out, you bastards!" It was Fallow's voice. No time to dawdle. He was already inside.

Goodbye, shoes.

Ellen kicked off her clunky footwear and climbed, following the sound of giggled laughter.

As she hoisted herself through the hole, Ellen found herself in a second cramped room. The floor was unfinished plywood, and the walls were the same. There was no ceiling—instead, the space rose up another story. Above, the walls were merely louvers, panels of horizontal slats of wood, many of which were cracked in places, letting in the snow. And beyond that, the interior spire of the steeple, a patchwork of wooden cross braces groaning as the wind tried to topple the structure.

Ellen stood transfixed. Tacked to the walls were scores of crude drawings. Some in crayon, some in charcoal—all of the same subject. A woman with a swirling face.

Ellen ripped one off the wall and looked at it in more detail. It had all the sophistication of a child's drawing, but she suspected no child had made it.

That swirling face. It makes you almost sick to look at it.

"What is this place?" she asked Jo and Huck.

The children didn't answer. They were busy peering out a small window that looked down upon the sanctuary.

She folded the drawing and wedged herself in between the two. Through the window, she found she had a bird's eye view of the scene below.

"It's Papa!"

"Quiet, Jo. He'll find us."

"You be quiet."

Fallow circled Willa, gesticulating wildly as he ripped off his coat and hat. It was like watching a play from the back row of the theater.

"It's time to send me, child," the circling man hissed.

"Where?" Willa asked.

Ellen watched in horror as the man struck the girl, sending her sprawling on the floor. Caught off guard, Willa released her grip on the stone and it skidded across the floor.

"To her, of course!" he said, retrieving the stone and raising it high. Ellen could see it glint, even from here.

"We can't go back to the circle until morning. And Whisper is gone. You killed him!"

"You need a circle? You *really* need a circle? Fine! I'll give you one."

Fallow lifted his wrist to his mouth and bit down. The man shook his head back and forth until his teeth pulled a strip of flesh free. Blood appeared instantly.

"What's he doing?" Huck asked. The boy was frightened, and with good reason.

"It's a trick," Ellen offered. "He's playing a trick on her." But she knew she hadn't sold the lie. And how could she, when the red evidence of Fallow's self-inflicted violence was streaming down his arm.

"Here! Here's your circle!"

The man stooped, pressing his wrist to the floor and circled Willa—painting her in with his blood.

"And as for your Whisper, he's still here."

Fallow removed his sweater. His face—Peter's face—had kept its continuity, but his body was another story. The skin was grey and rippling, as if infested by enormous larvae.

"They're *all* still here. Inside me. All the Blinders' dark companions. Every demon I fed upon while trapped beneath the earth."

A dark beak punctured his chest, and the bird struggled to break free before being drawn back inside the roiling flesh.

Ellen pushed the children aside and blocked the view. If the scene below frightened her, she could only imagine what it was doing to the twins. She redirected their attention to the drawing.

"Did you do this?" she asked. Both kids shook their heads.

"This is Papa's office," Huck said by way of explanation.

"Papa did it," Jo added.

She was about to press them further when she spied an orange extension cord snaking across the floor. Following it, she found a small card table tucked away in the farthest corner of the room.

When Ellen approached the table, she was shocked to find an old friend waiting to greet her. Sitting amongst a pile of drawings was the Norelco tape recorder she had bought from the burning, dancing man.

CHAPTER 43

Dodge wrenched open the shed door, and Peter stumbled inside, Curly draped over his shoulder. He laid the boy down on the cot.

"Close that door!"

The teenager tossed the crutches inside before wrestling with the wind for control of the door, finally pulling it closed. The storm, and the things in it, howled.

"Your back. How is it?" Peter asked Dodge.

"Better than your hand."

Peter grabbed at the collar of his shirt and ripped it off, winding the torn cloth around his wounded finger. Aside from the pain shooting up his arm, he had one thing on his mind.

"Can they get inside?"

"They won't go inside the church," Dodge said. "Papa says they *can't*, but—"

"Can they get inside this shed?"

Before Dodge could reply, a solitary hand slid through the solid metal door and grasped at air.

"That answers that," Peter groaned. "Get back."

The teen obeyed and huddled close.

Curly stirred on the cot.

Dodge knelt by his side. "You okay, Curly?"

The boy opened his eyes and drew back, startled.

"It's okay. We're safe," Dodge assured him.

Curly spotted the hand reaching through the door and shook his head, making it known that he did not agree with Dodge's assessment. He grabbed for his crutches.

A face pressed through the door, and if it weren't for the hideous way the man's nose hung open, a hatchet wound across its bridge, the absurdity of it all might have made Peter laugh.

Curly pounded a crutch on the wooden planks lining the ground.

"Down!" the boy said, straining to make sure he was understood.

Peter looked down. He had noted the planks when he had first wakened in this place. He stomped his foot on the wood, and the sound it returned was hollow.

"Stand back," he told Dodge as he quickly stepped to the side so one of the boards was free of their weight. He pried it up. Pitch blackness lay beneath.

"I'm not crawling down there!" Dodge cried.

Curly shook his head emphatically. "Down!"

Peter held out his hand to Dodge. "Give me your lighter."

"I don't smoke."

"Give it to me."

The boy pulled a pack of cigarettes from his pocket and pulled a lighter from the pack.

Peter held the lighter down the hole and flicked it to life. The flame reflected off a damp surface some seven or eight feet below. There were footholds dug into the side of the shaft. Someone had ensured passage below would not be a one-way trip.

The sound of tearing metal brought Peter to his feet. One second, the roof was there; the next, it wasn't. The full force of the storm reached in and batted him aside while threatening to rip the rest of the shed apart.

That's it. Stay here and die or get in the hole.

"Think you can help get Curly down to me?" Peter shouted over the roaring wind.

"Yes!"

"Good."

And with that, Peter descended.

The shaft was deeper than Peter had expected, and some of the handholds offered less-than-perfect purchase. He dropped the final few feet to the bottom and looked up. Dodge was staring down at him, the sky churning above.

"Send him down!"

Dodge disappeared for a moment, then Curly's legs were dangling over the edge. Peter tucked the lighter between his teeth and grabbed the boy, hauling him down. He extracted the lighter and flicked it to life. The boy's eyes were wide.

"Dodge!" Curly complained.

"He's coming. Let's give him some room."

Peter hugged the wall, holding Curly close, while Dodge made his descent. In the glow of the flame, Peter could tell the teen was not happy about this decision.

"Now what?" Dodge asked.

Curly squirmed in Peter's arms, trying to wriggle free.

"No crutches?" Peter asked Dodge. The boy looked up at the mouth of the hole. Nope. The crutches were still up top.

Curly loosed a series of chuffs, urging Peter to his right. Curious what had so agitated the boy, he trained the lighter in that direction and found the hole opened up into a narrow tunnel in the earth.

"I don't like this," Dodge moaned.

As the light from the lighter fell upon the shaft, Curly spoke up. "In!"

"In there?" Peter asked.

Curly wriggled in the affirmative.

"I can't go in there," Dodge said, hanging his head. "I'm freaking out as it is."

"Stay here," Peter said, one hand around Curly's midsection, the other holding the lighter aloft like a mini torch. "And don't let any of those things down here."

"How am I supposed to do that?"

Peter shrugged. "Pray?"

With that, Peter and Curly slipped further into the earth. The air grew humid, and the temperature rose.

The tunnel was barely five feet high, and Peter had to walk with a stoop that did nothing for his grip on the boy, the throbbing in his hand or the ache in his back.

Maybe it's a shortcut into the church.

But no. They soon came to the end of the road about three yards from where they started.

"Dead end, Curly."

The boy didn't reply at first. His eyes were locked on the tunnel wall, his mouth working its way toward a single word.

"Mama."

Peter held out the lighter. Staring at him, embedded in the earthen wall, was a hollow-eyed skull, the dome of its forehead split.

"Praying didn't help."

Peter turned. Dodge was at his elbow. Farther down the tunnel, a pale man with a twisted neck dropped into the hole.

Another specter joined him. And another. Soon, the tunnel was crowded with the dead.

Well...that's that.

Curly reached out and placed a hand on the skull. With his other he grasped Peter's injured hand. Pain rose exponentially for a moment, and then...

The tunnel was gone. Curly and Dodge were gone. The approaching horde of spirits were gone.

All that remained was the woman with the straw-colored hair.

CHAPTER 44

The Norelco was definitely in better shape than the last time she had seen it, when it was setting off the smoke alarm and Rita's wrath.

Next to the recorder sat a stack of tape boxes. Ellen began quickly rifling through them.

Where is it? Where is it?

"Don't touch. Papa won't like that," Jo said.

Ellen ignored her. The second she spotted the recorder, a plan had popped into her head.

She located the tape she was looking for.

Hymns (30 min).

She quickly checked the recorder for power and then threaded the tape to a take-up reel.

A do over. Years from now, I'll be listening to this tape. It called me by name. Told me about Blind Rock. I'll just tape over it. Tell myself not to come. Maybe I'll pop back in my room like nothing ever happened. Like I never left Iowa City. Maybe…

Ellen grabbed the microphone and turned on the machine.

A choir exploded overhead.

She quickly hit Stop.

Looking up, she spied a loudspeaker she'd missed upon first examination. It sat wedged between two of the cross braces, pointed outward. A cord ran from the speaker down to the back of the recorder. Ellen yanked out the cord and tried again. This time, the choir gave a much quieter rendition.

Bringing in the sheaves!
Bringing in the sheaves!
We shall come rejoicing, bringing in the sheaves!

Ellen hit the Trick button and spoke adamantly into the mic.

"Ellen, this is Ellen. I know this sounds strange, but whatever you do, do *not* go to Blind Rock. Dad may try to get you to go, but stay far away from Blind Rock! You hear me? Do not go to Blind Rock. I repeat, do *not* go to Blind Rock!"

"Papa looks funny," Huck said staring down through the window.

Ellen quickly rewound the tape, making certain her message was intact. The hymn started up the same as before, and then came her voice, layered over the choir.

"Ellen...Ellen...Blind Rock...Blind Rock! You hear me?"

Shit.

The microphone must be broken. It only recorded part of what I said...

"Blind Rock!"

Ellen stopped the tape as she realized what she had done.

"Blind Rock!"

The voice she had heard back in her bedroom. The one that set her on her quest. It was her own. She had called herself to Blind Rock.

Behind her, the twins screamed.

Startled, Ellen whipped about, jostling the card table in the process. One of the legs buckled and the tape recorder fell to the floor with a clatter. The power cord split with a short pop, and a spark found fuel in a pile of portraits lying scattered on the floor, igniting the many renditions of the woman with the swirling face.

"No, no, no, no, no!" Ellen was about to stomp on the flame when she realized she'd left her shoes below.

The drawings went up as quickly as dry leaves. Ellen dashed over to the children and grabbed them by their arms.

"We've got to go."

"No!" Huck wailed. "Papa is—"

"We've got to go *now*."

She shoved them toward the opening in the floor. Jo helped Huck onto the ladder and the two descended, scrambling over each other.

Flames licked the walls, and the smoke grew thick. So much for hide-and-go-seek, but the alternative was stay-and-get-burned. Ellen grabbed hold of the ladder and followed the twins, leaving the Norelco to fend for itself in the fire.

Back down in the storage room, Ellen found herself alone once again.

I'm never *going to be a babysitter.*

She slowly peered out from behind the door and spotted the twins cautiously approaching the prone Willa. The cause of their trepidation was all too clear.

Fallow was at the far end of the church where the altar once stood—a minister addressing an absent congregation. His transformation from old to young had been unnerving in and of itself, but the evolution now taking place was more disturbing yet.

His skin wasn't quite doing its job of holding his insides in. There were places where the flesh had split, revealing dark, squirming things beneath. Like eels in a net. His face had changed as well, features stretched wide, forcing him into a predatory grin. All the color had drained from his cheeks, and his eyes sank into his head.

"An audience?" he hooted as he spied Ellen, his voice decaying as well. "Why not? I've always been a good storytell-tell-teller! Sitting in my booth reading books. So I could bring home the ba-a-a-con! For her." He raised the stone high. "For her!"

He stepped into the circle of blood.

"Send me," he ordered Willa.

"I…"

Such was Fallow's anger, Ellen thought the man was going to blast apart, his inner demons bursting free from the remnants of the man who contained them.

"Send me-ee-ee!"

And with that, Fallow tossed the stone into his mouth and swallowed.

CHAPTER 45

The woman with the straw-colored hair lay across from Peter in the field, her battered head wet and glistening in the moonlight.

The sudden shift left Peter momentarily disoriented. He was back in the killing field, the stalking grounds of the man with the knife.

"Where's my boy?" the woman whispered.

"I don't...your boy?"

"He's out there alone. He can't manage alone. He's crip—" She flinched in pain. "He's alone."

"Your boy. He's disabled? He uses crutches?"

The woman nodded vigorously.

"He's with me. He's safe." One truth; one lie.

The woman's eyes blazed. "You stole from us! Our dark companions. Our salvation!"

"I didn't..."

"Down in the earth. You stole..."

"No."

"...life!"

The woman lifted her blood-stained hand. Another's fingers intertwined with her own. Peter raised his head and discovered a chain of bodies littering the field, washed ghastly blue in the moonlight. Scores of the dead and dying gripping each other like a horrendous game of crack the whip.

"They buried us…"

"I'm sorry."

"And yet we lived. We held on. Each sharing their gifts, their companions with the other. Until *you.*"

Fallow had said he fed. Said he *gorged*. Robbing these people of their chance to survive.

"You!" a choir cried out. "You! You! You!"

"It wasn't me!" Peter cried. "But I'm sorry! For your pain and your loss. I'm…"

The woman with the straw-colored hair extracted her hand and laid it on Peter's face. She peered at him through dying eyes.

"No…not you. Not you at all."

"No."

"Where's my boy?"

"He's with me."

"Where's my boy?"

"He's safe."

She leaned in. "Tell him I love him."

The woman exhaled one last time, and Peter rode her breath across the darkness and the years until he stepped back from her skull embedded in the earth.

"They…They're leaving," Dodge said, incredulously.

Peter looked. The spirits were retreating back down the tunnel, rising like embers through the hole. The last to leave was the woman with the straw-colored hair. She remained a moment to gaze upon the boy Peter held in his arms. Then she too vanished.

Peter pressed his mouth close to Curly's ear.

"I've got a secret for you."

The boy wriggled expectantly.

"Your mother told me to tell you she loves you."

Curly sobbed. "I 'ove you, too, Mama."

Peter had another secret, one he wouldn't share with the child. He and Hannah had never rented a cabin in the Longfellow Mountains. In fact, they'd never been to Maine at all. It was something they always said they'd do, yet never managed to follow through on. And the moment Hannah told him she was pregnant? They were riding the ferry across the Hudson River into New York City.

I've always been a good storyteller, he thought, the hint of a grin tugging at the corner of his mouth. *Enjoy the stone, Fallow. I hope you choke on it.*

CHAPTER 46

The look of twisted glee on Fallow's face told Ellen things had just gone south. If that man—more monstrosity than man by this point—considered downing the stone a victory, then heaven help them all.

"Yes!" Fallow hissed. "Mountains! I see her. She's wearing a ball-ball-ball cap. Beautiful. She's beau-u-utiful!"

A tremor ran through the lurching man's frame, as if the menagerie of crawling horrors that made up his body experienced a collective jolt of electricity.

Ellen looked to where the two little ones stood trembling by the tall girl, their eyes glued on the man in wonder and horror. And well they should—it wasn't every day you watched your papa devolve into a squirming nightmare.

"Beautiful. Beau-u-u…"

Fallow's voice caught in his throat, and his eyes flew open.

"No. No!"

The man doubled over and retched. Black and orange bile poured from his mouth, splattering on the wooden floorboards. Black and orange—a Halloween spew.

"A trick? A trick!" Fallow roared. "She's not there. She's not there! A trick! A fucking trick!"

Willa rose, clutching Huck and Jo tight, and slowly backed away from the blood circle. Fallow reacted instantly.

"Wher-ere-ere do you think you're going? Send me."

"I can't!" Willa shouted.

Fallow lurched forward. Mouths opened up across his torso, angry and snapping and eager to bite. He pointed a stub finger at the little ones.

"Send me or I'll chew-chew-chew them to bits! To bits! Chew you *all* to bits!"

Willa stepped forward, his betrayal making her brave.

"Where's Papa? What have you done to him?"

"*I'm* Papa. And I say—"

"No, you are not. Just look at you."

The demand threw Fallow off guard. He raised his arms and found they were now made up of glistening worms, black and writhing, burrowing into each other.

He laughed.

"Papa. Peter. Old skin. Best shed."

The man in the circle ripped off the last shreds of human flesh, discarding them like old clothes. The last to go was the face.

"You want him? Here! Have him."

Fallow tossed his still-grinning face at Willa. It landed at her feet with a splat.

"Now…send me!"

The church groaned in response under the force of the wind. The change in pressure drew a swirl of embers from the little window set in the rear wall. The fire in Fallow's office was quickly becoming a full-fledged blaze.

The side door rattled, dead hands pounded the walls, a cacophony of wails filled the air. And yet, the storm of spirits remained outside.

"Scream all you want!" Fallow called to the howling wind. "I drank you dry. Down in the earth. I fed-fed-fed on you! You're nothing but cries and whispers. You're nothing but the bree-ee-eeze! Fly away and let me finish this!"

The smoke from the fire had curled down into the sanctuary, making it suddenly clear to Ellen if she stayed much longer, she was in serious jeopardy of joining the dead. The dead who were, even now, pounding on the door for admittance.

I think you should let them in.

The pounding grew louder, so much so Ellen could feel it in her chest.

I think you should let them in.

It threatened to set her heart galloping like a wild horse headed for a cliff.

"I think you should let them in."

The memory arrived with such force that Ellen's breath caught in her throat.

Her father stood in the middle of the living room, looking down on her. Ellen scooted over to let him sit next to her on the sofa.

"Let who in?"

Her father looked about stealthily, but Ellen knew he had no cause to worry. The way her mother had stormed out of the apartment, it would likely be a couple hours before she cooled down.

"Who, Daddy?" she asked, nudging him.

Her father pulled a paper from his pocket. It was crumpled and pieced together with tape. It was the page she'd written with Dad's typewriter. The story about Treat.

"I won't have this nonsense in my house, do you hear?" Rita had shrieked when Ellen showed her the page. "Can't you be normal for once?"

"Mom threw it away. She ripped it up and threw it away."

"And I un-threw it away," her father said.

He handed her the paper. A secret between the two of them.

"What you did here? It's called automatic writing. Or maybe, in this case, typewriting. It's something my mother, your Grandma Marx, used to do. And her sister. They'd jot down things folks—dead folks—wanted to tell them. Me? I maybe felt a thing or two, but I never heard a peep. But you…"

Her father leaned in close. He took her chin in his hand.

"Your mother is never going tell you what I'm about to tell you. She would rather you got rid of what you have. Like a cold. But you know what, Spooky?" he said, tapping the page. "This *is* normal. For you, anyway. And if someone reaches out to you from the other side, someone who needs your help, well…"

He leaned back, carefully considering his next words.

"I think you should let them in."

Ellen inhaled smoke. Her lungs screamed.

Let them in.

She swooned, fearing she would faint.

Let them—

Screw it. Forget Mom and her hateful words. Forget the therapists who tried to fix her. Forget all the kids at school who laughed and insulted her behind her back. In all the wretched mess of humanity, there was only one person she truly trusted. Just one.

Dad.

"Okay!" Ellen said, choking. "Okay…"

With that, she stumbled to the church door.

"No!" Fallow cried.

Ellen threw all her weight behind the door, fighting the wind to swing it open wide. A crowd of the dead awaited her.

"Hey," Ellen said, staring down the throng of hollow-eyed horrors. "Come on in."

The ghosts accepted her invitation, drawing on her gift and her will, solidifying. Shadows becoming ice and ice becoming flesh. And in a great rush, the Blind Rock dead poured into the church and descended upon Fallow. He may have said something before the ghosts embraced him, before they dug into him, relieving him of life, but if he did, Ellen didn't hear it.

She was too busy passing out.

CHAPTER 47

As Peter rose from the hole, the scent of burning lumber and tarpaper hit his nose. The church's steeple was on fire.

"Oh, God. Is there anyone in there?" Peter called to Dodge.

Huck and Jo's sudden appearance answered his question—the children tumbled through the open door and into the snow. Willa followed, dragging the girl named Ellen.

Peter stepped forward, but Dodge stopped him in his tracks.

"I'll go. You stay with Curly."

"But—"

"Look at your hand, dude."

Peter looked. The climb out of the hole had started the bleeding anew—his hand was a crimson claw.

"Willa!" Dodge shouted as he leapt into action. The boy sprinted across the field, passing the twins on his way to Willa's side. Together, they hauled Ellen away from the burning church.

Peter sat down in the snow, nursing his hand while pulling Curly close. One of the boy's crutches lay nearby, and Peter retrieved it and handed it to him. The boy wriggled upright, marveling at the blaze.

"Papa?" Curly asked, his teeth starting to chatter from the cold.

"Yeah, Curly. I'm pretty sure he's inside."

The boy watched as flames traveled the length of the roof's peak—bright yellow and orange against a purple-black sky.

"Good," the boy said. And nothing more.

As the little ones approached, it was Huck who this time won the race.

"Everything's on fire!" Huck announced.

"We didn't do it," Jo insisted.

Dodge and Willa joined the group and set the still unconscious girl in black next to Peter and Curly.

"Fallow?" Peter asked, looking at Willa.

The girl didn't say a word, but perhaps it was her silence that convinced Peter the fire in the distance was consuming more than just the church.

A thundering crack rolled across the field, and everyone turned toward the blaze. The spine of the church's roof sagged, then crumbled, bringing down the steeple. The whole structure folding in on itself.

A plume of black smoke rose from what was quickly becoming Illinois's biggest bonfire, and from the cloud of soot and ash, shrieks of terror, of joy, of release. And rising above it all, Peter thought—no, *knew*—he saw a bird rise into the heavens.

"Bye-bye, church," Jo said.

"Bye-bye," Huck echoed.

The girl in black sat bolt upright. "Is it over?"

"It's over," Peter assured her.

Ellen rose, brushing off snow. "Now what?"

He wasn't sure if the question was directed at him, or if the girl was asking the universe in general. In any case, he had no answer for the girl nor for the rest of them. Now what, indeed? Being the lone adult, he felt the pressure to come up with a plan. But all he seriously wanted to do was to lie back in the snow and sleep. To dream himself back to *her*.

"That's what," Willa said, pointing across the field toward town. The first dim pulses of red dotted the horizon as sirens rose like distant, howling wolves. The cavalry was coming in the form of the Maple City Fire Department, and their questions would be even harder to answer than Ellen's.

"I think I should leave," Peter said, rising. "Best they find you here alone. I'd only raise eyebrows."

"Leave and go where?" the girl in black asked brusquely. "That circle is broken. I should know—I tried it."

"She's right," Willa said. "I'm sure I could draw something forth. But without my Whisper? I couldn't send you anywhere. That was his trick, not mine."

As soon as the words were out of Willa's mouth, her eyes lit up. She reached out for Peter.

"Come with me."

When she offered no further explanation, Peter took her hand.

"You all stay here," she said to the group and to Huck and Jo in particular. "Keep Curly company."

Willa led Peter away from the others, and he went willingly. The flashing lights in the distance were not so distant now. Whatever the girl had in mind, it had better be quick.

She stopped at the edge of the frozen pond. Kneeling, she peered up at him.

"What?" Peter asked.

273

"My Whisper used to tell me secrets. He told me one a while back. One I had a hard time believing. But now…I don't know. Maybe he was right."

"A secret. About me?"

"Yes."

"What was it?"

The girl simply studied his face. Then she dug into the frozen earth and pulled out a smooth, flat stone. She held it up to him.

"Do you remember skipping stones with me?"

"Yes, I do."

Willa rose. She placed her hands over his.

"I want you to place yourself into the stone."

"Place…?"

"Turn off your brain—brains are stupid. Place your heart into the stone. Everything you love. *Everyone* you love. Place it all inside."

Headlights swept across the field, momentarily distracting Peter. A truck had pulled off the highway, drawn by the fire.

"Do it, Peter."

Peter closed his eyes and gripped the stone.

Hannah. The woman who sometimes smiled when she was angry. The one who made unintended puns and told him nonsense in her sleep. His best gal, his best friend. The girl of his dreams.

"Have you done it?"

Peter nodded.

He felt fingers touch his forehead, but he kept his eyes closed. Willa was drawing secret words on his skin.

"One stone spits into two, two into four. Skip the stone, Peter. Send your heart across the ice."

Peter felt the stone grow warm in his hands.

"Send it skipping in all directions," Willa said.

"And then?" he asked, finally opening his eyes.

The girl smiled. "Choose one."

Peter turned toward the frozen pond. Holding the stone in his bloody hand, he wound up...

Hannah

...and skipped the stone. The stone split. And then it split again and again, his heart following each and every one, pulling him thin, until...

A single stone skittered across the ice and dove into the snow on the far bank.

Peter had chosen.

And Willa stood alone at the edge of the frozen pond.

CHAPTER 48

Ellen looked about at the other kids shivering in the snow. They stared back warily, as if seeing her for the first time.

"Your head's bruised," Dodge said, pointing to the knot on her forehead.

"Yeah. I noticed."

"So, what's your deal?"

"My deal?"

"Yeah. Where'd you come from?"

"I told you. Iowa." Some people never listened.

Silence settled back on the group as Huck and Jo amused Curly with their butterfly trick.

When the tall girl returned, she was alone.

"They're going to come get us now," Willa said, pointing her words toward the little ones. "It's okay. They're coming to help. But we aren't going to make butterflies or tell them about Whisper or anything like that, right?"

"Why not?" Huck asked.

"Because, Huck," Jo warned.

"Because…" Willa said, staving off the squabble. "Because the people who are coming. They aren't family, are they? Those things we do, those are ours. We'll keep them to ourselves, right?"

"Right!" Jo said, jostling her brother.

"Okay," Huck said, waving away the last of the butterflies.

"Right," Curly crooned.

"Right," Dodge said.

Everyone turned to Ellen.

"Why are you looking at me?" she complained. "I'm not part of this."

Willa leaned in and looked her square in the eye. "The ones in the snow. You opened the door for them."

"So?"

Willa tilted her head. "I think that makes you 'part of this.' Maybe even more than you know."

A loud honk interrupted them. Ellen looked to the source—an extended truck parked at the side of the road, the words Department of Public Works stenciled across the side.

A man got out of the truck and picked his way across the field toward them. Ellen sensed the tall girl bristle at first, then relax as the man drew closer. He was a burly man and slightly out of breath. The nametag on his coveralls said *Big Bear*.

"Holy cow, look at you all out here in the cold. Is there anyone inside?"

"No," Willa said before anyone else could answer.

"Thank God for that. Why don't we get you somewhere warm. Can you help me get them to the truck, miss? I think we should get everyone over to the hospital. To get checked out, at least." This last, he directed to Willa.

"Yes, of course."

Dodge tried to help Curly up, but the boy shooed him off, managing with one crutch instead of two. Willa took the little ones by the hand. She looked back to Ellen.

"Are you coming?"

But Ellen's attention was elsewhere. Not on the raging conflagration or the big man helping Curly into the cab of his truck or the wail of the approaching fire engines. Her eyes were on the car pulling off to the side of the road.

"You go ahead," Ellen said. "I think my ride is here."

A puzzled look came across Willa's face, but before she could reply, Huck and Jo were dragging her across the field.

"I get to ride up front!" Jo squealed.

"It's called shotgun," Huck said.

"Shotgun!"

Ellen stood shoeless in the snow, toes wiggling, waiting to see if she'd gotten it right. And when the driver of the Plymouth got out of his car, she knew she had.

Dad...

CHAPTER 49

Ellen approached the Plymouth Satellite before the driver had an opportunity to speak. She lifted up a wet, stockinged foot.

"I just escaped from that fire. I don't have any shoes and I'm cold and I'm scared."

The man quirked his head, a motion all too familiar to Ellen. It meant she had sparked his curiosity.

"Then I supposed you'd better get in the car."

She dashed over to the Plymouth, opened the door and was inside before the man was. Smooth jazz played on the radio—her father's favorite and her *least* favorite.

As soon as the man was behind the wheel, she shot out her hand.

"I'm Ellen. Ellen Gooding."

"Good to meet you, Ellen. I'm Frank."

"Just Frank?" Oh, how she wanted to hear him say his full name.

"No. My name is Francis William Dante Marx. Starts out stoic—"

"And ends with sparks!" Ellen giggled, finishing his thought. It was part of their regular routine…no, *would be* come 1995 or so. Until then, she'd have to savor the look of wonder on his face.

"Right… But you can call me Frank."

"Okay. Frank."

"That's a nasty bump on your noggin. Does it hurt?"

"A little."

"Think we should go get you checked out? At a hospital?"

"Yes, I do, Frank. Follow them," she said, nodding toward the truck. "That's where they're going."

The Plymouth steered back onto the road, following the truck containing Big Bear, Willa and the other children. Snow was falling, and Frank turned on the wipers.

"That's some fire. I saw it all the way from the highway. You're lucky to be out in one piece."

"Yup. I'm lucky, all right," Ellen said.

She looked back at the burning church through the clutter of books, file folders and dry cleaning in the rear seat. The last of the structure was down for the count, looking much like it did when she had first seen it after crashing Riggs's Jeep, save for the hellish glow signaling its death throes.

"Why's your car so packed?" Ellen asked.

"I'm on my way to a new job. In Iowa."

"At the university, right?"

The man chuckled. "What are you, a mind reader?"

Ellen simply switched the radio from jazz to country, filling the silence with something less offensive to her ears.

The car swerved slightly on a patch of ice, and Ellen braced herself. One tumble off the road was enough.

When she looked back at her father, she had the distinct impression that, like the radio, he too had changed channels. He inhaled sharply before speaking.

"Hey, Spooky."

Ellen shivered. "Hey, Dad."

Her father—still the version she'd only known from old photographs—stole a glance her way.

"Can't stay long. This takes a bit of doing."

"I miss you, Dad," Ellen blurted out, jumping straight to the point.

"I miss you, too."

"Why did you go away? Why did you have to die and leave me alone with Mom? She doesn't like me. She wants me to be normal. I *can't* be normal. I don't know how! I miss you. I miss you, I miss you, I—"

Francis Marx took his daughter's hand in his and squeezed.

"If you were normal, would we be able to see each other right now? Have the chance to say goodbye?"

"No…"

"Then I'd say normal is pretty overrated."

"Yeah?"

"Yeah."

Ellen squeezed back. "I don't want to say goodbye."

"And you think I do?"

"No."

"What should we do instead?"

Ellen thought hard. The truck ahead of them was exiting off the highway and into the emergency entrance of the Maple City Hospital. A light snow was falling, turning the scene into a snow globe.

"We should say, 'See you later.'"

"'See you later?'" Her father smiled. "I like the sound of that."

He pulled the car over to the curb, just fifty feet shy of the entrance. He threw the Plymouth into park and turned to Ellen.

"Should I go first?"

"Yes, please," Ellen said, tears falling with abandon.

"Okay…"

Her father leaned over and kissed the top of her head. Ellen closed her eyes tight.

"See you later, Spooky."

"See you later, Dad."

Ellen hung onto the moment. Hung on and stretched it out as long as she could, for she didn't know which version of her father she'd find once she opened her eyes.

Her father whispered in her ear.

"You might want to look under your mother's bed."

Ellen's eyes shot open.

She was no longer sitting in the Plymouth's passenger seat. In fact, she was no longer in the Plymouth at all. She was behind the wheel of Riggs's Jeep, tipped sideways in the ravine. Bright sunlight had replaced the snow, and her father…

There was no sign of Francis Marx to be seen.

Ellen struggled to be free of her seatbelt and managed to shove open the driver's side door. As she climbed out of the Jeep, she was welcomed by the sharp bleat of a siren.

Sitting in the middle of the road ahead of her was a patrol car from which stepped a uniformed officer. The woman gave Ellen a nod.

"Well, young lady, I'm guessing you have neither a license nor registration."

Oh shit. I'm back…

CHAPTER 50

The scent of antiseptic and aftershave hit Ellen's nostrils, making her cough. The doctor with the cheery, chubby face pressed an ice pack against her forehead. Her bruise sang with pain.

"No sign of concussion. She'll be sore for a few days, but if you keep ice on it—"

Rita rose from her chair next to the exam table. Her expression was one Ellen knew quite well. She was livid.

"What in the world were you thinking?"

"Why don't we give the child a moment to gather her wits?" the doctor suggested.

"Why don't we give the child a moment to talk to her mother? Hmm, doctor?"

The doctor slipped out, leaving Ellen and Rita alone in the examination room.

"You are so…I don't even know where to start. You run away, you *lie* to me. You wreck a car…a car?"

I'm back. I'm in big trouble, but I'm back.

"Are you even listening to me?" Ellen's mother had never laid a hand on her in anger, but at the moment it looked like she wanted to shake the living hell out of her daughter.

"Yes."

"Good!"

The doctor poked his head back into the room.

"Ms. Gooding? That officer would like to have a word with the girl. Now that she's—"

"Yeah, yeah. Now that she's okay and you can't make any more money off her. I hear you." Ellen's mom motioned for her to get off the table. "Come on. Let's go see if you're heading off to juvie."

Officer Meltzer—the woman who had found the Jeep—was soft-spoken, and she knelt to speak to Ellen at her level.

"I'm going to ask you and your mother to come with me down to the station to clear a few things up, okay?"

No mention of juvie. No mention of the crashed Jeep. Maybe things weren't as bad as they seemed.

But when Ellen arrived at the police station and saw Riggs's worry-reddened eyes, she realized that yeah, things were pretty bad.

Pat Porter was also there, standing by Riggs, as was another man Ellen didn't recognize—a gentleman in a track suit who looked like he'd rather be anywhere else. All three looked at her expectantly.

It was the stranger who spoke.

"Honey, my name is Don Whittaker. I used to be the big cheese around here before they put me out to pasture. Now they only call to interrupt my workout routine."

"Hello," Ellen squeaked.

"Eli here tells me Mrs. Flynt accidentally locked you in the library overnight, is that so?"

Ellen looked to Riggs. Riggs looked down.

"Yes. I got locked in."

"Fine. And when you took Eli's Jeep—"

"I was trying to get home. Because I was scared…from getting locked in."

Whittaker nodded, having gotten everything out of her he needed. Or all he wanted.

"I'm going to recommend to the library board that Alice Flynt take a little vacation. She's got some health issues that are obviously clouding her judgment. I don't buy it for a second Eli did anything nefarious. A history of fifteen parking tickets and disturbing the peace does not a felon make. I'm inclined to let him go." He looked to Officer Meltzer. "Sorry. Force of habit."

"No, I agree," the officer said.

"Yes!" Riggs yipped. Pat placed a hand on his shoulder to silence him.

Whittaker turned to Rita. "As for the Jeep, let's call it a joyride and leave it at that. In exchange, you and your daughter promise to steer clear of Maple City next time around. Sound good to you, Mom?"

Rita ground her teeth. "Are we free to go?"

"Yes, Ms. Gooding," Officer Meltzer said.

Ellen's mother grabbed her by the hand and led her out of the room. Ellen glanced back at Riggs one last time. He flashed her a thumbs up before turning to Pat.

"Think you can give me a ride over to Themanson's Garage? I gotta get a tow."

* * *

Mother and daughter drove home. Past the town square, the Crossroads Motel, the Primeland processing plant and its noxious fumes. Heading west across the prairie on Route 67, Iowa bound.

"Mom, I—"

"You seriously do *not* want to talk to me right now."

Ellen zipped her lip.

After two hours on the road, they finally pulled off at the Iowa City exit, neither one having said a word.

CHAPTER 51

It was still only early afternoon when Rita banished Ellen to her bedroom. Her final instructions to her daughter were, "The *only* reason I want to see you out of this room is if you need to use the bathroom. You hear me?"

Ellen heard loud and clear.

She also heard her mother cleaning up her mess over the phone. Explaining things to a confused Aunt Tuffy, arguing with the hospital billing department, eating crow and begging Dr. Rankin for a second therapy session for her daughter. And once the calls were over, Ellen heard the telltale sounds of the liquor cabinet being opened and ice tumbling into a glass.

For the rest of the afternoon and well into the evening, Ellen's mother commuted between the living room and the kitchen. One drink led to a second, two movies led to a third. Ellen listened for hours until the channel surfing slowed and the trips to the freezer for more ice grew less frequent. It was nearly eight when they stopped altogether.

That's when Ellen ventured a look into the living room.

Rita Gooding lay passed out on the sofa in front of *Chitty Chitty Bang Bang*. One minute, Dick Van Dyke was cheerily flying his motorcar through the clouds, the next, a pitchman was hawking a juicer.

Now or never.

Ellen eased back down the hallway, past the bathroom and into her mother's bedroom.

The room was twice her bedroom's size and had a large water stain on the ceiling. A lone chest of drawers covered in loose change and bills sat to one side of the bed, above which perched a round mirror her mother had picked up for five dollars at a yard sale.

Ellen caught her reflection in the mirror, startling herself.

Come on, come on!

She quickly hunkered down next to the bed and ran her hand underneath. Shoes, shoes and more shoes—most purchased used at two dollars a pair.

She was just about to switch over to the other side when her hand came in contact with something other than footwear. She ran her fingertips across it, trying to guess at what she'd found.

A blast of music from a particularly loud commercial echoed down the hall, and Ellen knew she couldn't risk remaining out of her room for much longer. She grabbed the thing under the bed and hauled it out.

The beige case made her heart skip a beat.

It was her father's manual typewriter. Rita hadn't sold it on eBay after all.

Lifting her prize by its handle, Ellen scooted down the hall and dove into her room, swinging the door shut behind her.

She scrambled onto her bed, pushing aside the piles of books she'd used to amuse herself during her detention. Now she had something she could really sink her teeth into. She had Dad's typewriter.

Ellen ran a finger over the *F.M.* that adorned the case. Francis Marx. She lifted the cover as carefully as if it were a coffin lid. Perhaps her father had left her one last message, one that had just been sitting there under her mother's bed for God knows how long. But when the cover was off and the device was revealed, she found no final missive. Just an empty roller where a sheet of paper should be.

"Let them in."

Dad's words, but her voice.

Ellen leaned over to her nightstand and pulled out a spiral notebook. She ripped out half a dozen pages and set them beside the typewriter. Extracting the top sheet from the rest, she fed it into the machine.

She flicked the ink option to red and closed her eyes. She tried to clear her mind and found it more difficult than she had expected.

Clear your mind. Mind your manners. Mind over matter. Mad as a hatter…

"Shush!"

She placed her fingers on the keyboard as gently as one would touch a Ouija board's planchette, and breathed.

Let them in.

Slowly at first, then gaining speed, Ellen's fingers began to tap away at the keyboard.

```
Still buzzing with excitement, Peter
exited the elevator…
```

CHAPTER 52

Still buzzing with excitement, Peter exited the elevator, walked briskly through the lobby, threw open the glass door and stepped out into the bright, New York spring day.

He had nailed the audition. One hundred percent. Sure, he'd been nervous at first. He'd never narrated an audiobook before, but the casting director had put him at ease.

"Just tell me the story like you'd tell it to a friend over a campfire," she had said.

And it had worked. Damn, it had worked like gangbusters.

He unchained his old bike from the lamppost, glad to see it still had its tires. He hopped on and steered skillfully into downtown traffic. Yellow cabs swerved and honked, delivery trucks braked and blared, but Peter wove his way past all of them. He was on top of the world. He was untouchable.

As he passed Union Square heading south, the traffic thinned. No more taxis to dodge. It was smooth sailing as far as the eye could see.

He steered past a road construction sign and gave wide berth to an open, steaming manhole. He let muscle memory guide him home as he mentally spent his first paycheck.

I'm getting a new bike, Peter thought. First chance I get.

As he passed the next intersection, leaving Union Square behind, a bird walked out of the ground floor of a building to his left and stopped to watch him as he rode by.

What the...?

No. It wasn't a bird. It was a man.

How could he have mistaken him for a—

The impact of hitting the parked delivery van cut Peter's thought short, and the world went suddenly black.

* * *

"Are you okay?"

Peter sat up. The frozen pond was gone, in its place a hot street and the roar of a bustling city.

"I think so," he stammered.

"Oh, my God. Your finger!"

Peter glanced down at his hand. The wound he'd received from the knife-wielding man was bleeding freely. And lying on the ground between his sprawled legs was...

A finger. His finger.

Instinctively, he reached for it.

"No! Don't touch it. Wait here. Wait!"

The person at his side bolted, leaving him alone with a mangled bicycle and mangled hand.

Feeling a bit nauseous, he looked up instead of down. Skyscrapers loomed overhead. The bright blue sky was a crisscross of contrails. A picture-perfect spring day.

Perfect, Peter thought, except for the fact that I have no fucking clue what's going on.

"Okay, I've got some ice. Let me just..." A hand reached between his legs and plucked the severed digit from the ground. "Oh, God."

Peter turned toward the voice's owner. A fetching woman with olive skin and untamed curls knelt next to him, holding his finger in a pint glass filled with ice.

"Can you get up?" she asked.

Peter nodded and proved he could.

"Come inside. I'll call 911."

The woman dashed ahead of him, holding the pint glass out of her line of vision as she disappeared through the open door of an Irish pub.

Peter glanced up at the sign. Michael's Pub.

I've always liked that name, he mused.

The woman was the only person in the joint. She was busy placing a call with the pub's landline.

"Busy? Are you kidding?" She hung up and tried again.

Peter sat at the bar like a regular customer, eyeing up his finger sitting on ice in the pint glass on the bar top.

"Is that the happy hour special?" he asked, nodding toward the macabre drink.

This made the woman snort. "Whoa. That is dark. You have got to be in shock."

"Probably."

She tried the phone again.

"I'm Peter, by the way."

"Nice to meet you, Peter. I'm Hannah."

"I know."

She flashed him a smile.

"You wanna shut up and let me make this call, Peter?"

He listened as Hannah spoke to the 911 operator. Marveled at her beauty and feistiness and strength. He had skipped the stone across the pond, and it had made it to the other side.

He was home.

Friday, June 27, 2003
Iowa City, IA
Ellen Gooding

CHAPTER 53

Ellen had just finished reading what she had typed when
Rita burst into the room.

"What the hell's all the racket?"

At first, Ellen hadn't a clue as to what her mother was
talking about. Then she looked down at her hands, still poised
over the typewriter, a small stack of typed pages strewn about
it. She laid her hands at her side, like a musician finished
playing a sonata.

The moment her mother's eyes landed on the typewriter,
her face went red.

"You went poking around in my room, didn't you?"

"Mom…"

"Answer me."

Ellen stared at her mother. Not with fear or anger, but with
pity. She could see what the years had in store for the woman.
More regret, more bad choices. And eventually, self-imposed
isolation, hiding amongst her garage sale finds from a world
out to do her wrong.

Ellen would weep for her, in the end. But not tonight. Not
right now. Instead, she would stand her ground. Or sit, as the
case may be.

"Yes, I poked around. Dad wanted me to have it."

"What did you say?"

"I said Dad—"

"Are you seriously giving me sass, you little freak—"

Tap.

One of the typewriter's keys hit the page.

Her mother blinked. "Give me that damned thing."

Tap.

"You want it?" Ellen asked. "Come get it."

Tap-tap.

Rita Gooding stepped forward, and as she did so, the typewriter kicked into hyperdrive.

Tap! Tap-tap, tap-tap-tap.

TAP!

Tap-tap. TAP-TAP!

TAP!

Ellen folded her arms, letting the typewriter do the talking. When it let loose with its final keystroke, her mother looked her squarely in the eye. And Ellen could tell Rita was scared.

"Go to sleep."

"Goodnight, Mom."

Ellen hoped the typewriter would send her mother out of the room with one last *Tap!*, but it remained silent as the woman slipped out the door.

Ellen looked down at the page, curious if the keyboard's tantrum had resulted in anything of note.

There was no new message, no tirade in ink, just one simple revision the ghostly typist had thought appropriate.

Friday, June 27, 2003
Iowa City, IA
Ellen ~~Gooding~~ Marx

Ellen reached into the drawer and retrieved a permanent marker. Setting the typewriter's cover in her lap, she proceeded to make her own alteration, changing the *F. M.* on the front to *E. M.* with a single, careful stroke of the pen.

When she was done, Ellen placed the cover back on the typewriter and put the typewriter under her bed. She got under the covers and switched off the light on the nightstand. Shadows of tree branches covered her ceiling, thanks to the street lamp outside her window, waving gently like skeletal hands.

Ellen grinned and closed her eyes.

AUTHOR'S NOTE

I started writing this book before the pandemic hit. The day New Jersey locked down, so did my creative spark.

For months, I didn't write a word. Instead, I busied myself filling our freezer with food, sourcing masks and hand sanitizer, throwing myself into my audiobook work. I put my head down and dealt with the day-to-day grind.

And then Ellen came to save me.

I woke up one morning with a profound sense of guilt, the feeling that someone who had been waiting patiently was no longer content to remain silent. If I had to put words to the complaint, I believe it would be…

"Great. You finally come up with a story centered around me and you leave me hanging. Just great."

Her annoyance was palpable.

I jumped back into the story. Every day, as the news from the outside world grew worse, Ellen stubbornly demanded my attention.

Today, I sit with a stack of printed pages that wouldn't be here if not for her. I owe her a debt—not just for helping me finish this book, but for reminding me to keep trudging along no matter the obstacles.

Ellen is a real pain in the ass. And for that, I will always be grateful.

Love you, Spooky.

Chris Sorensen
October 11, 2020

THE NIGHTMARE ROOM
BOOK ONE SYNOPSIS

New York audiobook narrator Peter Larson and his wife Hannah have recently lost their son Michael to cancer. When the call comes from Peter's sister that their father (nicknamed Big Bear) had to be placed in a home, Peter and Hannah pack their bags and head off to Maple City, Illinois, intending to move into Peter's father's house and start life afresh.

After settling in at the Intermission Motor Lodge, a lawyer informs them that the house has to be sold to pay for Big Bear's care. However, it seems Peter's father owns an old farmhouse he bought at auction. Upon visiting the rundown place, the couple decide to make a go of it.

Peter sets up a recording studio in the basement; Hannah lands a job bartending at a local dive called the Blind Rock Tavern where she works under one of Peter's high school buddies, a charming scoundrel named Riggs.

As Peter settles into a recording groove, strange things begin to happen. A tangible darkness always seems to be watching. His son's voice appears on the audio tracks, and with it come snippets of long-repressed memories about the boy's illness. Peter erases the audio and tries to move on, but when he comes face to face with the ghost of a grey man on the stairs beating a young boy, he realizes that the house is haunted.

Having narrated a series of books on hauntings, he calls upon the author, who is semi-local. Peter sneaks away to Iowa City to meet Ellen Marx, a stoic, abrasive young woman who tells him point blank that a demon has latched itself to him.

She offers assistance, but in the end, Peter must face the demon himself.

Back at the farmhouse, Peter has a vision of the grey man and his wife with a newborn. The woman (Willa) had an affair with Big Bear, and when the grey man (Albert Carver) finds out, he drowns her in a pond behind the house. But not before Willa commands a dark spirit to keep watch over her child.

Peter is dumfounded. The ghostly boy he's been seeing is himself. The hauntings are visions of his past growing up under Albert Carver's roof.

In the end, Peter confronts the demon in the basement, learning that the entity, despite its dark nature, has protected him his whole life...even from his own memories. The demon (Whisper) reveals the truth he has kept hidden from Peter. Unable to bear his son Michael's suffering, Peter gave the boy an overdose of morphine. A mercy killing.

The revelation breaks Peter. As the past and present merge, he sacrifices himself to Whisper, allowing the young version of himself to move forward in time without the burden of his mother's protective curse. In so doing, he grapples with Whisper until the two become one—an amalgam (The Messy Man)—before vanishing into the ether.

As the story wraps, we see Peter and Hannah arrive at the Intermission Motor Lodge as they did at the beginning. Only this time, their son Michael is with them. Peter's sacrifice was not in vain.

And yet, from the corner of the motel room, a shadow watches the young family. Watches and waits...

THE HUNGRY ONES
BOOK TWO SYNOPSIS

Jessie Voss is the new owner of the Crossroads Motel in Maple City. She's initially wary of the place's ugly history—a local man shot up the place a number of years back, killing scores before turning his shotgun on himself. But Jessie is eager to throw herself into a project, and she and her best friend Steph go about transforming the dilapidated old motel into the revamped Intermission Motor Lodge.

While preparing for the soft opening, a young family arrives in desperate need of a room. It is the Larsons (Peter, Hannah and their son Michael) hauling everything they own from New York City. Jessie senses the family could use a break and offers them a room.

Michael's parents are beleaguered—Peter's father has dementia and they must figure out his care—but the boy loves motel life. The pool, the vending machines, the cow statue on top of the still-to-open restaurant portion. The one thing he could do without are the ghosts of the shotgun massacre.

Before the soft open, a stranger (a man named Wood) visits Jessie, introducing himself as a travel blogger. As she'd already broken the seal with the Larsons, Jessie offers him a room. Once safe inside his room, the man sets a duffel bag filled with old bones on the bed and waits. At the witching hour, a dark creature (Sister) rises from the bag with two companions, sniffing out the spirit of the woman killed during the massacre. And when they locate her, they eat her.

The night of the soft open, all hell breaks loose. Michael spies the ghost of a young girl and follows her. Sister pursues the ghost as well, and soon have both Michael and the ghost girl cornered in the laundry room. Just before Sister strikes, a protective shadow rises up before the children. It is Peter/Whisper amalgam from the previous story (The Messy Man), keeping watch over Michael.

Jessie, who has witnessed multiple ghostly appearances, wants to shut the motel down, but Steph won't permit it.

Meanwhile, Wood bargains with Sister—she hungers for Michael, a child who shouldn't exist. Sister attempts to steal Michael's soul, but The Messy Man spirits him to the past, to the evening of the massacre. Now, Michael must manage to evade the gunman and save the young girl while being pursued by Sister.

Back in the present, Ellen Marx shows up on the scene, having dreamed about the motel. She spells out the situation to Jessie and Steph, and Jess agrees to drug herself in order to venture into the spirit world. In non-corporeal form, she aids Michael in his escape while The Messy Man dispatches Sister.

The Messy Man deposits Michael back in the present, before the soft open. No longer will he be bothered by Sister or the ghosts. And The Messy Man? The demon half of the duo races through the ether, dragging them both back *home.*

Peter lands in the center of a stone circle in the middle of a snowy field. A girl stands before him, dressed in homespun clothes. Whisper, now freed, flies to her and perches on her shoulder. Before we leave him there, we learn the girl's name: Willa.

Chris Sorensen is the author of *The Nightmare Room, The Hungry Ones, The Messy Man, The Mad Scientists of New Jersey* and has written numerous screenplays including *Suckerville, Bee Tornado* and *The Roswell Project*. The Butte Theater and Thin Air Theatre Company of Cripple Creek, Colorado have produced dozens of his plays including *Dr. Jekyll's Medicine Show, Werewolves of Poverty Gulch,* and *The Vampire of Cripple Creek.* Chris has narrated over 200 audiobooks (including the award-winning *Missing* series by Margaret Peterson Haddix). He is the recipient of three AudioFile Earphone Awards, and AudioFile singled out his performance of *Sent* as one of the 'Best Audiobooks of 2010'.

Chris thanks Stephanie Hilliard, Gretchen Douglas, Nick Sullivan, JoAnne Sorensen and Deborah Graybill for their invaluable input.